CRITICAL ACCLAIM FOR TREVOR SCOTT

"[Scott] is an expert at thoroughly deceiving the reader, drawing us into a seemingly unsolvable plot just as he fascinates us with action that is non-stop . . ."

— *The Midwest Book Review*

"Technothriller fans looking for an alternative to Clancy will find Scott a somewhat smaller-scale but perhaps even more authentic alternative."

— *Booklist*

"A damned good writer."

— *David Hagberg*
author of *High Flight* and *Critical Mass*

JAKE ADAMS
INTERNATIONAL THRILLERS
by Trevor Scott

Fatal Network

Extreme Faction
[coming July 2005]

FATAL NETWORK

A JAKE ADAMS
INTERNATIONAL THRILLER

TREVOR SCOTT

new york
www.ibooks.net

DISTRIBUTED BY SIMON & SCHUSTER, INC.

FATAL
NETWORK

1

KOBLENZ, GERMANY

The turbid waters of the Rhine crept higher than normal along the stone barrier from heavy rain and melting snow. The confluence with the Mosel River pushed equally high as the two rivers met with a thundering crash. The few barges that risked the high water moved slowly upstream, or faster than normal down, apparitions of steel with running lights for eyes.

Charlie Johnson crouched in the darkness against the Monument to German Unity, skirting the bitter wind from the exposure of both rivers. He flipped the collar of his overcoat closer to his neck and then shoved his gloved hands deep into his front pockets.

Footsteps came and went as couples braved the bow-like point of the German Corner. The water was far too high and the wind far too fierce for anything more than a quick look and then a quickened pace back to their cars. And the darkness allowed no view. But just to stand at the very end of the

German Corner, leaning forward against the metal chain, the Rhine to the right and Mosel to the left, made it feel as though the power of a great ship was behind them, moving swiftly through the river. Obscurity did nothing to diminish that feeling of power.

His contact was late. Something must have gone wrong. He could just leave and return to the warmth of his car and his Scotch. He was getting too old to hide in the shadows. Too old to stoop in the stench of squalid alleys, or even these fine bricks lining the Rhine. He should just take his military retirement and go fishing like all his old comrades had.

A man with a long black coat walked along the outer edge of the cobblestone point until he reached the tip. The man never looked over his shoulder toward Charlie or the monument. His neck was scrunched down as a turtle would do to hide from a predator, the ear-flaps from his hat lowered to slow the wind's bite.

Finally, the man Charlie had been waiting for. He rose stiffly from behind the monument and walked cautiously toward the man in the dark coat. He stopped within a few feet of his contact. The man still had not turned to see who was coming. Who could be that confi-dent? Then the man turned slowly.

"Gunter!" Charlie said. "What are you doing here?"

Gunter Schecht grinned wickedly. He was not used to answering questions from anyone, directly. His steely eyes glistened like a cat's ready to pounce on its prey. Pushing his massive chest outward with each breath, he appeared more like a bear than a man. His stiff, square jaw jutted out from an otherwise round face almost as a caricature.

"I heard I might find you here," Gunter Schecht finally said, barely above the roar of the two rivers.

Only one person could have told Gunter he would be there. And he would have never talked without... The thought lingered in Charlie's mind. Without dying? "What does the boss need now?" Charlie asked, his voice crawling slowly with each word. "I thought he had everything he wanted from Teredata for now."

"He does. But now you think you can freelance and sell to another company?"

"I wouldn't do that," Charlie pleaded. He felt the cold leaving his body, as if his blood were seeping from every pore.

"Then why are we here having this conversation?" Gunter said, smiling callously.

Charlie's shoulders tightened and a hot flush of anger spread through him as he realized the probable fate of his real contact. He had heard that Gunter had a tendency to go overboard. Kill first and not bother to ask questions later. "You can't blame a guy for trying," Charlie finally said.

"Have you ever seen the North Sea?" Gunter asked, moving a few steps closer to him. He was now at that uncomfortable distance reserved for lovers or enemies. And Gunter was not inclined to love anything.

"Yes, a long time ago. But..."

"Well I'm going to give you a chance to see it again. That is if you don't get hung up on some buoy cable or bridge piling."

Charlie turned his head to search for an escape route, but Gunter's two friends had quietly approached behind him with guns aimed in his direction. Gunter was a large man, but his two men dwarfed even him. The largest one went well over three hundred pounds, and of that great girth much of it was fat. But enough muscle remained to make him a forbidding sight, especially in the dark. His 9mm automatic looked like a toy in his thick right hand. The smaller man was somewhat soft about the middle also, from a dark point of view, but his Uzi made him look much larger. They both glared with mock solemnity at Charlie.

Charlie turned to look at Gunter, and he too had pulled an Uzi from inside his long coat and had it directed at him. Charlie Johnson had no retreat.

"Americans are too greedy, Charlie," Gunter said. "You had everything you needed, but you wanted more. I hate greedy thieves. You're right, we have everything we need from your company, for now, so we no longer need you. Don't let the fish bite."

A faint thud was barely audible over the roar of the two rivers as the metal pipe struck the back of Charlie's head, instantly knocking him to the ground. The fat man quickly wrapped a thick plastic bag over Charlie's head and tied it around his neck, ensuring all the air had escaped first. The other man tied his hands behind his back and his feet together, and then tied a rope connecting his hands to his feet. Then both men unzipped their coats and removed a sand-filled pouch from their waists. Each bag weighed over twenty pounds and was attached by velcro strips. In seconds, the pouches were around Charlie's waist and securely fastened. Then with one quick motion, the two men swung the wrapped body over the chain and into the fast-moving Rhine. Only a slight splash echoed back through the darkness.

* * *

Herbert Kline stooped behind the half-moon stone wall that partially enclosed the Monument to German Unity. Gunter's men turned and looked in his direction, but could not see him in the darkness. What kind of men were these? Kill a man as easily as ordering a beer. No conscience. No humanity. He shuddered slightly and then drew a small smooth flask from his inside coat pocket, popped the worn cork from the top, and quickly downed a mouthful of schnapps.

The three men turned and walked back along the Rhine to the tree-lined pathway that led to a street where a blue Fiat van was parked. The three laughed either out of enjoyment for the hideous crime just committed, or to act as though nothing had happened. And then the laughter and footsteps ended. Two doors slammed and the van pulled away.

Herb had worked with Gunter on a number of cases over the years. From the first time they met, Herb despised Gunter. He was too arrogant and too willing to openly criticize and ridicule without all the facts. The world had few saints and far too many tyrants. Sure, Herb wasn't a perfect, sterling performer, but at least he was honest on the job and with himself. Sleeping came easy for him. He could retire in a year or so with a clean conscience. Gunter had no conscience.

BONN, GERMANY

Back in the relative comfort and security of his office at the headquarters of German Customs, Herbert Kline sat at his cluttered desk with his hands over his face, rubbing the fatigue from his eyes. He started to reach for his smooth flask and realized it hung with his coat behind the door. Instead, he pulled out a gold, metal flask of schnapps from the lower right desk drawer. As he poured himself a small glass, he looked deep into the textured stag on the side of the flask. He had received the flask as a gift while working on a case in the Black Forest. He had stopped the illegal trade of clocks made in Taiwan and re-labeled and sold to tourists as Black Forest originals. That was one of the highest points in his career with German Customs. Now he languished in the obscurity of a bureaucracy he had come to hate.

With a quick gulp, the schnapps slid down his throat and warmed his whole body. The chill of the Rhine and the brutal men would soon be forgotten.

Unlocking the center desk drawer, he pulled out a thick manila folder and stared at it for a moment. Perhaps more schnapps. He quickly poured and gulped another glass full. The folder on Bundenbach Electronics was getting thicker each day. The players had also increased, not only in number, but in intensity. Shit! Retirement was far too close to start making waves now. Why couldn't this case have come years ago when it would have meant an instant promotion, or at least the admiration and esteem from his peers? If God was just, then why had he succumbed to the mediocrity of

this existence? What exis-tence? This was only life
in its most submissive and acquiescent form.

After the schnapps, the office seemed even smaller. The flask quickly ran out, but the main bottle in
his file cabinet was still nearly full. On his way back
from the cabinet, he stopped in front of the window
overlooking a darkened Rhine River three floors
below. He swung the window open and leaned
against the sill. The frigid air swiftly swept in and
enveloped Herb almost as completely as the
schnapps had. He took in a deep breath and savored
it as a pipe smoker would a puff of his favorite
blend. The river was there. He could hear its torrent
churning and awesome power even from the distance of a soccer field. Charlie Johnson, the poor
bastard, could be by anytime now.

He closed the window and went back to his desk
and the thick file. The file that could never be officially filed. The file that had gotten Charlie Johnson
killed. The case file that he had stumbled on when
German Intelligence decided it had nothing to do
with state security. The file that nobody else wanted
or he wouldn't have had.

The boss said he wanted a thorough report. Not
the normal sloppy mess he was accustomed to getting from him. So he wasn't some ass kisser who
was more concerned over graphs and charts than the
basic facts. Did that make him inferior? Less com-
petent?

Finally, he slid the contents of the folder onto an already jumbled desk. There were statistics sheets and handwritten memos on Bundenbach Electronics and Teredata International Semiconductors. Import and export data. Transcripts from conversations with the mole before he was found riddled with holes, his mouth shot wide open.

Why kill Johnson? He's the supply link. Did they have everything they needed? He may never know. Gunter might have just gotten bored with Johnson and needed someone to feel superior to.

Another shot of schnapps.

2

PORTLAND, OREGON

Jake Adams sat in the plush white chair waiting as patiently as he could. He crossed his legs and straightened out the small cuff on the gray dress pants. He always wore a suit when meeting prospective clients, and then promptly discarded it as soon as possible. He gazed down at his brown leather shoes, Italian leather. When his former girlfriend, Toni Contardo, insisted he buy them, he was hesitant of the expense. It turned out she was right. It paid to buy quality.

He glanced at his watch. One fifteen. Milton Swenson was a man who despised impertinence in others, but who regarded himself immune. Jake knew this from interning at Teredata International Semiconductors in college. But years had passed since those days, and he had not even heard from Milt in over three years. Why Milt had summoned him now was a mystery of sorts. Jake was pretty sure it had something to do with his new business, but with Milt Swenson nothing was really certain.

When the large wooden door to the office finally opened, Jake could hear Milt instructing his secretary that he was not to be disturbed. Following Milt closely, Steven Carlson, the second in charge, plopped down in a white matching sofa across the room.

"Jake, I'm glad you could make it," Milton Swenson said as he approached with his hand stretched outward.

Jake stood and shook his hand firmly. "I was intrigued."

"Please, have a seat," Milt said. "I'm sure you remember Steve Carlson."

Jake nodded and tried to force a smile. Carlson turned up the right side of his mouth in his version of a smile. "Yes, I do," Jake said. He remembered his constant badgering.

Milt appeared more serious than Jake recalled him being. His thin, blonde hair, that which still remained, lay disheveled over his bald pate. Bags under his eyes showed lack of sleep. His normally impeccable suit hung haplessly over a flaccid physique.

"What can I do for you?" Jake asked.

Milt sat on the edge of his large oak desk. "I've got a problem I think you can help me solve."

"Shoot."

"You worked for Air Force Intelligence in Germany."

Jake crossed his arms and sat back. Air Force Intelligence, the CIA, and various other agencies on loan. "That's not really a secret."

Milt Swenson finally let himself smile. "Jake, I've followed your most recent career here in Portland, and think you're just the person who can help me out of a particular jam my company is in."

Jake considered Milt more seriously now. "What kind of jam?"

Milt gazed toward Steve Carlson and then back to Jake. "An employee of ours in Germany is missing," Milt said. "I'd like you to go over there and find him."

"Have you talked with the German Polizei?"

"Yes, but they said they can't do much for us at this time."

"How long has your guy been missing?"

Milt paused. "About four days."

"Four days!" Jake shouted. "That's all? Hell, maybe he just picked up some fraulein and took her to Monte Carlo."

Milt shook his head. "I don't think so. Charlie Johnson is a responsible man. He runs our program in Germany. He doesn't just take off with some girl."

Jake looked at Milt's troubled face, and then glanced briefly at Steve Carlson. Milt had given him a break in college. He felt somewhat obligated to help him. "I'll do what I can, Milt."

"Great!"

"But if you've checked into my work, you know I don't usually handle missing persons. I mostly check into company security breaches and computer crimes."

Milt nodded. "I know. But I need someone who still has contacts in Germany. Someone I can trust to be discrete."

Jake thought for a moment. "Why is discretion so important?"

Milt looked at Carlson again, who was now combing his fingers through his beard. Milt finally said, "Our contract in Germany is important to our government." He paused for a moment. "Charlie and his guys are retrofitting some new avionics gear to the Air Force F-15. We've developed a new chip that's faster than anything on the market. We plan on using the chip commercially in the near future, but a contingency of our goverment contract required us to test the chip in Europe against NATO defenses. If the chip works as advertised there, it'll work anywhere." He hesitated for a moment. "A successful retrofit would give us a huge advantage when we bid for the Joint Strike Fighter contract."

Jake looked over at Steve Carlson. He was now

trying to pick unseen objects from his fingernails with a bent paperclip. "Still, what does Charlie Johnson's disappearance have to do with your government contract?" Jake asked Milt.

"Maybe nothing, maybe everything," Milt said. "That's what I want you to find out."

Something was wrong with his logic. He had to know more than he was telling him. "All this is great background information, Milt. But what are you failing to tell me?"

Milt Swenson smiled slightly. "I could never keep anything from you, Jake," he said. "A few months ago our testing was running smoothly, no problems. We looked like we'd finish ahead of schedule. But then a few weeks ago the chips started failing at an unacceptable rate. We were all baffled. We shipped over replacements for those that failed, in fact they were even a more advanced version."

"Did you check out the old chips to see what happened?" Jake asked.

Milt glanced at Steve and back slowly. "Charlie told us one of his guys mistakenly destroyed them in the base incinerator while getting rid of some classified data," Milt said.

Jake nodded. "So you think there was really nothing wrong with the chips and Charlie may be hawking them to someone else?"

"Maybe."

"The discretion you're asking for could land my

ass in jail," Jake said. "I take it you haven't notified the government?"

"I have nothing to report," Milt said emphatically. "The chips are officially destroyed."

"And the chips themselves aren't really classified, but restricted from trade," Jake said.

"Right. But the avionics contract is classified," Milt conceded. "So, we're not really required to report a leak in our own chip technology unless it involves the avionics system."

Jake thought about it for a minute, looking carefully for some sign or reason to trust Milt and Steve. Milt's logic was straddling the fence a bit. But Jake was used to borderline propriety. Since going private, he found himself swaying in the breeze on that fence more times than not.

Jake rose from the chair. "When do I leave?"

"As soon as possible," Milt said. "I have tickets for you to leave tonight on Northwest Flight 125 to Frankfurt. I've made copies of the personnel files on Charlie Johnson and his men. You can read them on the plane."

"Anything else?" Jake asked.

Milt hesitated. "Unfortunately. A delegation of the Senate Armed Services Committee will visit us here in two weeks to observe our progress on the retrofit. We've had nothing but glowing reports in the past, and I was hoping to give them a similar report. As you know, budgets can be cut at any time.

They could make or break our contract bid for the Joint Strike Fighter."

"Two weeks! That's not much time," Jake said. "Have you also heard about my fees?"

"Yes," Milt said. "I'll double your standard fees and your expenses to cover the foreign travel. This is extremely important to us."

"Sounds good."

Jake and Milt shook hands, and then Jake nodded with Steve Carlson on his way out the door.

As he left the modern glassed building in the heart of Portland to retrieve his car, he couldn't help feeling nostalgic returning to Germany. He knew he'd have to report his findings to the U.S. government if he found the restricted chips had been sold to another country. Before hearing about the chips, he would have guessed his first theory correct. A girl. But Milt's concern was far too grave for simple solutions. And something in the back of his mind told him that Milt was still holding back information. Regardless, he would definitely need the full two weeks.

3

BIRKWALD, GERMANY

A persistent fog had frozen overnight turning trees into crystalline works of art and transforming rolling green hills into a convoluted tundra.

Jake Adams cranked over his rental Audi A4, and as the engine slowly warmed, he thought about the personnel files on the Teredata tech reps he was on his way to talk to. After arriving at Frankfurt International yesterday, he acquired a new CZ-75 9mm automatic pistol with a few boxes of ammo. Then he headed straight for the Gasthaus Birkwald, perched on top of a hill in the Eifel region of Rhineland-Pfalz. Jet lag had caught up with him, though. So he spent the rest of his arrival day and the evening in the Gasthaus eating, drinking good beer, and sleeping. But mostly sleeping.

Jake shifted in the wide bucket seat, strapped the shoulder harness across his black leather jacket, and clicked the seat belt in. As he waited for the heater to clear the windshield, he looked into the rear view mirror at his tired brown eyes. Red spiders streaked the whites. He hadn't bothered to shave; dark stubble crackled as he scratched the right side of his face. He ran his fingers through his dark brown hair. How did it get so long?

He looked across the street and noticed a blonde woman sitting erect in a small red Ford Fiesta. She glanced over at Jake and then quickly forward again. She was a beauty. Silky blonde hair. High cheek bones. It was strange, though. Her car was running and parked on the opposite side of the road facing the wrong direction. Then she quickly pulled away from the curb and sped off.

The windshield now clear, Jake signaled, pulled out onto the main road that dissected the small village, and took off in the same direction as the blonde.

Shortly, he rounded the last corner before entering the village next to his, and quickly down shifted into second gear. Then he saw the blonde again. He slowed down even more for a better look.

As he slowly passed the blonde, she smiled. Jake found himself smiling and then looking over his shoulder and in his rear view mirror as the distance grew between their cars.

He wondered why she turned around and sat at the intersection. She was probably on her way to work and forgot something at home. Yet, it did make him a bit suspicious. He moved slowly through the gears now, taking the corners smoother.

* * *

A dark blue Fiat van with three men sat among a group of thick pine trees with a view of the winding German country road. The driver, a robust man with high brow ridges and thick black eye brows, worked feverishly to keep the windshield defrosted. The engine ran at idle, but the breathing of the three men fogged the windows.

Gunter Schecht sat next to the passenger door with his 9mm Uzi cradled across his wide lap. "Dummkopf!" Gunter yelled at his driver. "How do you expect to complete this job if you can't even keep the damn windshield clear?"

The driver grumbled under his breath. The middle man, not quite as stout as the driver, his eyes closed, smiled broadly.

Gunter had briefed his men on Jake Adams. He only hoped they took him seriously.

"He's coming," said a soft, female voice over the Fiat's radio. The three men made last minute preparations. On Gunter's command, they all chambered rounds.

Jake fiddled with the Audi's radio trying to come up with a station that played classic Rock and Roll, but the rolling hills bounced the FM signal every which way but to his antenna.

He shifted into fifth gear after clearing a small hill, and once again took his eyes off the road to search for a station. He looked up for a second and noticed a blue van a kilometer ahead pull from a small dirt road. Shifting down to fourth gear, anticipating he would have to pass the van, he looked at his radio again.

As Jake looked up again, "Shit!" He slammed on the brakes and clutch simultaneously as both arms tightened to the steering wheel.

The car quickly decelerated.

He jammed the stick toward first gear, but it wouldn't slide into place.

Flashes from the guns flickered furiously without noise.

He dove to the passenger seat, straining against his seat belt. His feet slipped from the clutch and brake and stalled the Audi with a great lurch forward.

The windshield shattered and thousands of tiny pieces of glass rained down on Jake's back.

The van sat broadside in the road, with three men crouched next to it. They continued to empty their Uzis into the front of Jake's car from fifty meters away. Only the sound of lead hitting metal and glass broke the silence.

"Son of a bitch!"

Jake brushed broken glass from the seat and worked his way back behind the wheel.

He peeked over the dash. Three men. The largest man quickly opened the front door of the van and squeezed behind the wheel. The other two were changing the clips in their guns.

Jake twisted the keys and the four cylinders cranked over but didn't start. He tried again. This time they kicked in. He cranked the wheel, jammed the gas pedal to the floor, and popped the clutch. The Audi's tires dug in, but he couldn't make a full U-turn without first coming to a stop, putting it in reverse, and then forward again.

Just as he pulled the gear shift back into second, a new barrage of 9mm slugs shattered the back window and the trunk of his car. He crouched as low as he could. By the time he hit third, he was down the hill and out of range.

His car was riddled with holes.

He drove to the first crossroad, took a right, then sped toward an isolated spot between two villages and turned down a small dirt road. In a few hundred meters of bouncing dirt road, he cranked the wheel and smashed into a group of small bushes. He removed his newly scratched leather briefcase from the floor of the passenger side, and abandoned the Audi. Then he quickly ran two kilometers to the nearest town.

When he finally had time to think about what had just happened, he sifted through his mind for a reason. The blonde was obviously a lookout. But who were the three with the silenced Uzis? They knew where he was staying and where he was going. But how? He'd have to think about that. In the meantime he needed a new car.

BITBURG AIR BASE, GERMANY

Jake Adams showed the gate guard his ID and the rental contract for his new Volkswagen Passat. The rental company had sent it from the Frankfurt Airport after he reported the Audi missing.

His papers were in order. The stern-faced guard waved him on base. Jake knew the routine from his days as an officer in Air Force Intelligence. In fact, he had been stationed near Bitburg for three years.

He drove slowly to the end of an old hangar near the flight line. The corrugated metal building, painted Earthtone brown, had been slapped up in the 50s to provide maintenance space for U.S. fighter aircraft. It had long since been replaced by hardened individual shelters that resembled long concrete igloos. The old hangar would have been condemned if Teredata had not needed the space.

Teredata International Semiconductors was a subcontractor on nearly every aircraft in the Air Force and Navy arsenals. Charlie Johnson, until his mysterious disappearance, ran a team of five men, all ex-Air Force technicians, on the new avionics retrofit to the F-15s at Bitburg. The project was on the cutting edge of technology. The Top Secret security clearances required by the tech reps proved that.

Jake sat in the parking lot for a moment to think. In a situation like this he always felt like an actor preparing to perform on stage, so his first impression was important. He hoped someone would know where to find Charlie, but realized he was probably dreaming. A quick fix wasn't in the cards on this trip. The three men with silenced Uzis had just assured him of that.

He got out and walked toward the building, stopped outside the metal door to the hangar for a moment, and squeezed his left arm against his 9mm automatic. It was always a comforting feeling knowing it was there.

He entered the small office at the North end of the old hangar. The man sitting behind the large gray metal desk was Blaise Parker, second in charge of the Teredata Bitburg operation.

The man glanced up at Jake, but didn't look him in the eye. His long gray hair stuck up in places. His white shirt with red and blue vertical stripes bulged over his belt. He appeared more as an unsuccessful car salesman than one with a great deal of technical information.

"I'm Jake Adams." Jake reached out to shake his hand. "I'm sorry I was...delayed. I assume Milt Swenson mentioned I'd be coming by."

Blaise Parker still refused to look him in the eye. Parker, like Johnson, had over twenty years prior service in the Air Force before Teredata hired him. Both men knew the F-15 inside and out. Nothing unusual showed up in his background.

"Mr. Swenson sent a Fax saying someone would be coming by," Parker finally said in a slow southern drawl. "He didn't mention your name. It's not like Charlie taking off like this. I've known him for ten years, and he's never been late for work, let alone gone for days."

"So, you're the one who contacted Milt?"

Parker nodded. "Yeah, I told the security police and OSI, but they said they don't have jurisdiction over civilians."

That was true. The Air Force Office of Special Investigations worked with the German Polizei on matters dealing with military personnel on or off base—mostly drug cases. The security police only handled base security and minor infractions like DWIs. "And the Polizei?" Jake asked.

Parker finally shifted his gray eyes at Jake. "They said they'd look for his car, check the local morgues, and that's about it."

"They could find him. But in the meantime, I'll be looking for him. I'll need a list of all his associates and friends in Germany. Local hangouts. Favorite habits he has. Anything that could help."

"Sure." Parker thought for a moment and then scribbled on a piece of scratch paper. "This could help."

Jake scanned the note. "This is it?"

Parker nodded. "He likes the huge schnitzel at the Gasthaus Birkwald. He stops there every night on the way home from work."

"Anything else?" Jake asked. "Any German friends?"

"No. He's a loner. Once in a while we all get together, but that's about it."

Jake realized he didn't have much to go on. "What about the other Teredata tech reps?"

"I've talked to all of them. They have no clue. They're all out working on a bird in the hangar. If you'd like to ask them yourself, I'll go fetch 'em one by one."

Jake thought for a moment. "Sure. But first tell me about the recent failure rate of the chips."

Parker looked up quickly. "I don't know how to explain it. It just started happening."

"Do you have any of the bad chips?" It was a question Jake already had the answer to, but it was worth a shot.

He shook his head. "Nope. Charlie destroyed them."

Now that was interesting. Charlie told Milt that one of the other reps destroyed them inadvertently. "If another one fails, make sure you hang on to it," Jake said, although he didn't expect that to happen.

"I will! Mr. Swenson already briefed me on that."

Parker let Jake use the office to talk to the rest of the tech reps, but as he suspected, they were of little help. Charlie Johnson was a loner. He worked hard, but the consensus unanimously pointed to his being a basically boring individual after work. Time would tell if that theory held up.

Back outside in his car, Jake realized that Blaise Parker and the other tech reps would probably be of no further help. He already knew that Charlie Johnson frequented the Gasthaus Birkwald. That was the reason he took a room there. Maybe Charlie's apartment would reveal something. He started the car and headed toward Charlie Johnson's apartment on the outskirts of Koblenz.

4

USS THEODORE ROOSEVELT

As the massive carrier turned into the wind, salt spray showered over its bow. High, dense clouds hid the glow of the early January stars. The Mediterranean was dark and desolate.

Kurt Lamar braced himself against the starboard catwalk, waiting for the first jet lights to appear over the horizon. Leaning against the gray metal barrier, he glanced down at the choppy waves nearly seventy feet below. The forty knot winds over the deck, cold and bitter, reminded him of his early morning deer hunts back home in Wisconsin. The first red and green aircraft lights flickered in the distance from the stern of the ship.

The muffled voice of the Air Boss sounded: "On the flight deck, all hands get into a complete and proper flight deck uniform. Clear the port catwalks; standby to recover aircraft. A-7 at one mile."

The aircraft's lights got closer and closer until the outline of its wings and fuselage could be seen. The sucking of intake air and roaring of engine exhaust, laboring toward landing speed, finally reached his ears. Kurt could tell now from the tail markings that it was an A-7J from his squadron.

The engine screeched as the pilot slowed his aircraft more and descended toward the heavily pitching deck.

Moving his legs further apart for stability, and grasping a metal railing, Kurt flexed his muscles, and his heart pounded with excitement and fear. He could never get over the feeling of helplessness involved with watching flight ops.

With a crash, the tail hook grabbed one of four arresting cables. The tires and struts of the rear landing gear compressed under the tremendous weight of the aircraft. The nose gear, hitting the metal deck last, also compressed, jerking the pilot forward in the cockpit. The arresting gear cable reeled out over sixty yards before the A-7 came to a halt.

Within seconds the pilot retracted his tail hook, the cable reeled back in its place, and the plane taxied toward the bow to be launched again. The flight deck crew directed the aircraft forward and attached its launch bar to the catapult.

The Jet Blast Deflectors rose from the deck behind the A-7. The pilot pushed his throttle for-

ward sending hot, foul exhaust over the deflectors
and high into the air.

Kurt watched the meticulous crew prepare the aircraft for launch.

The pilot saluted the deck crew, the cat officer
signaled the pilot, and the jet roared to the bow and
soared up and away from the ship and into the darkness. Only the faint, fading flames of exhaust disturbed the night.

Kurt had seen enough to satisfy his curiosity.
Although he was a veteran, it had been nearly two
years since his last flight deck experience. When he
became an officer with the Naval Investigative
Service, he thought he had given up that dangerous
vocation. But he knew it was his prior experience
that led the NIS to select him for this mission.

Carefully, Kurt stepped down the metal ladder,
swung the latch secure on the hatch, and opened the
heavy metal door. All of the deafening flight deck
noises were muffled with the slamming of the hatch
behind him.

He worked his way through a maze of passageways and compartments until he reached the shop
that he'd call his home—at least until his investigation was complete.

Inside he was still a stranger. The Electronics
Technicians had crossed the Atlantic together, but
were far from shipmates. Over thirty men worked
out of a small twelve-by-twelve compartment in

two twelve-hour shifts. Kurt had asked for nights, which allowed him time for his real mission there.

Leo Birdsong was the only friend he had made. They had become close in such a short time. Kurt knew that often happened with sailors. Kurt dreaded the day when he'd have to tell Leo the truth about why he was really there.

"About time you got your ass off that deck," Leo said.

Kurt flipped his goggles up and removed his helmet. "I love the smell of jet exhaust in the evening," Kurt said.

In the two weeks they had known each other, they had entrusted each other with a lot of their background. Leo, who grew up in Denver, had joked that he must be the only Black man who had never tried grits. But he also knew that not many Black men could ski like him. Kurt had opened up as well, not telling lies, but not telling the whole truth—more like selecting bits of information from his youth and prior flight deck experiences.

"Fuckin' A," Kurt said. "No matter how many times I watch flight ops, I'll never get used to it. It must be twenty degrees up there, but the fuckin' exhaust will still curl your hair and fry your ass."

Leo laughed. "Shit. You're gonna start lookin' like me."

Kurt sat next to Leo. He was flipping through a Skiing Magazine, dreaming about the Alps and the ship's first port of call in Genoa, Italy. Kurt wanted to ski with Leo, but he knew he had work to do while in port.

"Did you get to see Corsica this afternoon?" Kurt asked. Working nights for nine days while crossing the Atlantic, and another six since entering the Mediterranean, Kurt longed for a daylight view of the aqua blue Ligurian Sea and the rocky Corsican coast.

"No. I couldn't drag my butt out of the rack," Leo said.

"I just had to see the sun," Kurt explained.

Leo nodded. "Need my beauty sleep. You're only twenty-five now. You keep this shit up, and you'll start looking like those thirty-five year old lifers who look sixty." He quickly flipped his eyes toward an obese man laying in a crumpled heap among a large pile of clean rags.

Kurt smiled. The man who nearly everyone had learned to hate in a short period of time, Petty Officer First Class Shelby Taylor, snored loudly over the muffled flight ops on the deck above. His face was a contorted mess. His cheeks a cross between that of a chipmunk and a bulldog. Some in the shop believed Shelby could sleep on command. Even while standing. But nobody complained. There was far more harmony while he slept.

Kurt needed to talk with Leo privately. He knew they would be free to speak below decks in the hangar bay. The large, cavernous area where most of the maintenance took place without being exposed to the elements, hummed with power carts that allowed technicians to simulate flight postures in search of electrical problems. Normally, the night shift performed maintenance on the A-7 weapon and avionics systems. But this night they were flying, so half the crew did maintenance and the other half was on the deck waiting in case one of the aircraft had an avionics problem.

"Let's go to the hangar," Kurt said.

Without answering, they both got up and departed through the hatch and out of the compartment. Kurt was really an Ensign, but wore the rank of a Petty Officer Second Class. Leo was a Petty Officer Third Class.

When they reached the hangar, they applied auxiliary power to one of the A-7s. Leo got inside the cockpit and partially closed the canopy. With the power on and the cockpit ajar he could lean into the cockpit and speak to Leo without anyone else hearing them.

"What do you think of Shelby?" Kurt asked.

"Shelby's a cock sucker."

"Besides that," Kurt laughed. He already knew that Leo, and most everyone else, hated Shelby.

Petty Officer First Class Shelby Taylor was Kurt's prime suspect in the disappearance of numerous computer chips, manuals, and avionics components.

The NIS had been alerted by a young supply sailor whose records failed to balance. The sailor had narrowed the disappearing items down to the A-7 squadron, since it was the only unit using the new avionics equipment. The NIS quickly had the sailor transferred before the Mediterranean cruise began, and placed Kurt in the light attack squadron to find out where the high tech components were going.

"Shelby Taylor is a sleaze ball," Leo said. "I've known him for about a year; that's about three hundred and sixty-five days too long. He's a clap-infested dude. I wouldn't trust him as far as I could throw his fat ass."

"So, you like him then," Kurt said with a smile.

Leo turned power on to the cockpit and the Heads Up Display lit up like a Christmas tree. He then began playing with the moving-map display—a navigational tool on the right console.

"You'd like to fly one of these beasts, wouldn't you?"

"I wouldn't mind, but I've seen some of the assholes who work on these things," Leo said, flicking on more switches.

Kurt was trying to find a way to get more information on Shelby's activities. Leo was Shelby's assistant when ordering supplies, but Kurt had already cleared Leo from any wrongdoing. But had Leo noticed anything strange?

"You know we traced the problem on the 06 Bird down to the Nav-Weapons avionics box," Kurt said.

"I ordered a new processor from supply, and when it didn't come in after a few days, I gave them a call. They said they were all out...that Shelby had wiped them out last week. But I checked our work orders and supply bins and can't find even one."

Leo gazed up at Kurt. "That's not the only thing missing. Shelby's taken me out of the supply business," Leo said. "When I questioned him on it, the son of a bitch just said 'Don't worry Bro, let me take care of supply this cruise'."

"What do you suppose he's doing with the stuff?"

"Shit if I know. Maybe he's selling the shit to the Russians."

Kurt didn't answer. That was a possibility. The avionics components were part of a classified retro-fit. The chips that ran the entire system were even restricted from trade to NATO countries.

Leo hesitated for a minute while he played with the onboard computer. "Last week I went to run down a spark through the forward black box," he said, pausing for a moment, not sure if he should continue. "I went to get the manual to trace the schematic—it wasn't there...you know where we normally keep them. So I ask Shelby if he knew where it was. He said our sister squadron had it, and we'd get it back in a few days. I told him I didn't need the damn thing in a few days, I needed it now. He told me to shut the fuck up and work on something else."

"That's strange," Kurt said.

"Well it's back on our shelves now," Leo said, "and our sister squadron didn't have the damn thing. They've got their own. And, I called...they didn't borrow shit from Shelby."

Kurt fiddled with a few dials. Shelby must have taken the manuals down to a copier. But they were so thick, he could only make a few copies at a time without arousing suspicion. That would have taken a few days. The manuals are only classified Confidential and NATO restricted, but someone wanted them as though they were Top Secret.

Kurt left the hangar bay and returned to the shop to prepare for a stint on the flight deck. He donned his deflated life vest, helmet and goggles, and tool pouch, and proceeded to the catwalk with Leo following closely behind. One of the first things a good flight deck crewman learns about night operations, is to proceed slowly; stand by on the catwalk until his eyes have a chance to adjust to the darkness. Kurt knew this, so he instinctively stood and watched flight ops for about ten minutes before ascending the final metal steps to the dark, hard iron non-skid surface.

On the bow, just ahead of Kurt, an F-14 hit full afterburner, sending a set of flames back to the Jet Blast Deflectors, and then was catapulted forward and up away from the ship as a rocket launching out into space. Kurt kept his mouth shut and covered his nose with his hand to repel some of the nasty exhaust. But he knew his hand was never enough. After each shift, he would blow globs of black from his nostrils.

Kurt had heard once that flight deck work was the second most dangerous job in the world; only coal mining was worse. But he would have gladly been in some West Virginia mine on dark nights like this.

He remembered that when he had first worked the flight deck, he was virtually without communications. He got used to certain hand signals. But sometimes those were ambiguous in tense moments. He was grateful now to have a four-channel head set. He could talk to his shop, flight deck crew members, and pilots on the deck. He could also listen to the Air Boss in the Island Tower and the pilots in the air. Once the pilots were airborne, they switched to a different frequency. He could hear them, but not talk with them.

Kurt was standing by with Leo in case a pilot had a problem with one of his electronic systems. He knew he could troubleshoot most anything on the spot, and fix many things without replacing parts to keep the launch on schedule. Often the problem was just a circuit-breaker that had not been properly actuated by the pilot on preflight.

"Kurt, how many birds we workin'?" Leo asked over his headset.

"We've got one fired up aft, and two airborne,"

Kurt answered. "The one aft might not go. They think it has a hydraulic problem."

"At least it's not our problem," Leo said.

One of Kurt's A-7s flew low over the deck but didn't land. Its engine roared to keep it airborne at such a slow speed, its landing gear dangling like an eagle's talons.

Kurt switched to the airborne frequency to find out what might be wrong.

"See anything?" came a voice from Kurt's radio. He recognized the voice of a pilot from his squadron.

"It's really too dark to tell if your gear is locked or not," said the LSO, a pilot who stands in the aft, port catwalk and relays safety information to landing pilots.

"Permission to bingo," said the pilot.

A pause of static.

"Bingo to primary," said the Air Traffic Controller.

The primary diversion site for their current operating location was Camp Darby, a U.S. Army post near Pisa, Italy.

Kurt switched frequencies and relayed the information to his shop. The pilot had complained that his landing gear down and locked indicator wasn't lit. If the aircraft tried to land on the carrier and its gear collapsed, it could mean one hell of an accident. The pilot and flight deck crew had a much better chance of escaping injury if the aircraft landed on solid ground. Kurt surmised it was probably just a faulty indicator, but was pleased that the pilot wanted to take the safest route. He had experienced a few flight deck accidents, and they usually involved death.

"That's the Bingo King," Leo said.

"Ah, that's the guy," Kurt said. "The squeamish rookie you told me about." Leo thought he was afraid to land on the carrier, especially at night, because he diverted his aircraft to shore more than any other pilot he'd known. Maybe Leo was right.

CAMP DARBY, ITALY

The A-7J landed smoothly and taxied to just outside of an old U.S. Army hangar. There were six Blackhawk helicopters outside the hangar on the flight line.

The pilot brought his aircraft to a halt and cut power. He popped the canopy, collected his flight bag, and reached outside to the fuselage to release the steps and ladder. After climbing out and closing the canopy, he descended to the tarmac. Then he opened a large panel on the port side of the A-7, pulled a circuit-breaker on an avionics panel, and removed a large flight bag from between two black boxes. He quickly closed the panel and walked toward the hangar.

The inside of the hangar was dark; only a few red overhead lights attempted to illuminate the large space. The pilot set the bag he had taken from inside the panel and placed it under a work bench next to a 55-gallon drum of dirty rags. He then departed through the opposite side of the hangar and hiked toward Post Billeting for a room.

A man in civilian clothes emerged from the shadows within the hangar and picked up the flight bag. He unzipped the bag and felt inside. Satisfied, he zipped the bag and left the hangar. The man gently placed the bag in the trunk of his Fiat Uno and slowly drove off the Post.

5

BIRKWALD, GERMANY

The afternoon sun had made a rare January appearance, but had now passed over the Eifel Hills and was on its way to the Atlantic.

Jake drove his rental green Passat slowly into town, pulled to a stop more than four blocks from the Gasthaus Birkwald, turned off the lights and waited.

The streets were nearly vacant. The street lights had come on, what few there were, but they did little to brighten the small, six-block town. An occasional car would come bolting in from the countryside, quickly decelerate, and turn into a side street, a driveway, or the Gasthaus Birkwald.

Jake had just come from Charlie Johnson's apartment on the western outskirts of Koblenz. His second floor one bedroom sat within easy hearing distance of the junction of Autobahn 61 and 48, two very popular routes. Autobahn 48 runs pretty much north and south, which eventually leads to Trier, Germany's oldest city, before dumping into Luxembourg. Autobahn 61 heads toward Bonn to the North, and ends near Heidelberg in the south, with quick connections to Frankfurt. It would seem strange for Johnson to live such a long distance from the air base.

But driving wasn't measured in distance in Germany. Time was the important factor when there were no speed limits on the outer Autobahns. Jake had found out nothing new at Johnson's place. The Chevrolet he had shipped to Germany wasn't in his garage, and his landlord, who lived on the first floor, said he had not seen him for days. He allowed Jake to walk through his apartment to be sure. There was nothing in there to indicate he wouldn't be returning.

That was a bad sign. If he was on the run, selling computer chips, he wouldn't have left a thick wad of Deutschemarks lying on the nightstand.

On a Friday evening, strange cars entering Birkwald weren't uncommon. Jake knew that people came from kilometers away for the substantial Schnitzel served at Birkwald's only Gasthaus. Charlie Johnson was a big eater, and Birkwald was just a short distance out of his way before reaching Autobahn 48 on his way home. It was only five o'clock; most Germans ate much later, so Jake

knew the Gasthaus crowd would consist mostly of
beer drinkers. But it was about the right time that
Charlie would normally pass through. Jake didn't
expect to find Johnson, but maybe someone had
seen him recently.

After about ten minutes, he started his car and in
the darkness slowly pulled forward and onto the
cobblestone street—then turned his lights on. He
cruised past the Gasthaus. He was a bit cautious
after the morning encounter. Flying bullets,
although infrequent, always put him on edge.

He pulled the Volkswagen around the back of the
building to the guest parking area. It was a paved
area with unnumbered slots. There were only
twelve rooms in the Gasthaus, and only four occupied. The parking lot was equally vacant. He was
fairly certain that the three men in the Fiat van
wouldn't try to hit him at the Gasthaus. If they had
wanted to, they could have done that last night as he
slept soundly following the twelve-hour flight.

Jake entered through the back door with a guest
key. He pushed on a timed light that gave him two
minutes to reach the second floor and into his room
without going off.

This time he stood outside the door until the light
went out, and then he quietly slipped through the
door. Inside, Jake clicked on a small desk lamp and
scanned the one-room apartment. It had a full-size
bed, a small desk with a phone, a tiny stove and

refrigerator, and a bathroom with a tub, a sink and a water-preserving toilet. Everything appeared to be as he left it in the morning.

He had to call Portland. He punched in Milt Swenson's private number.

"Hello," came a voice on the other end.

"It's Jake."

"How's it going?" Milt asked.

"I went to Charlie Johnson's house. His landlord confirmed he's been gone for over five days. His car wasn't there either. I also talked with Blaise Parker at Bitburg. He doesn't know much except that Johnson has never been late for work in the ten years that he's known him."

"What about the police?" Milt asked.

"I haven't talked with the Polizei yet. I'll have them keep an eye out for his car. There aren't too many Chevys in Germany. They'll probably have me look at the morgues."

"Morgues?"

"Yeah, it's a possibility. I've got a friend who might be able to help me. I'll talk to him in the morning."

"What about the other tech reps?"

Jake wasn't sure how much to tell Milt. "Johnson told you one of his tech reps destroyed the bad chips, but according to Blaise Parker, Johnson got rid of them."

"Shit! Was Johnson selling them?"

"I don't know, but someone wants to keep me from finding out. Three men and a cute blonde tried to cut my stay in Germany short with enough lead to sink an aircraft carrier."

"What?"

"That's what I'm wondering. I just got here. Didn't even ask my first question. And someone tries blowing me away. How the hell'd they even know I was here?"

"Who do you think they're working for?"

"I don't have a clue. It could be a number of companies or governments," Jake said. "As you've said, the technology is an important breakthrough." Then Jake thought for a moment. "What if Johnson already sold the chips to someone else? Wouldn't whoever is buying these chips have everything they already need?"

"No! They can test the chip in an electronic environment and say, Yeah, this is one fast chip, but they still don't know how we make it so fast. I can't even tell you that, Jake. Only a handful of people at Teredata know that information."

"So, Charlie Johnson could be trying to sell something that isn't his?"

"Right! Charlie doesn't know enough to really hurt us. But we still can't allow these chips to be out in the market, because eventually someone could give away the rest of the formula."

"What next?"

"Find Charlie Johnson," Milt said. "We need to know who he's selling out to."

"Hey, Milt, I have someone shook and willing to blow me away," Jake said. "Do you want me to push further and see who I can shake from the bushes?"

"Don't take any extraordinary risks, Jake."

Jake was used to people asking him to take risks, and sometimes he even took them without being asked. But he didn't like people taking pot shots at him. "No problem, Milt. I can handle myself."

"I know! That's why I hired you."

There was a pause on the line.

"Give me a call if you find anything," Milt said.

"Sure." Jake hung up slowly.

His stomach growled as if on cue to him hanging up. He went to the small bathroom, splashed some water on his face, and then pulled his shirt off over his head and replaced it with a fresh one.

Back out in the main room, he looked at his automatic pistol in its brown leather shoulder holster draped over the back of a chair. Reluctantly, he left it behind.

Downstairs the bar was crowded, a prelude to Fasching, the German equivalent to Mardi Gras. The carved wood faces on the walls stared at Jake as he entered through the door and took a seat at the end of the bar with his back against the wall.

He drank a beer and ordered his meal from the bar. Then, in his best German, he started asking people if they'd seen Charlie Johnson, flashing the man's personnel photo at each person.

Finally, the owner, Brunner Weiss, motioned for him to have a seat at his table. Weiss was a stout and brusque man with the thick forearms of an ancient seaman. His pipe was notched permanently in the side of his mouth. He ruled over his realm from the family's corner booth. He never had to say a word. A nod of the head, a crooked pointing finger, or a blink of the eye would send the waitress in the proper direction as if a whip had cracked.

Jack took a seat across from the man, dropping his beer on the oak table. He studied Brunner. "Do you know Charlie Johnson?"

The old man nodded. "Ja, he hasn't been by in a while."

"I heard he came here a lot," Jake said.

Brunner nodded and sucked on his pipe.

"Did he have any friends here?"

The old man shook his head. "No, he sat alone most nights. Once in a while with me. He ate his meal, had a beer and some scotch, and then left. It was common with him. He isn't a talker."

Jake stayed in the bar for a few more beers before heading upstairs. But he learned nothing about Charlie Johnson.

* * *

Gunter Schecht waited outside the Gasthaus for a reply to his license plate inquiry. His cellular phone finally beeped and the woman on the other end informed him that only one car was registered to a rental company, the green VW Passat. "Danke, Gurt," he said, and then smiled.

Gunter was parked down the alley with only a tunnel vision of the Gasthaus parking lot through overhanging shrubbery and vines. He pulled a small transmitter from the glove box of his Mercedes, felt it over carefully in the darkness, and placed it in his leather coat pocket.

"Let's go Adolph, time to earn your keep." Gunter said to his long-haired dachshund that had been sleeping in the passenger's seat.

He clipped the leash to the dog's collar and entered the outside darkness for an evening stroll. Only a dim yellow light shone across the small parking lot. When Gunter reached the rear of Jake's car, he pulled back on the leash and Adolph stopped and sat. Gunter quickly placed the transmitter under the bumper of the VW, and then returned to his car.

"You're slipping, Jake Adams," he said softly to himself.

6

USS THEODORE ROOSEVELT

The sea was like a pool of crude oil and the bow cut through in darkness leaving only tranquil, flowing swells in its wake.

Flight operations had subsided for the evening, but a third of the ship's crew worked on through the night.

Kurt Lamar had left Leo Birdsong below decks with the intention of going to midnight chow. Kurt wanted to check on the Bingo King's flight records. He knew the Ready Room would be nearly empty by now.

Inside the Ready Room only a young sailor sat reclined in a high-back pilot's chair on his four-hour fire watch. He didn't even question Kurt when he came in through the metal hatch as if he owned the place, pulled the flight logs from under the counter, and flipped through them as if he'd been doing it all his life.

"So, you've got the watch, eh," Kurt said. "I used to hate this watch. The only thing that kept me awake was reading crotch novels. And then I'd get so horny I'd want to whack the weasel."

The sailor looked like he was right out of boot camp. He couldn't have been nineteen.

"I read MAD Magazine," the sailor said, not even looking up. "The parodies are totally excellent."

Kurt found what he was looking for. With a quick glance, he memorized all the dates and locations that Lt. Budd, the Bingo King, had flown. Could that be right? He flipped through a few other records. Leo had been right. Lt. Budd did divert a lot. He closed the files and headed toward the hatch.

"Hey, take it easy," Kurt said as he left.

The sailor just laughed and took a bite from a Snickers bar.

TRIESTE, ITALY

The late evening sky had cleared and the generous stars would have brought tears to Galileo's eyes. The faint headlights of a lone Fiat Uno sped down the Autostrada and exited at the Porto turn off. The street lights were blinking yellow, taunting the driver to maintain his speed. But the driver knew the Polizia would question the contents of the bag in his trunk, so he slowed his car to the speed limit.

He turned north along the seawall and marina, past the large shipping docks, to the fishing boats in a haggard part of town. He got out, put on a peacoat and a watch cap, and retrieved the bag from the trunk and started walking down the pier. A large rat scurried in front of him. Undaunted, he swung with his right foot to kick it. The rat simply dodged and burrowed under a stack of nets along the edge of the pier.

In the second to last slip, a three-man crew was making last minute preparations to shove off a small fishing boat from its moorings. The man with the bag hopped aboard without skill or grace and entered the small cabin.

The Italian-flagged Bella Donna departed on schedule as it did every morning. It slowly worked its way out of the port and past the break water as did scores of similar fishing boats working the Northern Adriatic waters of Italy and Slovenia. They all left with high hopes and returned with luck for some and barroom stories for others. The conflict of war over the years had hindered but never stopped the age-old fishing life.

The Bella Donna chugged slowly through the darkness, and the smooth water barely rippled past its stern. The sun was still a few hours away from appearing over the limestone hills. After about fifty minutes, the engine stopped and the inertia with it. The boat slackened to a halt and rocked for a minute before standing nearly dead in the water.

Within a few minutes, the red and green running lights of another fishing boat approached the Bella Donna from the southeast. Its engines slowed and it gingerly slid by within three feet. The man with the bag timed his jump just right, but landed wrong in the Slovenian-flagged fishing boat, and twisted his ankle, falling to the wooden deck in a bundle and with profuse swearing.

The Bella Donna continued on to its fishing waters. The Slovenian boat picked up speed and began its return trip to the port of Koper, Slovenia.

GENOA, ITALY

The large carrier came to a tired halt and dropped both anchors nearly a mile from the city of Genoa.

A few hours later, a small backpack over his shoulder, Kurt got onto a liberty launch and went ashore.

Once ashore, Kurt found the nearest cab, a yellow Fiat. "Parlare Inglese?" he asked the driver.

"Si, a little," the cabby said. "Where you go?"

"Christopher Columbus statue," Kurt said.

The cab jerked away from the curb and the cabby quickly flipped through the gears. Kurt wanted to tell the driver in his most pure Italian that he'd like to leave Italy in one piece.

He gazed at palm-lined boulevards passing by.

Parks and gardens were more green than he remembered.

The cab weaved in and out of traffic at a relentless pace. Kurt found himself holding on tightly to the door's arm rest and wondering why he hadn't remembered the crazy drivers.

The cab pulled up across the street from the statue of Genoa's hero and America's discoverer. Kurt paid the man and headed for the closest espresso bar. The streets were crowded with Saturday drivers, the sidewalks lined with afternoon shoppers. The sun was as high and bright as it could possibly be for that time of year. Kurt wished he had brought sunglasses. The night shift had sensitized his eyes to light.

The sun had also warmed Genoa to nearly forty-five degrees. Kurt sat at an outside table with coffee. He was nearly a half-hour early. It would give him time to observe the area, think, and develop his plan of action.

He tried to remember every word his boss had told him. His only written instructions were in case of a dire emergency; he would hand them over to the commanding officer. Even those instructions were ambiguous. They consisted only of a name and a number in the Washington, D.C. area, but looked official with the government seal. Kurt had tried the number himself before the Roosevelt had left Mayport, Florida. His boss answered with a simple hello. Kurt returned the hello, and they both laughed. His boss said he would have done the same thing—any good special agent would.

The oral instructions had become more uncertain with time. Kurt continually ran them through his mind to keep from losing the slightest detail. His shipboard duties were clear; review documents and question sailors. Those duties had led him to at least one guilty sailor named Shelby, and probably a squeamish pilot who was only buying time before jumping ship to a lucrative airline job. Well, Kurt would change his plans. He'd make sure the guy would become the friend of some huge Marine at Leavenworth.

His investigations ashore were to be even more intense than aboard the ship. That was unfortunate, for he really wanted to enjoy himself once in a while. The women were beautiful and the wine superb, and Kurt knew he would find little time for either. In Genoa his contact would be an American.

Kurt spotted a man with blue Levis, untied Nike basketball shoes, and enough camera equipment to drown him if he fell in water over three-feet deep, walking up the sidewalk. He began firing off shot-after-shot of the Columbus statue. He fit the description.

Kurt finished his espresso and scooted between traffic. He walked up to within five feet of the camera-happy man and looked up at the stone face of Columbus.

"Do you think he was the first to discover America?" Kurt asked, not looking at the man.

The man continued to focus his zoom lens on Christopher's face. "No! The Vikings had him beat by a long shot," came a soft woman's voice with an Italian accent.

Kurt quickly turned to take a closer look at his contact, and sure enough she was a woman. And not just a woman, but an extremely attractive woman with her hair tucked up under a dark blue beret. Kurt moved closer, and the woman handed him one of her cameras and kissed him on both cheeks. They both started walking down the sidewalk.

"Kurt?" the woman asked.

"Yes...Kurt Lamar."

"I'm Toni Contardo."

Kurt didn't know what to think of this woman. She sounded more Italian than American.

"So, how long have you worked Italy?" Kurt asked.

"Actually, I work most of Europe," Toni said. "But my specialty is Italy for obvious reasons. You might say I prefer the beaches and the sun of the Riviera over the Alps and the lowlands. An assignment to England would really piss me off. How about you?"

"I'm from Wisconsin," Kurt said. "So trees and lakes are just fine with me. To tell you the truth, I've never been to England, but I probably wouldn't like it either."

Kurt's NIS boss, Captain James Murphy, had given him the subjects that he was to discuss at first, from Columbus to a mutual disdain for England. After that he was on his own.

"So, what do ya know, kid?" Toni asked.

Well for one thing, Kurt thought, I'm twenty-five...hardly a kid. Besides, you look only about thirty yourself. "First of all, who do you work for?" Kurt asked.

"Same as you. Murphy," she said. "You might say I'm on loan to the Navy. Kind of a designated hitter."

"But, who do you normally work for?" Kurt probed.

"Okay, kid, I guess you have a right to know a little more," Toni said. "I'm CIA."

"I see. Has Murphy briefed you on how much we know?" Kurt asked.

"Yes. In fact I flew to Washington to discuss it with him," Toni said. "I want to assure you that you're the only person aboard the Roosevelt who knows what's going on. We just couldn't trust the on-board NIS team. We don't know who knows what, so we didn't want you ending up as shark-bait half way across the Atlantic."

"Well, I sure as hell appreciate that," Kurt said.

"So, what have you found out, kid?" Toni asked again.

"I'm sure Petty Officer First Class Shelby Taylor is involved," Kurt said. "He's been ordering parts and failing to document anything. He's misplaced technical manuals for days only to have them show up later. I think he's the lowest man on the rung though; he doesn't have the brains to be anything more."

"What's missing?" Toni asked.

"Computer components mostly, but from some of our newest avionics packages with some pretty hot chips," Kurt said. "The Europeans don't even have this technology."

He walked beside her down a sidewalk toward a garden with palm trees and ivy-lined walls. Flowers would have been everywhere in the summer.

"Shit! That's what we were afraid of," Toni said. "What's he doing with it?"

"I'm pretty sure he's loading it somewhere on one of our A-7s," Kurt said. "Then the pilot diverts from the carrier to shore and downloads the stuff at that time."

"There's a pilot involved too?" Toni asked. "Who is it, kid?"

"He's a lieutenant in the squadron. Named Budd...Stephen Budd. The other pilots have nick-named him Wiseguy." Kurt said. "You know Budweiser."

"Cute. Why do you suspect him?"

"I've gone over his flight records. He diverts his aircraft a lot. In fact, he's done it twice already on this cruise."

"But..."

"Wait! That's not all. Last night he bingoed to Pisa," Kurt added.

"But are you sure that's how the stuff is getting off the ship?" Toni asked. "I mean I trust you, but are you sure?"

Kurt thought for a minute. Christ, what did this woman want, a fuckin' signed confession? "No, I'm not positive. But I think we should check into it further," Kurt said. "Lt. Budd is stuck in Pisa for at least five days, since we don't leave Genoa until Wednesday, and flight ops won't commence until probably Thursday."

"Wait a minute, kid. What's this we shit?" Toni asked. "I work Italy alone."

"Well, I've got a four-day pass, and you need me," Kurt said. "I could check out the A-7 to see if anything is really wrong with it, before someone has a chance to mess with it."

Toni considered that. "So, kid...you ever see Pisa on a Saturday night?"

"No."

"Let's go."

7

WIESBADEN, GERMANY

Jake pulled into the Kaiser driveway, where red bricks were lined with small pines and yews. The grass was a luscious green. The white stucco house was accented by large exposed swatches of dark brown timber. The Kaiser's neighborhood reminded Jake of some of Portland's southern suburbs.

Gazing at the house, Jake remembered the first time he met the Kaisers. He had just resigned his commission in the Air Force and had remained in Germany for an extended vacation. He was still trying to decide who to work for.

A number of stateside companies had offered him employment due to his security clearance and military knowledge, but none of them could offer him overseas locations. And he wasn't ready to leave just yet. Then the CIA offered him a job that included stationing in Germany, but also working in Italy and other European countries. They wanted him mostly for his computer skills.

Jake jumped at the opportunity and took ninety days to travel Europe before going through his CIA training. On one of his travels, Jake was waiting for a train late one evening in Frankfurt when three Skinheads began harassing a young man and woman. The train station dock was isolated and dark, and Jake was the only person who could help. Jake was going to let the man deal with them, but then the Skinheads pulled knives. The Skinheads didn't even notice Jake walking up behind them. Jake took one guy out with a kidney punch, and another with a roundhouse kick to the jaw. The third decided to run.

Walter and Edeltrud Kaiser had been extremely grateful to Jake. They had asked him to dinner at their home in Wiesbaden, and he had accepted. His trip to Hamburg had to wait a day, but it was a small price to pay for a friendship that was nurtured over the years while Jake worked in Germany.

Edeltrud answered the door with a puzzled look on her face. She obviously recognized him, but he had changed, with his hair longer.

"Jake?" She grabbed his hand, pulled him inside the house, and gave him a big hug. "What are you doing here?"

"Hey, it sounds like you're not glad to see me?" Jake said. "I'm here on business, but I thought I'd mix a little pleasure in with my visit...that is if Walt isn't home."

"Jake, you haven't changed. Still have that dirty mind." She walked into the living room and offered Jake a chair. "Walter," she yelled upstairs. "Come see who's here."

Walter came down the marble staircase still in his white socks and buttoning his black stone-washed jeans. He was nearly as shocked as Edeltrud, but then Jake always had a penchant for showing up unexpectedly.

"Jake, I thought you went back to America for good," he said, his strong voice resonating down the stark stairs.

"Well, I thought I did too. Remember the last time I wrote telling you I had started my own business?"

"Ja, Ja," Walter nodded.

"Well a company in Portland hired me to find one of its employees over here."

"I'll get you men a beer so you can talk," Edeltrud said.

Jake watched her leave the room. She was even more beautiful than he remembered. Her straight blonde hair flowed over broad shoulders as her long tight legs propelled her like a ballerina.

"You're a lucky guy, Walt," Jake said. "You have a good job, a nice house, a beautiful wife and child...you should be very happy."

"I am a lucky guy, Jake. In fact, I have a new job.

I've been moved up into the investigative branch. No more drunk drivers."

That had been the worst of Walt's Polizei duties.

"Are you with the Federal Department here?" Jake asked.

"No," he said. "Criminal Investigations."

Jake smiled. "Good. Maybe you can help me then."

"I'll try."

* * *

Gunter's Mercedes had no problem keeping up with Jake's VW Passat. He sat two blocks from the Kaiser house playing the waiting game; waiting for Jake to make his next move, and waiting for his contact to call him back on his cellular phone. When it did fi-nally buzz, Mozart's concerto came to an abrupt squelch, and Gunter listened carefully and said only "Danke." The soft-voiced woman told Gunter who lived in the white stucco house. He stroked the long hair on his dog Adolph and smiled.

* * *

"Walt, the guy I'm looking for has been missing for almost a week now," Jake said.

Just then Edeltrud came in with two large beers.

"First one's on me," she said. "You'll have to fend for yourselves with the rest. Jakob wants me." She scooted up the stairs.

There was a long silence.

"What's wrong, Jake?"

Jake turned slowly and studied Walt. "I need your help."

"Sure. How can I help you, Jake?"

Jake went to the window and pulled back the patterned sheers. "Do you still have your computer set up the way I showed you?" Jake asked, still looking out the window.

"Yes. But why?"

"I need you to access the Polizei database," Jake said.

Walt paused for a moment. "That would be easy," he said, "but I can't breach the trust of my department."

"It's nothing like that. I just want you to run the license plates of this guy in a Mercedes who's been following me all morning."

Walt got up from the sofa and went to the window. "Is that all? That's no problem. Is he out there?"

"Yes, he's parked about a block down the street. He planted a tracking receiver on my car last night."

"Why don't I just go ask him?" Walt asked.

"No. I want the upper hand."

Walt took the license number and went upstairs. Jake had never told the Kaisers he worked for the CIA. Maybe that was a mistake. The man following him in the Mercedes was probably one of the three who filled his rental full of holes.

After a few minutes upstairs, Walt came down with a piece of paper. "A guy named Gunter Schecht, currently living in Bonn," Walt said.

"Shit!" Jake had known Gunter Schecht quite well. He worked for German Federal Intelligence and they had crossed paths while Jake worked for the CIA.

"You know him?" Walt asked.

"Sort of," Jake said, taking a long sip of beer. "We met a few times in Bonn." Gunter had a reputation within German Intelligence as a bit of a rogue. He was a proficient agent; almost too proficient. But Jake had a hard time believing German Intelligence wanted him dead.

Jake tried to change the subject. "Walt, thanks for the help and the beer. I should probably get going. I've still got to talk with the Polizei in Koblenz about my missing person."

"Give me his name," Walt said. "I'll do a computer check and keep an eye out for the guy."

"Thanks, Walt." Jake gave him a data sheet on Charlie Johnson, including copies of fingerprints and information on Johnson's Chevy.

Jake said goodbye to Walt and promised to come back before heading back to the States. But now he had to know why Gunter Schecht was following him.

The Passat cranked over with authority. Jake had
rented this car for its large size, but also for its
speed. It wasn't as quick off the line as a smaller car
like the GTI, but the top end was greater, and the
stability at high speed far surpassed the lighter
weight cars.

He drove out of the Kaiser neighborhood and
entered a crosstown Autobahn. Gunter was still a
few cars back. Then he turned North on Autobahn
60 toward Koblenz and picked up speed. Traffic
was light; just enough to make the drive interesting.
After he shifted into fifth gear, Jake looked at his
speedometer; 200 KPH. It had been a while, but
Jake made the conversion to MPH in his head. Not
many cars wandering into the fast lane this
Saturday, Jake thought.

The small cars in the right lane flew by as if
standing still. When a car did foolishly appear in
Jake's lane, he would flash his lights far enough in
advance to warn them back into the right lane.
Gunter's Mercedes persisted in Jake's rear view
mirror. He expected no less.

The two cars hastened toward Koblenz at well
over 120 MPH. Koblenz got nearer by the minute.
Jake wanted Gunter to think he was heading back
toward the Gasthaus Birkwald.

In Koblenz, Jake slowed just enough to exit South
onto Autobahn 48 toward Trier. He quickly picked
up speed again. A large blue sign prompted for an

exit two kilometers ahead. Just before the exit, Jake moved in front of a line of cars, slid onto the off-ramp and quickly decelerated. Gunter had just barely accomplished a similar maneuver and was still behind Jake coming down the ramp. Jake skidded his Passat to a quick stop, tires squealing, jumped from the driver's seat and pointed his CZ-75 at the Mercedes as it too was skidding to a halt just behind Jake's car.

Gunter must have recognized Jake. He got out of his car and put up his hands. They both smiled but said nothing.

Finally, Gunter broke the ice. "Still using that Czech garbage, Jake?" he asked.

"Yeah, and I see you still favor bumper drops," Jake said.

"I thought you quit the CIA," Gunter said. "Yet here you are back in Germany."

Jake glanced at the Mercedes. "I thought German Intelligence, and I realize that's a contradiction in terms, was partial to Beemers."

"I retired. And my pension was good to me."

Jake was still pointing his pistol at Gunter. He couldn't be sure if Gunter had a gun, but he had to assume he did.

"You've also put on some weight," Jake said.

"Why don't you put down the gun, Jake?" Gunter said. "We've known each other too long to point guns at each other."

Jake stood in silence. He knew Gunter hated to lose at anything. By discovering the transmitter, Jake had nearly emasculated him.

Gunter shook his head.

"All right, Gunter, let's cut the bullshit," Jake said. "We can either stand out here and wait for the sun to set and freeze our asses off, or you can tell me who the fuck you work for and why you were tailing me."

Neither said a word. The wind picked up, and Jake felt the chill across his exposed neck.

"Jake, you know the rules," Gunter said. "I can't tell you that." Gunter stood with his hands and arms extended as though standing before a mugger and declaring he had no money.

Jake knew he was getting nowhere. But he had accomplished what he wanted. Gunter now knew Jake was on to him.

"Here Gunter," Jake said, pulling a small transmitter from his left pocket and throwing it to Gunter. "Next time, have your dog actually take a piss."

Gunter stood next to his Mercedes, his hands cradling the transmitter. He was exposed to the rapidly cooling elements and the even cooler embarrassed realization of failure.

Jake got back into his Passat and drove away. Gunter didn't follow him this time. Jake didn't think he would.

8

PISA, ITALY

The drive had been as a majestic work of art with exhibits of marble on the face of the Apuan Alps near Carrara. Kurt thought the mountains looked ideal for skiing, but Toni assured him that it would be painful skiing down sheer marble cliffs.

The weather was also impressive. The crystal blue sky allowed the Mediterranean to remain nearly transparent and the rocky coast beneath unobscured.

Kurt had remained speechless for most of the drive. He had listened carefully for anything that could have been important, but more significantly, he had observed Toni carefully. She was as much a work of art as the marble cliffs above Carrara or the ocean to the West. With her hair out from under her beret, her black curly locks flowing over her shoulders, her beauty multiplied with each kilometer.

Pisa has no skyline. The Leaning Tower stands

out more from a distance than from near. Galileo's observatory overwhelmed Kurt. It was a landmark that he had seen a thousand times on TV, had evaded his previous visits, and now it was passing by to his left as though just another building in just another city.

Toni didn't even seem to notice the Tower or anything else around her. She was more content with singing along with a Verdi aria on the radio of her Alfa Romeo. She knew the words, and she wasn't half bad as far as Kurt could tell.

"So, kid, what do you know about Lt. Budd?" she asked, barely breaking stride with the aria.

For some reason, he had failed to realize the significance of that question. He had completed a sketchy background investigation of Lt. Budd, considering his resources, but just now realized that Lt. Budd also knew who he was, or at least who he was pretending to be. The lieutenant didn't really know him personally, but he knew that he was in his squadron and could become suspicious if he saw Kurt.

"He's from Florida," Kurt said. "Pretty standard Navy pilot...cocky, arrogant, flies hard and parties hard. Even though they call him the Bingo King, I think he only diverts to transfer information. His records show he won the bombing competition last time."

"So, we should be able to find him in the Officers'

Club tonight?" Toni asked.

"You can find him at the O'Club. He knows me, remember?"

"That's right," Toni agreed. "And you take a look at the airplane."

"Aircraft," Kurt corrected. "The Air Force has airplanes, the Navy has aircraft."

Toni shifted her eyes toward Kurt. Her beauty had probably allowed her to be right most of the time, Kurt thought. Most men would grant her that indiscretion in an attempt to seduce her mind if not her body.

The signs to the Army Post guided Toni's Alfa Romeo to a gate occupied by Italian and U.S. Army soldiers. Toni pulled out an ID card that looked somewhat strange to Kurt. The design was similar to his Navy IDs, but it was a color he had never seen before.

"What kind of ID is that?" he asked, after they were waved on post.

She shifted into second gear and then handed him her ID. It indicated she was a Public Health Nurse.

"You, a nurse? Give me a break," Kurt said.

"Why do you find that so hard to believe?"

He had to think fast now. "I mean you could be a nurse, but ah...it's a brilliant cover," he finally said smiling. "I mean who would suspect that a nurse is CIA?"

"Quit now before you dig yourself a deeper hole."

She drove to a small park on the East side of the post and stopped. She had made her way through the ambiguous streets as though she had been there before. The park was fairly large with huge evenly-spaced pine trees the only vegetation. The grills, picnic tables, and electrical outlets gave the place away as a summer campsite. With a glance to the opposite side of the site, it was clear why Toni had parked where she did. The sign in front of a building prompted: Visiting Officer Quarters.

Toni cranked her seat down to a reclined position, took off her seat belt, and closed her eyes. "I'm gonna catch a few Zs," she said. "I have a feeling I may be up late tonight getting a sailor drunk and taking advantage of him."

The sun still had nearly an hour before sinking out of sight to the West. Kurt needed to look at the A-7 before darkness so he wouldn't concern Army security. He figured as long as he stayed away from their Blackhawks they wouldn't care what he did to the A-7.

Kurt unzipped the small backpack he had brought with him from the ship, and pulled out a green flight suit. He unfolded it and laid it next to him. Then he pulled off his black boots and began pulling the oversize suit over his clothes. When the car began to rock, Toni opened her eyes and looked at Kurt with disbelief.

"What in the hell are you doing?" she asked.

"Well, you don't expect me to waltz out onto the flight line in civvies do you? The flight suit is all I could fit in my bag."

She shook her head as she closed her eyes and rested her shiny black hair against the head rest.

Kurt set a time to meet her later that evening. He thought she acknowledged him with a nod, but wasn't totally sure. He left her in her world of Verdi, nonetheless, as he closed the door and walked toward the flight line.

Walking out to the flight line with confidence, Kurt stayed well clear of the Army Blackhawks. When he got to the A-7J, he popped open the port access panel and gently lowered it on its hinges. Immediately he noticed something was wrong. The pre-set circuit breakers were not aligned properly. The pilot should have accessed the panel after flight to see if he had set them properly; if he truly had an in-flight emergency. If he had, then he would have reset them all to the standard in position. But instead, they were all out in their normal flight configuration. Normally, the technicians reset the circuit break-ers, but it's a standard policy for the pilot to do it if they divert. He may have forgotten, but he might have left them this way to show that the landing gear circuit breaker wasn't actuated.

He couldn't apply power to the A-7 to check it over further, so he had to rely on his intuition and make the assumption that Lt. Budd had passed some

information. Kurt knew some of what was transferred and who transferred it, but he still didn't
know why and to whom. Hopefully, Toni could help
fill in the blanks.

Darkness had started to make it dangerous for
Kurt to remain any longer. He closed the panel and
walked back toward the car.

* * *

Toni found the Wiseguy in the O'Club. He wasn't
hard to find. Lt. Budd had arrived in his flight suit.
Since he couldn't leave the post dressed like that, he
would have had to either buy a full set of clothes or
remain on post. He obviously chose to remain.

Toni had replaced the basketball shoes with
Italian black leather pumps. She knew her black
denim jeans accentuated her buttocks when she
tucked her white silk shirt in.

She walked through the bar with great aplomb,
ensuring that all could see what she had to offer.
Her hair shifted softly side to side over her shoulders with each step she took. She sat at the bar, two
stools down from her target, the only person in the
bar with a U.S. Navy flight suit, and ordered a glass
of Chianti. When her wine came, Lt. Budd put his
money on the bar and paid for it. The bait was presented, the hook set, and all that remained was to
reel him in. Toni could tell that he had a tremendous

head start on his drinking. She would be more cautious.

"Grazie," Toni said, hoping he'd still wonder if she was Italian.

"Hi! I'm Stephen Budd," he said with a slur as he moved one chair closer to Toni. "What's your name?"

This guy is really a piece of work, she thought. "Toni."

"Do you work on post?"

"No! I'm just visiting from Vicenza," she lied.

Lt. Budd looked at Toni, unsure what to think. His eyes were undressing her, but his words weren't coming. "Do you work there?" he asked.

"Yes. I'm a nurse at the Army post," she lied again.

"You're a nurse?" he asked with disbelief.

"Yes," she said, turning toward the bar to take a sip of wine.

"I'm sorry. It's not that I don't believe you. It's just that you're so...so beautiful," he apologized.

"Forget it," Toni said. "I hear that a lot. I mostly help deliver babies. Those soldiers don't seem to understand the correlation between sex and children," she added. She laid on the Italian accent to sound even more sexy.

"Have you been in Italy long?" Lt. Budd asked.

"About two years."

"Will you be at Darby long? I mean, maybe you

could show me around," he said, still slurring.

She sipped while he gulped. Shortly, they left together. Toni was sure she could handle him drunk or sober, but drunk was easier. His memory of her would also be blurred in the morning.

When they got to his room, he opened the door with great difficulty. Toni scanned the room for anything interesting. It was pretty empty. He wasn't planning on getting lucky—empty beer bottles and a half-empty bag of pretzels cluttered a small table by the window. The bed wasn't made. She noticed a small brown refrigerator in the corner of the room.

Lt. Budd sat down on the edge of the bed.

Toni strutted slowly to the refrigerator, every movement of her hips exactly as planned, every swish of hair perfectly choreographed. She bent over at the waist as she opened the small brown refrigerator door, and lingered there with her buttocks pointing directly at Lt. Budd. She pulled out two beers, opened both of them, and placed two small pills in his bottle. She looked over her shoulder. He hadn't missed a move. She turned slowly, pulled up a small chair, sat down on the edge, and slowly spread her legs invitingly.

"Let's have one more drink before we have mad passionate sex," she said, handing him his beer.

He eagerly took the beer from her and chugged about half of it. He lifted one leg to pull off a boot, but only got it half way off before the drugs took effect and he passed out flat on his back.

"Works every time," Toni said softly.

She quickly rifled through his desk drawers and flight bag. Just normal items. The room was clean. Then she looked at Lt. Budd, a contorted smirk on his face, in his Navy flight suit with the thousand zippers. One by one she checked each pocket. Finally, she found a small piece of paper with a number on it. She knew immediately what she had found. That was awfully careless. A pilot can remember hundreds of details, but can't even memorize one sequence of numbers?

* * *

Kurt was waiting in Toni's Alfa Romeo. She opened the door and climbed behind the wheel.

"It's about time," Kurt said.

"Ah, you miss me, kid?"

"No! I just have some information I want to share with you."

"Well I've got something too, but since you've been waiting so patiently, you go first."

"I checked out the A-7," Kurt said. "All of the avionics circuit breakers were at normal in-flight settings."

"So you've learned nothing, then."

Damn you can be a cold one, Kurt thought. Why not twist the knife after you stab me in the back.

"Actually, I've learned quite a bit. The settings shouldn't be normal. The pilot is supposed to reset all circuit breakers if he diverts. Sure he could have messed up and for-gotten, but I think he left them that way in case anyone wanted to check. If those are normal, then we have to do a complete electrical check of the system—from the sensor under the landing gear all the way up to the cockpit panel. That takes a lot of time."

"Good work, kid. I found something also. A telephone number."

"You spent that much time with him, and all you got was a telephone number?" Kurt asked.

"This could be important," she said. "It's a Rome number. I tried to call it, but there was no answer. So it could be a place of business. I'll have it traced in the morning."

Kurt thought for a moment. "But he has to know more. I'm sure we can make him talk."

She smiled.

The evening was young, and Lt. Budd would be under the influence of the drug for quite some time. It would be easy to get more information.

9

VARAZDIN, CROATIA

The drive through the Medvednica hills to the land beyond the mountains had been picturesque but mostly unobserved by the man with the green flight bag. He was surviving on adrenaline and nothing more. His swollen left ankle throbbed with pain from the jump to the fishing boat that morning.

The bag had now become an appendage. After reaching the old city, he walked with a limp along a narrow cobblestone street until he arrived at a Baroque house with a high metal gate out front. The gate creaked loudly as he entered and closed it behind him. The stone sidewalk was smooth from centuries of rain and human treading. The mansion had once been the palace of a wealthy aristocrat, but was now far from aristocratic. A once splendid garden was now overrun with weeds and vines and in dire need of a tender.

As the man with the bag reached the first brick step to the long front stairs, the large decorative wooden door opened. He entered and was led through a wide corridor by an old hunched-over woman who also walked with a limp. She showed him to a large study where two walls were completely lined with books. He sat down on a leather chair that had seen better days. Think plaster walls were chalk white. Oak trim that lined the windows, the base boards, and along the edge of the ceiling needed a coat of varnish. Some of the books were the only new items in the room. Many were old, passed down for generations probably, but a number were new and in many different languages.

In a few minutes, where the only sound had been that of a pendulum clock, a slight man with silver hair shuffled in and sat behind a large oak desk. His gray wool suit was of high Western standards. Italian.

Isaac Lebovitz looked at the man with the bag and collected his thoughts on how he wanted to begin his negotiations. He tapped his forehead with his finger in time with the clock on his desk. "I see you have the bag, Mr. Dalton," Isaac said. "I'm sure we can come to a reasonable agreement."

"Please, call me Jason," said the man with the bag. "I've come a long way and I'm tired, but we must take care of business."

"I agree," Isaac said. "Patience is not an American

virtue. Let's see what you've got."

Dalton unzipped the bag and removed a computer disk, a small wooden box, and a stack of papers. He stood up and plopped the papers on the oak desk.

"These are schematics and diagrams that will be helpful to your engineers and developers," Dalton said. He stood with his hands on his hips waiting for a response.

Isaac leafed through the pages quickly as a child tears into his toys at Christmas anticipating each new one and then swiftly moving on to the next. When finished, he looked up. "These will be very helpful. What else do you have for me?"

"The disk is also significant," Dalton said. "I got them from a different source. They correspond to international marketing strategy and economic forecasts, and could be even more helpful than any technical advantages you may receive."

This was a welcome bonus for Isaac. He had asked for this type of information, but wasn't sure if it was possible this soon. His Hungarian government had moved too slowly, frustrating him. He considered himself patient to a fault. But the time for patience had passed.

"I'll have my people look at the disk before we can come up with an overall price," Isaac said. "Could your people get the chips?"

Dalton opened the small wooden box. It was lined

with layers of foam with cut-outs where the chips were inset. With the precision of a surgeon, he pulled a small chip out of the foam with his thumb and forefinger. He handed the small chip to Isaac.

Isaac accepted the chip in the palm of his hand. He then pulled out a magnifying glass and viewed the chip as carefully as an Amsterdam diamond dealer examined a gem.

"This is the fast one you talked about?" Isaac asked, not an expert but trying not to be totally computer illiterate.

"Yes! Your company could become the Intel of Eastern Europe with this chip," Dalton said. "And the last of the information, of course."

Isaac smiled. That's what he wanted more than anything now. His headquarters was in Budapest, but once he shifted into full production, he planned on having facilities in all of Eastern Europe with marketing throughout Europe and the United States.

"Jason, you must be tired. My maid has prepared a room for you upstairs. Why don't you get some rest before we negotiate."

Dalton nodded in agreement, picked up his bag, which now only contained a few extra clothes and toiletries, and retired to the comfort of a feather bed.

* * *

Isaac Lebovitz rocked back and forth in his high back leather chair. The clock on his desk ticked loudly without bother to him. His hearing was diminished from the constant bombardment of German artillery during the long campaigns of World War II. His large stone house, passed down from generation to generation, survived that great war and many before. Even the scourge of Communism had not crumbled its foundation in poverty.

The information that Jason Dalton was selling far surpassed Isaac's expectations. Even though his English was far from perfect, having been taught first by American soldiers and then at Budapest University, he could tell that the management and marketing informa-tion could transform his company into a great East European conglomerate.

Isaac knew that this was the time to bring back the respect of his family name. Not only the wealth, but the esteem.

As the wooden door to the study opened, Isaac swiveled in his chair to see who had broken his thoughts. The maid had left for the day, so it could only be the American businessman.

"I feel like a new man," Dalton said as he limped in and took a seat. "Are you ready to make me an offer?"

Isaac studied the American. "Yes...but how is your ankle?"

"Sprained, I think. I guess I'm not much of a sailor."

They looked at each other as though a chess match had just begun—neither flinching an eyelid, the clock still ticking loudly.

Isaac broke the silence. "While you slept, I had my men check over the chips and the documents. We can use this information, but I need more."

"That's not a problem," Dalton assured him.

"The chips are impressive...better than anything I've seen in Hungary or through other sources."

"The Russians don't even have these yet," Dalton boasted.

That brought a smile to Isaac's face. For most of his adult life his country had languished in the backdrop of left-over technology from the former Soviet Union. Now he had a chance to push his country forward into a market-based economy with high technology.

"Not even the Russians?"

"No! In fact, the Germans and the Brits have shifted their emphasis to transputer technology instead of enhancing current computer technology. So, I'm certain they don't have a chip this fast either."

"Even if they do, that's not the point!" Isaac said. "More than just the technology, I want the Eastern Europeans to have what Western Europe has had for decades. The Russians denied us that affluence after the Great War."

Dalton rose from his chair and walked over to the book shelves. Some of the titles would have surely been banned at one time or another in Moscow or Budapest, but Yugoslavia, and more recently Croatia, had allowed more freedom.

"I want to help you and your country, but I need proper compensation," Dalton said. He paused for a second and then turned and looked directly at Isaac. "I don't want cash, at least not initially. I want a partnership."

Isaac raised his brows. "A partnership? This is a surprise. I assumed you would ask for cash. Isn't that what most Americans want?" he asked.

"I'm not your normal American!" Dalton blared, his hands talking as much as his mouth. "I like to take risks, gamble. If the stakes are high, so much the better. I've worked for a lot of companies that failed to take risks, and most of them are out of business. The strong ones, those that see an opportunity and grasp it, survive and thrive."

There was an uncomfortable pause as they stared each other down. Isaac finally smiled. "I like your attitude. The Communists told us for so long that we were nothing without them...we actually began to believe them. Most of the older people accepted the inevitability of Communism. Only the young people of your generation in our country decided that enough was enough. They want more for themselves and their families. The more they know about the West, the more they want to be like Western people."

"Have you read all of these books?" Dalton asked.

"Yes! It was either that or watch the latest techniques in collective farming on the television."

"Ah, I see."

He wasn't like a normal American, Isaac thought. The patience he was now showing was either a reflection of the sleep he had just received, or perhaps a true desire for a commitment. Nevertheless, it was refreshing.

"Would you like a drink, Jason?"

"Yes, please. Whatever you're having."

Isaac Lebovitz pulled a wooden panel down from behind his desk revealing a well-stocked bar. After a few seconds of mental debate, he selected a fine French Cognac and poured two snifters to the right level.

Dalton accepted his glass and twirled the contents allowing the aroma to rise to his nose. "Exceptional...as our partnership will be."

The growth of a new aristocracy pervaded the scarcely lit room with the warmth of a fine French brandy. And the clock slowly ticked on the desk with a patience that was soon to be overcome by the will of an old aristocracy with new ideas. Isaac sat back in his chair, smiled, and tapped the side of his forehead with his finger.

10

BONN, GERMANY

Jake Adams eased his rental Passat against the curb and cut the lights and engine. He had thrown Gunter Schecht a similar transmitter to the one he had found on his car. It allowed him to remain easily undetected far behind Gunter's Mercedes.

Thick dark clouds shrouded the gold-glassed headquarters building of Bundenbach Electronics in eerie darkness. Only a few lights on the top floor remained lit.

Gunter Schecht punched his card into a slot and a mechanical arm rose for him. He drove slowly into the underground parking ramp marked employees only.

Maybe Jake finally had a break in the case. He knew who tried to kill him, and now who that man worked for. But what type of work did Gunter do for Bundenbach Electronics? He made a mental note to check into that company late.

* * *

Gunter Schecht would have to face his boss alone. He used his credit card key to enter the executive elevator. He got off on the top floor and hesitated by a window overlooking the Rhine. The green grass that lined its banks were a stark contrast to the frozen Eifel Hills he had experienced yesterday morning.

Gunter yanked his pants up higher, tucked his shirt in, and snapped the bottom of his black leather coat. He entered the four-digit cipher code on an unmarked door, opened the door, and closed it behind him. The door led to a small, short passageway with a locked door on the other end. The walls were bare and the compartment reeked of stale cigarettes. Like all other passageways in the building, this one was monitored by closed circuit cameras. He looked up at the camera and tried to smile.

He knocked on the door three times. He couldn't remember if it was supposed to be three or four times, but he figured he was being watched anyway so why would it matter?

A large man, larger than Gunter's driver, opened the door. He said nothing as Gunter passed him. The man closed the door and propped himself against the wall next to it, guarding the exit.

Gunter sat down in one of two mahogany-red, leather chairs with gold studs. He wondered why under such tense circumstances he still found time to admire the quality of the textured leather, and the almost fresh fragrance it maintained. The boss must have smoked exclusively in that hallway, he thought.

"Would you like a beer, Gunter?" the boss asked, as he got up from behind his heavy wooden desk and went to a small cooler built into a bar in the corner of the large office.

"Yes, please. I could use one," Gunter said.

Even though Gunter knew he was the best man working special projects in the company, he also knew that no one was indispensable. The boss opened the large bottle of Bitburger Beer as if he were trying to seduce a Fraulein. His dark burgundy suit was tailored perfectly. He looked at Gunter with his light blue eyes like a hunter views his prey just before pulling the trigger. Gunter accepted the beer and took a large gulp.

"You know, Gunter, this project is the most important one we have going right now," the boss said, sitting down again. "In fact, it could change the way we do business for the next ten years. Only the strong will survive."

"I understand the consequences," Gunter said.

Gunter knew that his prior association with Jake Adams was important to the boss. His inside knowledge of Jake made him the perfect man for the job.

He would get the job done—whatever was asked of him. He retired from German Intelligence with a small pen-sion when Bundenbach Electronics offered him a substantial pay increase. But this had been the first time Herr Bundenbach had asked him to dissuade someone.

"You came a little too close to killing Adams," the boss said.

"He won't die that easily," Gunter explained.

"A little too close," the boss repeated.

Gunter stretched back in his chair and took another long gulp of beer.

"I know you're a professional, Gunter, but will you find it difficult to kill Jake Adams at some point?" the boss asked.

"No!" Gunter said callously. "Do you want us to continue?" Gunter looked at the boss for approval.

The boss glared at him, his hands in front of him as if praying. "Let's keep Adams alive for a while and see what he's up to," he said. "I need to know what he knows. Does he still work for the CIA? Find out! If he is working for Teredata, like we originally thought, then he'll have to go, of course. I can't have government agents dragging us down, and I won't be undercut or underbid by anyone. There's too much at stake. Our research staff has still not figured out the chips. So I still need Charlie Johnson for a while."

Gunter looked up quickly to the boss. "I thought

we had everything from him?"

"Let me do the thinking," the boss said. "Just find out about Adams for now."

"No problem." Gunter finished his beer.

* * *

Jake was just about to turn the keys to start his Passat when he recognized a man in an old blue BMW less than a block away. He thought his eyes were deceiving him, but at that distance he couldn't be mistaken. The BMW belonged to a German customs officer named Herbert Kline. Herb worked out of Bonn, at least he did the last time Jake saw him, so it should have been no coincidence that he was there. But why was he sitting out in front of Bundenbach Electronics? Kline had a reputation, earned or not, of being less than efficient. He was old enough and had worked long enough within the customs agency to be a secure, tenured bureaucrat. The agency couldn't fire him, and the criminals would rather keep him around alive with his incompetence than replace him with a talented newcomer. At least that had always been the rumor. With the limited exposure Jake had with him, the rumors were unfounded.

Jake needed to leave undetected. He had parked with the nose of his car just in front of a road that ended on his. Starting the car, he made a quick right

turn onto the side street. The Passat slowly gained
speed. Looking into his rear view mirror, Jake was
convinced that Kline had not seen him.

11

PISA, ITALY

Toni and Kurt drove swiftly along Via Bonanno Pisano catching a glimpse of the white marble leaning tower from time to time between buildings.

"I told you I'd show you Pisa on a Saturday night, kid," Toni quipped.

"Try Sunday morning."

"Close enough!"

She turned left on Via Volturno and crossed the Arno River. Kurt tried to keep up with the street names, but after crossing the river and turning left to parallel it, he lost track of where he was. The streets were poorly marked in this squalid part of town.

"Where in the hell are we?" Kurt asked.

"The Pisa most tourists don't see. Consider yourself lucky," she said with a smile.

Lucky or not, he knew they had a long evening

ahead of them. One that would bring him to the very
brink of his training.

The Alfa Romeo finally turned down a narrow
alley that was both dirty and wretched. After a few
blocks, when at times it appeared that the narrow-
ness would rip the outside mirrors from the car,
Toni pulled as close to one side as she could and
stopped. They both got out on the driver's side. Toni
pulled a key from her purse and opened a large
metal door. Then she opened the trunk, Kurt and she
quickly pulled Lt. Budd from within, and quietly
closed the trunk again. Kurt put him over his shoulder and carried him inside.

After the door closed, Toni turned on a small
overhead light that partially lit the sordid nature of
the tiny corridor. Chunks of wood and metal lay
strewn across the cement floor, and the smell of
urine and rat feces permeated throughout.

"Nice place, hey, kid? It reminds me of home in
New York," Toni said with a piercing echo.

"Is it okay to talk here?"

"Yeah, no problem," she said, fumbling through
her keys. "The Italians let us use this place. Most of
the people have moved out of this neighborhood.
Some developer wants to convert these buildings
into trendy apartments overlooking the river. But
we've still got a few more years to work out of here.
The funding has been slow, and the bureaucracy
even more so."

Toni opened the door at the end of the corridor. The room inside was a stark contrast to the alley and outer corridor. The furniture was old and worn, but it looked clean. The kitchen area had a metal table and chair set that could have been from the '50s, but it too was at least clean.

"Put him in the far back room and lock the door," Toni ordered.

Kurt carried him back, turned on the light and plopped the lieutenant in a small cot.

The room that Lt. Budd would now call home was designed to look like a prison cell. It had one small cot, a disgusting sink and toilet, and a cement wall. The wall was notched in groups of five marking off over sixty days for one visitor. The first few notches were deep and defined, but toward the end they were barely visible. The overhead light was actuated by a rheostat so its intensity could be overwhelming or virtually nonexistent. The door had a peep hole to look in, and it opened from the left side instead of the right. Kurt saw why when he noticed the walls in the hall were painted darker at the end than at the front, and a black curtain hung about midway down the hall to keep the kitchen and living room lights from interfering with the intended effects.

When Kurt returned, Toni had two cold beers opened.

"Thanks! I could use one," he said. "That's an interesting room you have there."

"Psychology is the most important aspect of a proper interrogation," Toni informed him.

"Is it totally sound proof?"

"Yes. He can yell all he wants, and we couldn't hear him out here. That goes both ways. We can talk freely."

Kurt had heard of such rooms in his training, but the Naval Investigative Service operated under more controlled conditions. All of their interrogation rooms were on Naval bases or air stations. He had never seen a shipboard facility since he was recruited to the NIS.

Toni quickly downed her beer. "Let's go, kid."

She had explained to him the tactics she wanted to use on Lt. Budd. At first it was hard for him to accept the use of drugs and electrical shock on a fellow officer. But the thought of selling out American technology sickened him even more.

Hours passed. The interrogations became more intense. Kurt's job was to monitor the whole charade from a small control room on closed circuit television. From time to time he would ask questions or make comments over a loud speaker through a muffled microphone. Most comments were in Italian, to make it appear that he was in charge and running the show. He could bring pain with a simple word bugiardo, or liar. The small electrical shocks were intensified in Lt. Budd's mind by a drug Toni had given him. He was in a lot less pain than he thought. She spoke to Lt. Budd in mostly Italian to confuse him, and then in broken English when she really wanted to know something.

The information came slowly. But Leo Birdsong had been right all along. Lt. Budd, the Bingo King, was squeamish at the least. The drugs didn't help his cause. Toni would administer one drug to knock him out long enough for her to change clothes. Then she gave him another drug to awaken him to make it appear as though another day had passed. All along he was on sodium pentothal to allow the words to flow more freely.

After nearly fifteen hours, Toni and Kurt had enough information on tape to keep their investigation going for weeks. Lt. Budd implicated Petty Officer First Class Shelby Taylor and two other men aboard the USS Roosevelt. The number Toni got from him earlier was to a place of business in Romean American is all he knew. In the end, Toni placed Lt. Budd into a deep narcosis.

Toni and Kurt had nearly dropped from exhaustion. They slept until evening, so they could return Lt. Budd to his room under the shroud of darkness.

Kurt woke to the sound of his watch alarm. Toni was sleeping on the sofa. He sat and watched her for a while. Her performance had been nothing less than spectacular. She earned an Academy Award as far as he was concerned. Her skin looked so soft; her high cheek bones and strong jaw were more

beautiful than he had ever seen. Finally, he shook
her to wake her up.

"Toni? We've got work to do."

"Jake, leave me alone," she said softly.

Jake? Who the hell is Jake?

Kurt shook her again. This time more violently.

"Toni! Get up," he said more loudly.

Finally her big brown eyes opened and looked
directly at Kurt.

"Kurt?"

"Yeah, Kurt, not Jake," he said, disturbed. "Who
the hell is Jake anyway?" He sounded more like a
jealous boy friend than he wanted to or had the right
to. "Never mind."

"No, it's okay. Jake Adams is a guy I know, or
used to know. I haven't seen or heard from him in
over a year and a half. We were close."

"Did you work together?"

"Not really." She paused for a second, smiled.
"He worked as an Air Force intelligence officer at
the Rome Embassy before he was reassigned to
Germany. He also worked for the Company after he
resigned his commission. He came to Italy a lot. His
specialty is computers. We had a ... relationship. He
left the CIA and Europe over a year ago."

Kurt went to the refrigerator and got a cold beer.

"You remind me of him a little."

"How's that?" he said and then took a big gulp of
beer.

"Well, I don't know. You look a little like him. Could we change the subject, kid?" Toni pleaded. "I've got a headache. I think it's from all the yelling I did in Italian. I think we got everything we need from him."

There was a pause.

"You were a pro in there," Kurt complimented. "I learned a lot, and I really appreciate that."

"Thanks. You weren't half-bad yourself."

They both seemed a bit uncomfortable.

"Let's go, kid," Toni finally said. "We've gotta get this Bozo back to the post before someone misses him."

Kurt went to the interrogation room, lifted Lt. Budd over his shoulder once again, and carried him to the car. It reminded him of numerous times in high school when he had to carry his friend home after a night of drinking. After setting him in the trunk, Kurt and Toni drove back to the post to return him to his room. In the morning he'd feel like a truck ran him over, but his memory would be non-existent.

12

BAD HONNEF, GERMANY

Jake found a room in a small town on the outskirts of Bonn. He brought only a small bag with a change of clothes and a suitcase with his equipment into his room. The suitcase resembled a metal camera case that he carried on the plane with him. It contained a lap-top computer with a fax modem enclosed in a firm rubber insert, and various other small electronic devices. The small tracking transmitter was still under the front seat of the Passat, so there was an open spot in the rubber.

It was nearly an hour past the time he was to call Milt Swenson. Jake punched in Milt's private number.

After a pause and a few rings. "Hello," said a voice from Portland.

"Jake Adams!" After he said his name he put his hand over the mouthpiece quickly and looked toward the door. He thought he heard a noise outside his room.

"Is everything all right?" Milt asked.

"Yeah," he said calmly. "I just thought I heard someone in the corridor. I've got some news. Bundenbach Electronics. Do you know anything about that company?"

There was a pause. "Yeah, I've heard of them," Milt said derisively. "But they're no IBM. Why do you ask?"

"They hired Gunter Schecht, a former German Intelligence agent, to follow me."

"Why would they do that?"

"I don't know, but I need some information," Jake said. "Could you run a background on Bundenbach and fax it to my modem here." Jake gave him the telephone number to his room.

"No problem," Milt said. "I should be able to get that in about an hour. Anything else?"

"No! If I need you, I'll call you there or at your private home phone. I won't be available much."

"Jake, what does this company have to do with Charlie Johnson missing?" Milt asked.

Jake thought for a moment. "I'm not sure. But I'll find out."

"Thanks, Jake."

Jake plopped the phone back in its crevice.

The information from Milt would be helpful, but Jake also knew he needed a German perspective on Bundenbach Electronics. When he worked in

Germany, he had access to numbers to various foreign government agencies and some private companies and banks. Most of the intelligence agencies and police, like the German Polizei, changed their access codes every three months. So he wasn't sure how many would work. Jake quickly linked his laptop computer to his phone line. The numbers were hidden on his hard drive in different places.

He'd have to work fast so he could free his modem and not miss Milt's transmission. Within a few minutes, Jake had accessed the German equivalent of the U.S. Commerce Department. He down loaded about ten pages of information on Bundenbach to his hard drive. That would take him a while to translate into English. He wasn't really sure what to look for. He hoped that whatever it was would jump out from the page.

After about a half hour of meticulously translating boring statistics on Bundenbach Electronics, Jake switched off the LCD screen, turned off the light in his room and went to sleep.

* * *

It had been one of the hottest days in San Remo history. The Italian Riviera was speckled with sun worshippers hiding under their colorful umbrellas. The afternoon sun had skirted its way around the balcony of Jake's hotel room overlooking the aquamarine Mediterranean. He stood against the twisted metal railing with only his tight white tennis shorts and his black sunglasses hiding his nakedness. The intense sun over the past week had tanned his body to a golden brown.

Jake glanced back into the room. A soft breeze fluttered the sheers next to the open sliding glass door. Toni lay asleep on the bed following long, passionate lovemaking. Sex had become a staple of life like a good wine and pasta or the smell of the wondrous San Remo flower gardens.

Other women on the beach below couldn't compare to Toni's natural beauty, Jake thought. Her perfectly rounded breasts, firm butt and long, tight legs would excite any man. Her curly, black silky hair flowed delightfully over her broad shoulders. She could have easily had a successful modeling career, but instead, the adventure of the CIA and Europe beckoned her. Jake was thankful. He smiled at her beautifully naked form.

Jake moved inside and slipped off his shorts. As he flipped off his sun glasses and threw them to a chair, he rolled onto the crumpled sheets of the large bed, slid his hand across Toni's smooth shoulder, and kissed her on the nape of the neck. She scrunched her neck and sighed.

"Um...again?"

He slid his hand down to her smooth, firm butt and then between her legs to her wet, curly mound.

"Yes!"

They had only two days left. They had to make the most of them.

* * *

Jake woke in darkness and disoriented in his new room. Sweat beads on his forehead chilled him—reminding him that he was in Germany and not basking in the Italian sun with Toni Contardo. Was she still working in Italy? If she had her way, that's where she'd be.

Jake switched on a small desk lamp. He looked at the phone on the desk. He still had Toni's number. Did she still live in that second floor apartment in Rome? Maybe he'd call her later.

He noticed his computer on the table had received a call. Sleep would be more difficult now, thinking of Toni. He'd have to read the information Milt had sent.

He logged into the new file. The first page was a basic prospectus of Bundenbach Electronics. What they produced. Profit and loss statements. There were no losses. In fact, if Jake was a betting man, which he was on occasion, he could invest in this company on the strength of this information and that from the German commerce department that had been translated so far. The company seemed too good to be true. Too squeaky clean to hire a guy like

Gunter Schecht. Another page caught Jake's eye; a list of subsidiaries, production facilities, and clients.

Bundenbach had a number of German government contracts; mostly for the Tiger II Panzer, the main German battle tank, and helicopters. No fixed-wing aircraft contracts. The majority of its business was commercial, though.

Jake had a number of subsidiaries to check into. He had a feeling that most of Sunday would be spent in front of a computer screen. Maybe it would rain.

* * *

The room was completely dark until Jake pulled the thick nylon cord to the right of the window allowing the early morning sun to seep through the rolladens and then totally engulf the tiny room. He felt the radiator below the window for a sign of warmth, but found none. He had forgotten to open the valve before he went to sleep. He needed food, but that could wait. Bells from a nearby Catholic church rang, and he counted them out to himself nine times.

His computer had become nearly as important as a seeing-eye dog to a blind man. He had found that with properly configured and operated equipment, his one-man investigation could accomplish as much as an entire group of agents in the past. But the camaraderie was sorely missed. Jake logged on to the small laptop computer and began accessing the information he had received the night before from the German Commerce Department. He tried to read about the subsidiaries of Bundenbach Electronics, the seemingly endless figures, but his mind kept drifting off to Toni Contardo and Italy. Things with pleasure.

The cursor on the computer screen blinked quickly on and off prompting Jake for more data. Back to Bundenbach.

Jake sifted through all the information on Bundenbach Electronics. He was looking for a common link or reason why this German company needed this particular information and technology. There had to be a reason. Sure the technology was important in itself, but was it so important to fill Jake's rental car full of holes? And why hire a guy like Gunter Schecht? The whole case was becoming an enigma. The CIA had trained him to piece together bits of information and draw conclusions to come up with a reasonable analysis of a situation. His specialty was human intelligence. One on one, he was among the best. But this case was puzzling. There could be a number of reasons why Bundenbach wanted the Teredata technology, but Jake was beginning to feel that economics was the most important factor. A national security issue would be attracting his old employer and German Intelligence.

Throughout the documents a few facts were disturbing. Bundenbach's research and development costs had decreased steadily over the past two years, and projections indicated that they would diminish even further. This could only mean one of two things. Either Bundenbach was getting ready to go through a stabilization phase to rest on its laurels, or they had fired a number of good researchers in favor of industrial espionage agents like Gunter Schecht. Had it become more cost effective to steal than develop?

That might be a good move for the short term, but a corporate death sentence for the long term. Without its own independent researchers, Bundenbach would simply become a clone company. Maybe that's all they wanted to be? No! Jake didn't believe that for a moment. Bundenbach had been far too shrewd in the past to allow that. Stealing technology was more of a Russian or Western technique. Could Bundenbach be transferring the technology on to the Russians? That made no sense.

The church bells rang twelve times. Jake went to the window and looked to the street below. Well-dressed Germans walked arm in arm toward the large Gothic Cathedral on the corner across the Goethestrasse at the base of his Gasthaus. The Germans didn't seem to care that they were late, he thought. The Priest could become impatient, but God would surely wait.

Now he had to move on to a new location. But where should he go? There were still too many questions unanswered. The more he dug into Bundenbach Electronics, the more its image had tarnished. At first glance, the company appeared flawless. But then you add a corrosive agent like Gunter Schecht, and the shine quickly faded. Bundenbach's shifting of funds away from research and development was at least a curious aberration.

Then he thought about the German Customs Agent, Herbert Kline, watching Bundenbach Electronics. He could be some help.

13

BONN, GERMANY

The banks of the Rhine were still swollen from days of near-freezing rain. The sun was little comfort, warming the inside of Jake's rental Passat, but helping little to warm the Sunday afternoon strollers along the west bank of the great European river.

Jake had checked out of the Gasthaus in Bad Honnef and driven to a popular park near the German government buildings in Bonn. He knew that Herbert Kline always came to this park on Sundays to feed the ducks and swans.

As if a meeting had been prearranged, Herb was sitting on a wooden bench with concrete end supports feeding those birds brave enough to waddle close to him. Jake quietly walked up behind Herb and stood within five feet of him. It sounded as though Herb was talking to himself, but Jake couldn't make out what he was saying.

"Guten Tag," Jake said.

Herb startled by hunching his shoulders quickly, and then turned his head to see who had disturbed his peace.

"Jake?"

Jake moved around to the front of the bench.

"I thought you went back to America?"

"I did, but airplanes travel in both directions," Jake said with a smile.

"What are you doing here?"

"Same as you. Trying to figure out what's going on with Bundenbach Electronics." Might as well get to the point, Jake thought.

Herb's eyebrows rose sharply with that revelation.

"Before you ask...I'm working for myself now," Jake said. "The money's better, and I choose the jobs and the hours I work."

Herb looked as though he was trying to digest the startling reality of Jake's sudden appearance, and what Jake had just said.

"What do you know, Jake?" Herb asked.

"I know that Gunter Schecht is still a slime, and his new employer is Bundenbach."

Herb smiled finally. "Okay. We agree on that." He paused. "I know he's been buying up some American technology for his new boss, but I don't know why, honestly."

Jake hesitated for a moment. "Do you know why this is so important to Bundenbach?"

"No!" Herb said. "Jake, I know people don't think I'm good at what I do, but I have been good. Far before you or your associates worked Germany. I was damn good—maybe too good. You've probably laughed behind my back like the rest of them."

"Why are you telling me this?"

"Because I'm sick of people not taking me seriously. I'm sick of people thinking I'm some drunken old fool. Well I'm old and I may get drunk a lot, but I'm no fool."

Jake sat down on the other side of the bench. He ran his hands through his thick hair. "I've never laughed at you, Herb, and I've never taken you for a fool. It takes a lot more courage and inner strength to stick it out with an inflexible bureaucracy."

"You think so? I think it takes great strength to stand up to the bureaucracy and say it's wrong. I haven't done that for a long time," Herb said.

Jake looked down at the dark flowing water. "Maybe we should work together on this case," he said. "I could use your help."

Herb was thinking it over.

"Herb, do you know that Gunter and his boys tried to blow me away Friday?" Jake asked.

Herb flicked his head up quickly. "No!"

"It's personal now. I'm a professional, but nobody shoots at me without some sort of return fire. Bullets or prosecution, that's up to the guilty bastard who tries it."

There was silence for a moment. Only the swishing of the Rhine and an occasional squawk from a
duck.

Finally, Jake asked, "I'm looking for an American
tech rep named Charlie Johnson. Works at Bitburg
Air Base for an American contractor named
Teredata International Semiconductors. I work for
the president of that company out of Portland."

After a few moments of hesitation, Herb finally
said, "Charlie Johnson is dead."

"Shit! Are you sure?"

"Yes. I saw Gunter and two others knock him silly
and throw him into the Rhine last week in
Koblenz," Herb said." I was tailing Gunter and his
men because I got a tip about Bundenbach buying
up some restricted American technology. Johnson
was selling something to Gunter. Jake, I keep looking down at the Rhine to see if I can see him floating by. I know it's impossible, but your mind does
strange things sometimes."

"Why did Gunter kill Johnson?" Jake asked." I
mean, without him the supply link is broken."

"Maybe...maybe not. Maybe Gunter found another supplier. Or maybe Johnson asked for more
money. Gunter doesn't need a good reason to kill,
not even a reason."

"Did you file a report with the Polizei in
Koblenz?" Jake asked.

Herb shook his head slowly back and forth.

"Why not?"

He started to speak and then hesitated. "Because I was pretty drunk at the time. I need to stay on this case. My boss would have pulled me and forced me to retire. Besides, the way Gunter and his men did it, they may never find the body. No body, no case against Gunter. Only the word of a drunken fool."

"So, can we work together on this one?" Jake asked, looking Herb straight in the eye.

Herb turned to look at the swollen Rhine and the hungry ducks, and then back at Jake. "Yes!"

14

PORTLAND, OREGON

Milton Swenson picked up the papers on Bundenbach Electronics from the oak coffee table and leaned back on the plush white sofa. He had personally accessed the Moody's network on his computer the night before and gotten this information for Jake Adams. What was Bundenbach up to?

The sharp sound of knuckles echoed through the large wooden door to the room. Before Milt could answer, Steve Carlson entered swiftly and sat down at the other end of the large couch. Milt could tell from his heavily wrinkled forehead and tightened lips that something was wrong.

"What's the matter?" Milt asked.

"I've been trying all morning to call Jake, but can't seem to reach him."

"He's not at Birkwald anymore," Milt said. "He called last night and told me he was scrapping the original plan. He found out who's been after our stuff."

Steve Carlson rose, partially crossed his arms, and stroked his full black and gray beard. "Well?"

Milt shuffled the papers together as a deck of cards and handed them to Steve. "A company called Bundenbach Electronics out of Bonn. I sent Jake the Moody's listing for background information."

He hesitated for a moment. "Never heard of Bundenbach. They must not be too big," Steve said as he handed the papers back without looking at them.

"I think they're an up and comer," Milt said. He paused and studied his old friend. "They could be making a move on the avionics market. Their electronics branch deals mostly in tanks and helicopters for NATO equipment, so they might be trying to compete in the next round of NATO aircraft development. Our new chips could give them a great advantage over the Brits and French."

Steve Carlson paced to the gas fireplace, picked up a beer stein from the mantle, looked at the bottom, and then placed it back in its original spot.

"Do you know where Adams will go next?" Steve asked, looking over his shoulder at Milt.

"No! He seems to think it's best if we don't know."

"I see."

"What's wrong, Steve?"

"I don't know. You know I didn't want to hire Adams. I'm sure we could have found out what was going on without him."

"I don't think so," Milt said, as he got up from the couch. "Not many people know Germany like Jake."

Even though Milt and Steve had worked together for years, Milt knew that Steve felt somewhat indignant toward him. But it was Steve who had given up his partnership status, started his own company, gone bankrupt, and then come back to him for a job.

"What's wrong, Steve?" Milt asked again.

Steve paced a few times near the flames of the gas fireplace trying to bring warmth to his body and what he was about to tell Milt.

"We've got another leak," Steve finally said.

"What?"

"I know. It sounds impossible. I feel like the little Dutch boy sticking his finger in the dike. But I just got a call from Washington. The Navy says someone is quickly snatching up our new chips for the A-7 avionics upgrade. They want us to halt the supply chain."

"I can't believe this shit is happening," Milt screeched. "How in the fuck can their security be that horse shit."

"If the Air Force finds out about our problems in Germany, they're going to ask us the same question."

Milt walked over to the bar and poured two glasses of gin. He plopped two Alka Seltzer in one glass and watched the bubbles and foam rise like some mad scientist's concoction. In a few seconds, he took a long sip.

"I still don't know how you can stand to drink that," Steve said.

"It grows on you. Give me the specifics on what the Navy had to say."

Steve hesitated for a minute, took a sip of his gin, and then began. "Well, first of all, one of our technical advisors from Florida was at a meeting Friday with a group of Navy brass. Some under secretary started spouting off about how our equipment was failing at an unacceptable rate, and how the American people are paying all this money to upgrade the aging A-7. So this guy won't shut up about it. Our guy is getting kind of embarrassed, because he doesn't know what in the hell this guy is talking about. He's heard nothing but praise about the new A-7 retrofit. And besides, as you know, the A-7 is only a test-bed for the Joint Strike Fighter. Finally, this other guy, a Navy Captain, comes over and tells this guy to shut his mouth."

"So, how did you find out we have equipment missing?"

"This Captain Murphy notices our guy is looking nervous, so he takes him aside and tells him we need to cut our supply of high speed avionics chips to the Navy."

"Did the Captain give any specifics on the location of the leak?" Milt asked. "I mean, it could only be from the Jacksonville squadron. But he must have mentioned some specifics."

"Actually, he said it's from the squadron detachment currently deployed aboard the USS Theodore Roosevelt. The ship is now somewhere near Italy," Steve said.

"Great! Now we have to try to plug two holes in two countries. I need to get the word to Jake, somehow." He pointed at Steve. "This is why I didn't want them to take the retrofit aircraft to Europe."

Milt sat slowly onto his white couch again. He watched the bubbles rise quickly to the top of his drink and appear to dance across its surface. He imagined his blood coursing through his body, upward, trying to burst through the top of his skull.

Milt got up impatiently and went to the floor to ceiling windows overlooking the city. He gazed down at the Willamette River over thirty stories below his penthouse office. He pondered how he had built Teredata International Semiconductors from scratch, and was now the Chief Executive Officer on the leading edge of computer technology. He pinched the stomach bulge that worked its way over his fifty dollar belt. He had been so athletic. How could he have let himself get so far out of shape?

Milt stared at the Portland skyline, but he wasn't really looking at the large glassed buildings. He thought about the wealth that the buildings represented.

Steve Carlson accompanied Milt at the window.

Milt peered at Steve critically. He noticed Steve had not fallen out of shape. His stiff posture, even through a soft, gray suit, exuded a strength and magnitude that resembled nobility. Even though Steve's hair had been speckled with streaks of silver, his finely-trimmed beard included, he still looked more like thirty than fifty. When the two had started Teredata in the 70s, Milt had no idea he would run the company one day. Steve had sold out nearly ten years ago to form his own company, but then he filed bankruptcy and returned to Teredata as Vice President of Operations. It had been uncomfortable for both of them for quite some time.

Milt pressed his hands against the large windows. He though about Jake taking all the risks in the case. Was he setting Jake up, or was he just too scared to explain to the government that they may have let the fastest chip ever produced slip into someone else's hands? He knew his only hope for any salvation over this sticky situation was for Jake to save his butt.

"Maybe we should have told Jake the whole story," Milt said, looking out the window again, watching the rain pelt the glass.

"Yeah, but if we had told everything, he probably wouldn't have taken the job," Steve said. "Why should he? The reason he quit CIA, I hear, is because he was asked to do things and take certain risks that he felt were unnecessary."

"That's not true," Milt said, looking back at Steve. "Jake has always been a bit of a rebel. Even from his days at OSU, he's always hated the bureaucracy of government. I read some of his editorials when he worked for the college paper. I was surprised when I heard he took a commission in the Air Force, and even more surprised to hear he worked for the CIA. Remember the summer he interned here? He couldn't understand why we produced so many memos." Milt laughed.

Steve smiled. "Do we give him more information?"

"Yes!"

The rainy day had allowed most of the city street lights to remain lit. Milt rarely saw the light of day in January, coming to work in the early morning darkness, and driving home long after the sun had set. He wondered if the sun was shining over his production facilities in Florida and Mexico.

Of course, it was.

15

ROME, ITALY

Kurt was finally starting to feel human again. He and Toni had spent Sunday evening in an American-style hotel along the Autostrada between Pisa and Rome. Sleep had been restful for the first time in two weeks since he hastily packed and hoped aboard the car-rier. In the past, he became accustomed to the slowly swaying rack on the aircraft carrier. But on those cruises he was doing a job with implicit dangers he had trained for. On this past Atlantic crossing, the dangers weren't as clearly defined.

The Monday morning traffic in Rome was far from appealing, but Toni didn't seem to notice a change from the nearly-vacant Autostrada on the Northern outskirts. She sat erect in her bucket seat listening to Rome's version of a morning drive-time talk show with contemporary rock thrown in from time to time to keep the drivers from switching the channel.

Kurt liked the way she was holding up after a few days on the road. She was obviously used to this wandering life.

"Toni, do you ever get sick of traveling throughout Europe? I mean, wouldn't it be nice to grab a hot dog and watch a baseball game?" Kurt asked.

Toni didn't answer.

"I haven't been here that long," Kurt said." So everything is new to me. I think it would take awhile before I got bored with Italy."

Toni turned her Alfa Romeo from the Autostrada at the Central exit heading toward downtown Rome. The traffic swarmed bumper to bumper. Brake lights flickered and horns blared as the clustered cars and trucks positioned for invisible lanes.

"Unfortunately, kid, it becomes commonplace," she finally said. "The first few years I'd be driving down some beautiful Tuscany country road listening to Vivaldi, and a strange feeling would come over me. I'd twist the rear view mirror and look at myself to make sure that it was me behind the wheel. And I'd say to myself, 'Toni, you're actually driving down some back road in Italy.' The people back in New York would never believe me. Most people from my neighborhood haven't gone beyond Jersey."

"Do you get back home much?"

"No, not anymore," she said. "I passed through JFK on the way to see Captain Murphy in D.C., but I didn't stay. My dad died when I was young, and my mom died a few years ago. I have a bunch of cousins and uncles there, but every time I stop by they ask me why I'm not married, and where are my bambinos. So I mostly stay away."

Kurt didn't want to push any further. She was the perfect expatriate. She was doing a job that was important, but went mostly unnoticed and was misunderstood by the average American. And she was good. The Navy was splattered with misfits anxious to get away from something or somebody. History hadn't changed that fact.

Toni turned down a one way street in the downtown region and drove a few blocks to a section with a tree-lined boulevard. Then she turned right into a wide two-lane driveway with a large metal gate with spikes and concertina wire on top. A concrete barrier protected the front of a guard shack. The U.S. Marine at the gate recognized Toni and waved her into the compound with only a cursory look at her credentials.

Toni and Kurt had entered through the back of the American Embassy compound. The entrance was reserved for diplomats, distinguished guests, CIA, and even Italian cooks and maids. The average guest used the more impressive front of the building.

With a key, Toni opened a large wooden unmarked door, and climbed a flight of stairs. At the top, a small marble ledge with neglected plants sucked up light from a wall of square glazed tiles. There was a thick metal door with a peep hole and a cipher lock. Toni punched in the right numbers and the door clicked open. Inside was a small unimpressive room with old gray metal desks that could have been left over from a Navy sale. The electronics equipment was state of the art though—the newest fax machines, computers, and secure telephones available. There was a large wall vault that Kurt could only speculate on its contents. Other than the desks, filing cabinets, a small safe, and the visible electronics equipment, the room was empty.

"Nice place, eh, kid?"

Kurt scanned the room one more time.

"And you thought working for the CIA was glamorous," Toni said with a smile as she crossed her arms.

"This desk looks familiar," Kurt said. "Wait a minute. I'm sure I threw this desk overboard at the end of my last cruise off the coast of Florida. Did somebody fish this out of the Atlantic for you?"

Toni laughed her first real laugh since Kurt had met her three days ago. It suited her well. Her smile pushed her high cheek bones even higher, and exposed her straight white teeth.

"You've got a good sense of humor, kid. This office could use that from time to time."

Toni unlocked the small floor safe and pulled out some papers from the front file with a red `Secret' cover sheet. After about a minute of sifting through the papers as a returning vacationer would her mail, she handed them to Kurt.

It was a message from Captain Murphy.

"Shit!"

"You can say that again," Toni said.

"I'll bet Murphy wants to have that Under Secretary for lunch. Why in the hell do they trust civilians with that type of information?" Kurt asked. After he said it, he realized that Toni was also a civilian. "I'm sorry, Toni, no offense intended, it just pisses me off that some drunk bureaucrat can leak this sensitive information."

"It happens all the time. I had a friend who was working in Poland who was exposed by a stupid statement from a visiting congressman on the intelligence sub-committee. They found my friend the next day; what was left of him."

"Where do we go from here?" Kurt asked.

"Well, for one thing you can't report back to the Roosevelt. We don't know if you've been compromised, but we have to assume that you have."

"I need to talk to Murphy."

"No problem. You can use the secure phone."

Kurt sat on the edge of the desk and punched in the number from memory.

The phone rang on the other end three times, and then Kurt recognized Captain Murphy's "Hello."

"Whisky One," Kurt said. He heard a click on the other end that sounded like the receiver being placed down, but was only Captain Murphy keying his phone to secure mode.

"Kurt, I'm glad you called," Murphy said. "I guess you got my message at the embassy?"

"Yes, sir!"

"I'm sorry about that Goddamn Under Secretary. I want that guy's balls. I had just briefed the Secretary on our technology breach that afternoon. That other bureaucrat had to be there because he deals with acquisitions and special programs."

"I see."

"Well, the Secretary pressured me on what my plan of attack was, who and what agencies were involved, and how much time I needed to wrap up the case," Murphy said. "I told them as little as possible without getting my butt in a sling, and I thought that was the end of it. Later that evening at a party the Under Secretary shot off his mouth."

"Sir, I understand the company rep from Florida knows about the technology transfer now," Kurt said. "Do you think they know about me and Toni?"

"Kurt, I can't honestly say. I got to the guy and shut him up as soon as I could, but I have no idea how much he gave away."

"So we have to assume the worst?"

"Yes! That would be most prudent," Murphy answered.

"I won't return to the Roosevelt then," Kurt said. "Sir, could you make up some bogus story and send it to my squadron on the ship?"

"No problem. I'll have a message sent from Naples saying you were placed in the hospital there after being hit by a taxi, and will be flown back to the states once you're stable."

"Thanks, sir. Is there anything else you need from us?"

"Yes! What have you two come up with?" Murphy asked.

Kurt thought for a moment. "Sir, Petty Officer Shelby Taylor is our low man, and Lt. Budd is our drop artist," Kurt said. "There are a few other minor players on board the Roosevelt, but we're still trying to reel in the main fish. Request permission to remain ashore and help Special Agent Contardo with the investigation here?"

"Permission granted, Ensign Lamar."

"Thank you, sir."

"Keep in touch every few days if you can."

"Yes, sir."

The line went blank on the other end.

As Kurt was finishing his conversation with Captain Murphy, Toni had logged onto her computer and was accessing the Italian Telephone Company with her modem.

"Well? Who owns that number?" Kurt asked.

"Patience, kid. Rome wasn't built in a day," she said sarcastically.

Toni's fingers whipped across the computer keyboard like a journalist's on deadline. Kurt watched closely until the telephone number popped on the screen followed by an address. They looked at each other in disbelief.

"Holy shit!" Kurt said. "Why in the hell is the U.S. Commerce Department involved in something like this?"

A smile came across Toni's face as she logged off the computer. She shook her head.

"What do you find so funny?" Kurt asked.

"I don't know. I guess it figures," Toni said. "A lot of times we end up running across the path of another agency. It can get frustrating. Especially if you've been working a case for a few months."

"But why would the Commerce Department run an operation like this?" Kurt asked.

"They aren't, kid. There must be a rogue."

Kurt sat down on a typing chair backwards and swiveled around a few times. "What is the Commerce Department doing with an office in Italy?"

"I don't know," Toni said. "They could be here to keep track of all the new American companies opening offices. They're all trying to carve a piece of the pie when and if the European Community unifies. Those companies with a strong foothold have a chance to make big bucks."

"How are we going to find out who's been stealing our technology?"

Toni patted Kurt on the back and then left her hand on his shoulder. "Stick with me, kid. As you've seen, I have ways of making them talk," she said.

Kurt looked up at Toni. Her eyes had a sparkle, he thought, that could tame the wildest beast. Kurt put his hand on hers.

16

GENOA, ITALY

Sirens echoed back and forth adding chaos to the normal sounds of rush hour traffic. Cars reluctantly pulled to the sides of the busy roads allowing the ambulance to barely squeeze by. Polizia on Moto Guzzi motorcycles weaved onward through the clustered maze that had formed.

What was once a tranquil sidewalk cafe, was now turned into a horrid scene of destruction. Glass table tops had been shattered and scattered over fifty feet like shrapnel. Bodies lay helplessly on the sidewalk with blood oozing and spurting from countless jagged cuts. A lone, old robust woman screamed and prayed aloud as she held her black rosary close to her chest, repeatedly crossing herself.

Polizia and Carabiniere cordoned off the area and started searching the buildings.

The ambulance crew arrived and started attending to the only survivor—a man in an expensive suit that did nothing to protect him against the blast and flying glass.

A middle aged man with dark curly hair in a black double breasted suit paced back and forth pointing and shouting orders. Inspector Bruno Gallano was Genoa's terrorist expert. He stood quietly by himself for a moment and scratched the five o'clock stubble on the right side of his face. Finally, he waved his assistant over to him.

"What do the people say happened?" Gallano asked his assistant in Italian.

"Mixed reports," said his assistant. "But it appears to be a terrorist attack by the Red Brigade."

"Why?"

"Electronic device with plastic explosives. Similar to the Rome Train Station. Only one thing is different. They used a remote control car."

"How?"

"Well, a remote control Porsche came from up the sidewalk there," the assistant said pointing up the street. "Nobody touched it as it weaved in and out of the people on the sidewalk. Then witnesses say the car took a right turn here and stopped under the table of four men. It was there for only a second before blowing."

The two men sidestepped all the debris and positioned themselves over the remains of four bodies covered by blood-soaked sheets.

"Any identification on these four?" Bruno asked,

lifting the sheet of one and viewing what was left of a previously healthy male, and then lowering the sheet.

"Yes! The glass and metal did a number on the fronts of their bodies, but their backs were pretty much intact. They all had wallets."

"Well?" Bruno said, becoming impatient. "Who are they?"

"All American sailors."

"Shit! That's all we need," Bruno said. "We've got the USS Roosevelt in port for its first visit, and we have a fucking international terrorist incident."

Bruno Gallano scanned the scene one more time to perhaps convince himself that it wasn't happening. But the reality of four American bodies lay at his feet. The three additional Italian corpses lay further away. Bruno knew that one death was as important as the next, but the Americans would be harder to explain. It changed things from a municipal problem to an international incident. He could do without that kind of notoriety, he thought.

"Have your men come up with anything yet?" Bruno asked.

"Not much. It appears that there had to be at least two people involved—one to drop off the car and the other to direct it from that building there," the assistant said pointing across the street to a large five story brick building with Roman arch windows.

Bruno looked up at the building and then back at

the Americans. "What's the connection here?" he said. "This isn't your typical American hang out. How could the Red Brigade know they'd be here at this time? Or did they really give a shit who they killed? The car stopped right under the table, though. So, whoever did this, had to know these guys would be here at this particular time."

Bruno's assistant just shrugged his shoulders.

"Who are the Americans?" Bruno asked.

"Let's see," the assistant said flipping through his note pad. "We have a Lieutenant Budd, a PO1 Albrecht, whatever that is, a PO1 Taylor, and a Seaman Phillips."

Bruno scratched his impending beard again. He stooped down and took a look at another American sailor. "Isn't that kind of a strange group?" he asked. "I mean, in the Italian military we never went anywhere with the enlisted men, yet here we have a lieutenant with three enlisted sailors. Is that significant?"

"I don't know," the assistant said. "Maybe we should ask the American officials when they show up."

Bruno's assistant had sent word to the USS Roosevelt as soon as he found out that American sailors had been victims.

"Inspector!" yelled a man from the third floor window of the building across the street from the bloody site.

Bruno turned and looked up. "Si, si."

"We found something."

Bruno instructed his men at the scene to leave the bodies where they were until the American authorities arrived. Then he and his assistant entered the old brick building and climbed the three flights of stairs. The stairwell was dark, and Bruno noticed that a bright sunny day would probably not change that fact. The hallway on the third floor had uneven hardwood floors and tan thick plaster walls in need of fresh paint. Two Carabiniere officers waited in front of a wide doorway.

Bruno breezed past the men and into a small one room apartment. Bruno stopped and scanned the room. A boy around eight years old sat on the edge of a small bed in one corner. He immediately looked up at Bruno with his dark overpowering eyes. Fear seemed to scream from each eye with recent tears streaking his dark cheeks. Bruno looked at the rest of the room to try to de-emphasize his presence and put the boy at ease. He walked to the window and leaned against the sill to observe the gory scene below. Had the boy seen what happened and was fearful of its tragic consequences, or did he know more? Bruno suspected the latter. He walked back over to the two Carabiniere at the doorway and escorted them farther into the hallway.

"Does the boy know what happened?" Bruno asked.

"Si!" said the older of the two officers. "We just got to this floor when the door slammed. The boy acted strange, so we asked him a few questions."

"And?" Bruno asked impatiently.

"He was sitting on the steps on the first floor of the building when a man came up to him and asked if he would like to make some money. Of course, he did. The man told the boy to meet him back here at four. When the man came back, he had a small case with him. He told the boy he needed to bring him to his apartment. When they got up here, the guy opens his case and pulls out a black remote control Porsche. Of course the boy's eyes lit up with joy when he saw that."

"Then what?"

"The man puts the car in a paper bag and tells the boy not to let anyone see it. He then instructed him to take the car down the block to the alley, pull it out and set it on the sidewalk when the church bell chimed on the half hour. It was timed so the boy would only have to stand there for about a minute or two."

"Can he describe the man?" Bruno asked.

"Si, inspector. The man was in his mid-thirties, well dressed, expensive black pants, a leather coat, driving gloves, and a black knit cap. But more importantly, his Italian was poor."

"What type of accent?" Bruno asked quickly.

The officer paused for a minute. "American."

Bruno put his hand up to his nose, stroked it, and then slid it down and rubbed the stubble on his face again. Either the Americans were trying to take their crimes to his streets, or one had joined the Red Brigade, Bruno thought.

"Where's the boy's parents?"

"He says there's only a mother who works days at an office a few blocks away. The boy decided not to go to school this morning. We think the mother walks the streets at night."

"Why's that?"

"The room right next door to this one has papers with her name on it. There's only a bed in there and a few skimpy outfits."

"You say nothing about this to anyone," Bruno said. "Do you understand? Not to your superiors, friends, wife, nobody!"

"Si, inspector," they both said.

"Take the boy directly to my office. Don't let anyone question him, or see you take him from this building. Any questions?"

They looked at each other, and then said: "No, sir."

After the men left with the boy, Bruno looked over the room. He knew he wouldn't find anything, but it was a force of habit. He found himself feeling sorry for the young boy and the situation he was in. He had to be frightened, it could be no other way. The room, the building, the neighborhood had all hardened him in some way. But he was still a child. And children still have fears, Bruno thought. He locked the door and headed back down to deal with the bodies still lying in the street.

17

BUDAPEST, HUNGARY

Over six inches of thick, heavy snow had fallen overnight. The city looked cleaner than it had in decades. Many of the older buildings, damaged during World War II, still hadn't received their restorations as promised, but progress had surely been made. To the thousands of people who had flooded the streets to protest the government's stagnant economy, it was as though a baptism had been performed by God himself upon the two million citizens of Budapest.

At his weathered, wooden desk, Isaac Lebovitz slowly paged through the volumes of information that the American businessman, Jason Dalton, had given him. The frequent chants for more jobs by the protesters below his office brought an occasional smile to his face. He knew that not long ago the people would have been silently whisked away to jail, or worse. But now the chants were tolerated;

the will of the people could no longer be stomped under foot. And Isaac intended to take advantage of this movement.

Isaac's men had printed page after page of computer data and bound them in hard cardboard binders to allow more easy reading. The marketing information was current; perhaps too current to allow his company to properly use this powerful information.

Behind his desk, a large cast iron radiator, with few paint chips remaining on its surface, clanked violently out of control. Isaac kicked it with the side of his shoe dropping more paint chips to the floor, but doing nothing to stop the noise. Things will surely change, he thought. No more second-rate anything.

The phone rang.

Isaac picked up the ancient black dial phone and simply said "Lebovitz."

His secretary, who had been with Isaac as long as the phone, told him that two of his men had arrived and wished to speak with him. "Send them in," he said, and then set the phone back in its slot.

The brass door latch swiveled, but the door wouldn't open. Isaac got out of his chair, flipped the binders closed, and shuffled to the door to unlock it. The papers weren't for all to view.

"Have a seat," Isaac said, sweeping his hand toward the two wooden chairs in front of his desk as he sat back in his chair.

Isaac searched the faces of his men for some answer. He knew he could depend on Stanislav Kirsac and Max Sardouf to follow his directions to the letter, regardless of how difficult the assignment. After all, they had worked for Isaac in Hungarian Intelligence for over ten years. But they weren't due back in Budapest for a week. They had all traveled together throughout Western Europe and Scandinavia in search of military secrets to please the Hungarian government and, more importantly, the former Soviet KGB. Anything they found that hadn't already been uncovered by the KGB was not only a source of great pride to Isaac, but nearly contemptuous to the KGB for not getting the information sooner. But what the trio had found on those frequent trips to the West, was an affluent people with a fervent lust for things. And their democratic European cousins got what they wanted, Isaac thought. That will change soon.

"How was Germany?" Isaac asked.

The two men sat side by side as one. The two could have passed as brothers, Isaac thought. Their high brow ridges resembled more Ukrainian men than their Croatian heritage. Even more than their pronounced foreheads, their continual stoic expressions in near perfect harmony, made them appear as only brothers could. They looked at each other, and then back at Isaac.

"One of our contacts is missing," Max finally said, more self-assured than Stanislav.

"Which one?" Isaac asked.

"The one from Bitburg," Max added. "We're sure he's dead."

Isaac leaned back in his chair. It wasn't as comfortable as the one in Croatia, but not much would be for a while.

"Who did it?" Isaac asked.

"We have our suspicions," Max continued. "We think he might have been selling to another country or one of the local businesses."

"Why?"

"Well...we saw him with Gunter Schecht."

Isaac paused for a moment. "Shit! I thought he retired last year?"

"He may be freelancing," Stanislav said cautiously.

"Can we replace our contact?" Isaac asked.

The two men looked at each other again. "Do we need one?" Stanislav asked more boldly.

"Of course we do," Lebovitz said, somewhat disgusted with the question. I'm glad I don't count on these two for their brains, he thought. "We might need more from Teredata...we should have all we need, but I'm not certain. We do need a good, reliable contact in Germany, though. Find someone close to the government in Bonn. We'll need some good inside information."

"Anything else?" Max asked as both men rose.

Isaac thought for a moment. Something wasn't making sense. Why kill the man in Bitburg? "I need to know who killed our Teredata contact, and why," Isaac said. "Also, find out who Gunter Schecht is working for. I don't like it when a guy with his reputation is involved. I don't trust that bastard."

With all the directions the men needed, they both nodded and departed the office.

Isaac slumped back into his chair and tapped the side of his forehead with his index finger. Somehow this must all come together, he thought. It will happen. The San Remo villa overlooking the opulent Mediterranean coast will surely be his. The overwhelming scent of roses will rise from the terraced fields and engulf his very existence.

18

BONN, GERMANY

The Audi A6 crept slowly up the residential hill and turned left onto a one block dead end street. There were only a few houses with large, meticulously landscaped yards on the block. Jake had selected a corner house due to its view of the road and Bonn. He pulled over to the curb and parked over a block from his newest apartment, and waited to see if he had any surprise guests. He had leased the house from an older couple for a month; an agreement that he would not keep. Using his best British accent, he had told his landlords he was just assigned to the embassy.

Jake was a bit superstitious about renting another Audi, since his previous encounter with Gunter and his men. Superstitions aside, he wasn't about to let Gunter take another crack at him. Changing cars daily was a small caution.

A few days had passed since Jake Adams and

Herbert Kline became partners. The weather had been uncooperative, raining constantly. Even a warm rain would have been welcomed, but this was the type that chilled one to the bone. Not cold enough to snow, but cold enough to freeze after it hit the ground. His windshield wipers swished across the glass, but left annoying splotches of ice right in Jake's view.

Jake was getting used to working with Herb. The computer remained an important source of information, but a human factor was refreshing.

Herb was old school intelligence. Hit the streets, work the contacts, analyze the reliability, and come up with a reasonable analysis. Herb's skill and intuition had been underestimated by Jake's colleagues at the CIA and German Intelligence. Most had seen the outside man, not the inner man. Only time and proper observation could reveal the innate qualities of a person, Jake thought.

Along with the change of cars, Jake had continued to move from hotel to Gasthaus throughout the Bonn area, frustrating Herb each time. His current house in the hills on the right bank of the Rhine offered a splendid view of Bonn's government office district and a distanced view of Bundenbach Electronics. Seeing the building had a cathartic affect on Jake. It wasn't necessary to remain so close, but it seemed to focus his vision on his mission.

The days had been filled with long hours in cars observing Bundenbach and Gunter Schecht. The time in the car had reminded Jake of his days with the Company. Jake had often felt guilty that he was getting paid to sit and observe someone going through their normal daily routines. When his observations actually turned into a significant piece of information, Jake would finally find satisfaction and accomplishment in all the waiting.

Everything looked in order. Jake drove forward slowly and pressed the button to the remote control garage door opener. The gray door crept fully open just as Jake's Audi slid through. He quickly closed the garage door and entered the house through an inside door.

Once inside, he checked the place for any disturbances. Nothing. He opened the Rolladens covering the windows and let in what little light remained in the overcast afternoon.

Jake looked down at the smooth Rhine out his back window. A coal barge loaded to the hilt slowly worked its way up stream toward Koblenz or Mainz. Jake couldn't help wondering about the fate of Charlie Johnson's body. He should have just retired from the Air Force and gone Bass fishing in Georgia like he had planned all along.

A small flat beeper attached to the inside pocket of Jake's leather jacket beeped three times. He quickly retrieved it. A red light blinked next to a number lit up on an LCD screen. Jake picked up the phone and dialed Herb's number. The system was working. Jake had given Herb his beeper number that could be accessed through a central switch and transmitted anywhere in Germany.

Herb answered the phone on the first ring. "Tag."

"Wie gehts? So, how about some dinner tonight?"

"Sounds good. The place we discussed?"

"Yes!"

"Is seven fine with you?" Herb asked.

"Yes!"

"See you then."

The line went blank. Jake looked at his watch; it was five o'clock. He still had over an hour before he was to meet Herb for dinner. All of their meeting times were actually an hour before the stated time.

The apartment Jake leased was furnished in a contemporary style. Black marble coffee table and end tables, brass lamps, and short dark gray carpeting. Jake plopped down onto one of the oversized white leather chairs. He was about to remove one of his Italian leather shoes by shoving the toe against the heel, but then he thought for a second and decided to undo the laces and set them gently next to the chair. Toni Contardo had bought him those shoes on a ski vacation in Cortina D'Ampezzo almost three years ago. "You buy quality leather and they'll last," Toni had said. He wondered if he should call her? They had made a clean and mutual break when

Jake left Germany, but if Toni found out he was back in Europe and failed to call...well, he didn't want to think of the consequences of Toni's Italian temper.

* * *

The entrance to the Spa on the outskirts of Bad Honnef was covered with wilted ivy and vines that stretched all the way across the brown brick front of the castle-like building. Even in the darkness, with only a dim lantern flickering shadows across the wall, Jake could imagine how beautiful it would look once the plush green leaves adorned it. He entered through the three inch thick carved wood door and walked through a medieval foyer with suits of armor and weaponry authentically placed. Inside was a natural atrium that at one time must have been open to the elements, but was now covered with a glass dome. Live trees and water fountains made the large area seem like full summer. Tables were spaced at great distances to allow discreet conversations. Herb had told Jake that couples who were having affairs often came here.

Jake took a table near a fountain and ordered a beer. It had been a long day, and the most productive since Jake and Herb had become partners. He hoped that things were finally coming together.

Herb showed up just as Jake's second beer

arrived. He sat down and took a long drink on the mug of beer. "Thanks Jake, you timed that just right," Herb said.

"You know Herb, in the old West I could have shot you for taking my beer?"

"I know. I've seen all the Clint Eastwood movies," Herb said, and then took another gulp.

"I have something interesting that happened today." Jake paused for a moment somewhat reluctant to tell everything. It wasn't that he didn't trust Herb, it's just that he hadn't told his client everything either. In fact, he hadn't even spoken to Milt Swenson for days.

"Well?" Herb asked. "Will you tell me before I die of old age?"

"Just drink my beer," Jake said smiling. "Okay...while I was following Gunter and his buddies around today, I recognized some people from my not so distant past. Gunter stopped for lunch at his normal Gasthaus at the normal time...he seems impervious. Anyway, I just sunk my teeth into a bratwurst and I noticed a brown Mercedes pull up across the street. Inside were two guys who looked Russian and could have been twins. I know those guys."

Jake motioned for the Fraulein to get him and Herb another beer. She nodded her head.

"Anyone I know?" Herb asked.

"I'm not sure if you've run across these guys. They're not Russians; they're Hungarians."

Herb emptied the last sip of beer from his mug. "No! How'd you run across them before?"

"Oh, they set up a minor spy ring a few years back," Jake said. "They coerced an Army and Air Force linguist to turn over some classified documents. It all started out innocently. The Americans were at a Frankfurt club and were asked to a German party. There were a few gorgeous blonde Frauleins that decided they wanted to be with them that night. Well, one thing led to another and it turned into an orgy with all four of them in one huge bed. The girls, or course, were very persuasive. After a number of nights of crazy sex, the girls convinced the guys to do certain things to each other. And, as you might have already guessed, all of the sessions were taped."

"I didn't hear about that case," Herb said.

"The Americans minimized the impact and shipped the two guys back to the States for prosecution. I'm sure their talents are not being wasted in Leavenworth."

"So, how were the Hungarians involved?"

"They set up the whole scam. The girls were actually Swedish, so you can understand the temptation. Really they didn't get much from our guys. Just a little operational knowledge that we quickly changed."

"So why are they checking into Gunter Schecht?" Herb asked.

"That's the puzzling thing. I just sat there eating my brat trying to figure that out. It could be a number of reasons. They could be trying to get a hold of some of Bundenbach technology. But they should know Gunter from his days with German Intelligence. And of course that could be a link. Maybe the Hungarian twins think that Gunter is still with German Intelligence and feel that anything that he's interested in must be important. I'm just not sure, though."

The Fraulein set down the two frothy mugs of beer and left quickly without the normal pause that American waitresses make in anticipation of a tip.

"Do you think that maybe the Hungarians are looking for work?" Herb asked.

"No! They were checking out Gunter from a distance just like I was. One of them got out of the car and went into the bakery for a few Brotchen and coffee, but he never ventured far and always kept an eye on his partner in case he needed to move out quickly. I've had some time to think about those guys, though, and something is different about them. I can't think of what. I thought it might be the car. But the Hungarians have used Mercedes in the past, so it can't be that. I don't know what it is, but it's bugging me."

"Maybe their clothes. What were they wearing?" Herb asked.

"Pretty standard off the rack German clothes. Last year's contemporary. Green plaid pleated pants. One wore a mustard colored shirt with a thin black tie, and the other wore a magenta shirt with what looked like a thin green tie. Nothing really out of the ordinary."

Jake sat back in his chair and looked at his mug of beer in front of him. What in the Hell was different about those guys? Their brow ridges still made them look like Neanderthal Man. Their shoes? No! Jackets? They weren't wearing jackets.

"That's it!" Jake said. "They weren't wearing jackets."

"So? How is that important?" Herb asked.

"It was only about thirty-two degrees, that's zero celsius. Even that isn't overly strange for those guys. But what might be strange, is that these guys have never gone anywhere without their Glock 19s. Their 9mm's are like a baby's pacifier. If they don't have them, they cry all the way to the Frankfurt Consulate. I don't know how they could have hidden those guns without their standard issue brown leather jackets."

Herb took another sip of beer, and then glanced at Jake. "I still don't understand how that's important."

"Okay...you said that Charlie Johnson was doubling back on Gunter and Bundenbach Electronics. Well, just maybe Johnson was selling out to the

Hungarian twins. Gunter finds out that Johnson is working both sides of the track, and cracks open Johnson's retirement nest egg."

"But why not kill off the Hungarians instead?" Herb asked. "I mean, then he could still have Johnson supplying him with Teredata's computer technology."

"That's true. But maybe Bundenbach had all they needed from Teredata and just wanted to cut off the supply to a competitor and cover up all the loose ends at the same time."

Jake could see on Herb's face that this was beginning to make sense, but surmised that there were also loose ends in Jake's reasoning.

"But why is not having their guns significant?" Herb asked.

"I don't know for sure. But I'm guessing that the Hungarian twins are no longer sanctioned by the Hungarian government. Therefore, they'd have a tough time bringing guns into Germany. As you know, the airlines have really tightened security since the bombings, and they probably didn't drive. Their car was a rental. The borders are also tightening up with the swarm of immigrants into Germany. The border guards must be going nuts, but I'm sure they are more thorough now than they have been in years. So I think that the Hungarian twins are either freelancing or working for some other government or company."

"They might have wanted someone to think they weren't armed," Herb said.

Jake sipped his beer. "True! But habits are hard to break. It's sort of like buckling your seat belt. You don't realize you're doing it."

Johnson's death was finally starting to make more sense. But what goals were Gunter and Bundenbach trying to accomplish? Why did they want the Teredata technology? Jake knew he'd find out with time.

Once the beer started to take effect, Herb and Jake switched subjects to upcoming soccer matches and the strength of the teams. The waterfall continued to flow, and the conversation continued on into the night until Herb took a cab, and Jake took a room on the second floor.

19

ROME, ITALY

The early morning rush hour crowds pushed and shoved squeezing more people onto the already packed subway train at Rome's Central Station Metro stop. Kurt Lamar strained forward making sure that his subject didn't pile on without him. Kurt was just slim enough to allow the doors to close in front of him. His subject, with a gray tweed cap looming cautiously above the crowd, had made a similar maneuver at the other door of the same car.

Kurt looked around for something to hang onto as the train lurched forward. It wasn't really necessary; Kurt couldn't have moved if he wanted to.

Kurt had been watching the U.S. Commerce Department's Rome bureau chief for three days. He normally drove a small red Fiat to work each morning, but this morning he was deviating from that practice.

The Metro train stopped at every terminal and opened its doors. Not many departed, and there was no room for additional passengers. Those left waiting on the cement platform for the next train looked disgustingly at their watches as the subway train slowly pulled forward and proceeded quickly into the darkness of the underground tunnels. Kurt realized now that most of the commuters were probably heading to the downtown business district.

Kurt was still not perfectly familiar with Rome. He could get around without becoming totally disoriented, but keeping track of another person in this busy crowd was something altogether different. The only advantage he could see was that the commerce department had only set up shop less than a month ago, just after Christmas. His subject was probably not overly familiar with Rome either, and Kurt was sure that he had remained unnoticed. And then there was the gray tweed cap that appeared somewhat out of place and more suited for a convertible drive through the English countryside.

The train stopped again. This time the majority of the passengers off-loaded, pushing their way toward the stairs to the street above. The commerce man was in the lead. His cap bobbed up and down and back and forth in an almost comical, uncoordinated fashion.

Cutting the distance between him and his subject, Kurt moved to within a meter of the commerce department official. Kurt was familiar with close surveillance tactics, but the Naval Investigative Service had hired him more for his technical expertise than any other reason. And the NIS had not had a reason to assign Kurt to such duties...until now.

Captain Murphy had told him during his initial briefing that he could run into situations that would require him to act from instinct. Kurt knew that this was one of them.

At the top of the stairs, the man made a quick turn around the railing and doubled back on the street above. The man glanced back with indifference at the crowd that had been following him since departing the train.

Kurt was so close at that point that all his subject could have seen were those followers still on the stairs.

The sidewalks were as a river flowing through an autumn forest with all the people leaves that had fallen from the trees along the banks. When the leaves touched, they bounce off to a path of less resistance. Kurt hated cities because of this indifferent contact, but, at the same time, enjoyed the anonymity of that impersonality.

After two blocks, the man entered a store. Kurt walked past, memorized the name of the store, and then stopped three stores down for espresso at a stand up counter. He could still see the front of the building the man had entered. With the quick glance, Kurt had seen that the store sold mostly office supplies, typewriters and business computers.

The waiting game wasn't one of Kurt's favorite pastimes. What could he do, read the menu on the wall? Espresso was so named for its quick brewing and expedient consumption. Kurt could hardly coddle or linger with it. His intention was to appear Italian. The language was no problem. And his dark hair fit the mold. Most Italians stopped at the counter for a quick jolt of espresso and then departed to work. He knew that the longer he remained, the less Italian he would appear.

Cars zipped by honking their horns at daring jaywalkers and slower cars. Scooters weaved in and out of traffic. Buses spewed plumes of exhaust as they slowed with the flow of traffic and then pulled forward quickly.

After about ten minutes, the man with the tweed cap came out of the store carrying a brown leather briefcase. Kurt thought the case looked new, but it made no sense. He could have just as easily gotten a briefcase from a store closer to his home or work, and spared himself the early-morning rush hour Metro ride. Besides, the commerce man had been carrying a case for the last couple of days. Kurt got up and followed the man.

The man hailed a taxi, pointed vehemently to the cabby, obviously having a problem with the language, and finally departed the curb.

Kurt grabbed a cab also, and followed the man back to the Commerce Department office. As he sat and watched the man with the gray tweed cap enter the old brick building, he noticed the cab driver watching him in the rear view mirror. He gave the cabby Toni's address. Time to regroup.

* * *

Toni Contardo crossed her legs and felt her black leather skirt slide up exposing the majority of her long slender leg. She took a sip of cappuccino. The fresh coffee and cream warmed her all the way down, and she knew she had made the right decision to wear a skirt on a cold January day.

A man with hair to his shoulders came from the back bathroom and took a seat across from Toni. They must appear as an odd couple, Toni thought. The tight skirt, expensive silk blouse, and black leather pumps labeled Toni as perhaps upper middle class, whereas the man across the table wore faded blue jeans with holes, and a T-shirt with a cubed man kicking a soccer ball advertising the World Cup.

"Buon Giorno," Toni said, as she reached across the table and placed her hand on his.

"Buon Giorno." he said, his dark intense eyes searching Toni's body seductively. "Mio caro amico, Toni. Come sta?"

"Good. And you?"

The man shifted his shoulders back and forth and gestured with his hands open and palms facing upward. "Could be better I'm sure, but I can't really complain. After all, I'm still alive."

Toni took another sip of cappuccino, giving her time to think of her line of questioning. The internal rehearsals had been thorough, but were never the same when sitting across from a dangerous man. He left himself open for this one, she thought.

"I heard you and your friends were busy in Genova a few days back," Toni said, smiling and searching his face for a reaction. "That was an inventive way to kill people."

"Si! I wish we had thought of it. The problem is, we don't go after small fish like that. I would have blown up the captain of the ship. Besides, most of our group was at a soccer match in Florence at the time. As far as I know, we have no activity planned. Anything like this happens in Italy, they naturally assume we did it. Shit, it could have been the Mafia trying to give us a bad name. Then that idiot Giorgio finds out about the bombing and takes it upon himself to call in responsibility for it."

Well, now that's interesting, Toni thought. If the Red Brigade didn't blow up Lt. Budd and his guys, then who in the hell did?

"I'm sorry, Nicolo, but I'm sure that my family wasn't involved," Toni said. The Red Brigade thought that Toni was a member of the Sardoni family, one of the most brutal in Italy with worldwide crime connections. The CIA had planted the right information to give credence to the ruse. She knew that the information she received from the Reds had been indispensable over the years.

Looking down at her watch, Toni quickly finished the last of her cappuccino, said good-bye to Nicolo with a pat on the shoulder, and walked gracefully out of the cafe.

* * *

Kurt quickly rose from a lying position on the Victorian style sofa with the sound of a key at the door.

Toni came in carrying a small black attaché case. Kurt had departed earlier in the morning, before Toni got up and left in her short leather skirt. He couldn't help staring at her perfectly long legs, and well rounded buttocks. Did she only dress that way when she wanted information, or did she enjoy driving men wild?

"Well? How's it going, kid?" Toni asked.

"Just great. I think I'm getting used to your couch."

Toni came over and sat down in a matching chair next to Kurt, set the attaché case on an ornate wood coffee table, and slid off her shoes and set them under her chair.

"Did you find out anything?" she asked.

"Yes. But I don't know what."

"What do you mean?"

"Well, I followed the commerce chief."

"Kirby Stanley...the third."

"Yeah. I followed him on the Metro from his house to a small store downtown. After about ten minutes, he came out carrying a briefcase similar to the one on the table there, only it was brown and a little bigger. The store sold mostly business computers and office supplies."

"So, you want to know why in the hell he went all the way downtown to buy a briefcase?"

"Exactly! I mean I'm not stupid enough to believe that he bought that briefcase. I think he picked up something from someone in the store."

"So, what do you think was in the briefcase, kid?"

Kurt got up from the couch, put his hands in his pockets, and paced over to the large window that overlooked a beautifully landscaped courtyard three stories down.

"Before you answer, I want you to know that I went across town for this leather skirt, so it is possible that a briefcase is just a briefcase."

Kurt paused. "I've got this strange feeling, Toni. There's more to this than just computer chips and avionics technology."

"I agree," Toni said. "But what do you think is going on?"

Kurt turned and looked straight into Toni's dark rounded eyes.

"I've been lying here thinking about it for a couple of hours, and I just have this hunch that something bigger is taking place. Do you ever get this feeling that something is going to happen, and then something does happen? And then you don't know if what you were just feeling was an anxiety of uncertainty, or an actual premonition. You have no way of knowing...may never know. That happens to me sometimes. It's happening to me now."

Toni clicked opened both locks on the attaché case simultaneously, and popped the case wide open.

"What do you have?" Kurt asked.

Toni looked at him with a fiendish smile that must have driven her parents crazy.

"I received a diplomatic pouch from our courier this morning," she said. "Some interesting stuff on the Commerce Department men and their mission."

Kurt moved back and sat on the edge of the sofa nearest Toni.

"It answers a few questions for us," Toni said. "For instance, why the U.S. Commerce Department even has an office in Italy. According to the orders given to Kirby Stanley and his men only a few months ago, they're supposed to have a two-part agenda. Aid U.S. companies currently operating in Europe, and help East European countries move toward market-based economies."

"You've lost me. What in the hell does this have to do with ripping off computer chips and selling them to the bad guys?"

"You know how you said you get strange feelings when something's about to happen? Well, I've got a feeling. I think these guys, or at least someone at Commerce, may have a hidden agenda."

"Wait a minute," Kurt said. "Did you say they were to aid U.S. companies currently doing business in Europe?"

"Yes!"

Kurt thought for a moment. "You mentioned it to me a few days ago. The economic unification of Europe. You said those U.S. companies who don't get a foot in the door soon could be out in the cold and lose whatever European market share they have."

"That's right! And the abstract of this Commerce Department statement of intent explains it further." She looked at some papers. "Congressional limitations on the transfer of high technology to NATO or other European countries will be adhered to without exception. So, someone has found a way to bypass the limitations."

Toni threw the report back into the attaché case. Rising from the chair, she began swearing and yelling in Italian. Kurt could understand most of it, but some of the expressions were clearly slang that he had failed to come across. He could tell that she had no use for bureaucrats. It reminded him of the time she interrogated Lt. Budd.

Finally, Toni composed herself enough to open a large bottle of Chianti, pour a glass, and take a long sip before sitting down again.

"That was interesting," Kurt said smiling. "Feel better?"

She didn't answer. Instead she took another sip of wine.

Kurt didn't want to push his luck, so he picked up the report on the Commerce Department and began reading it.

"All right, I'll tell you what the report says, kid." Kurt quickly dropped the report.

"Stanley, the main man, is basically a yes man," she said. "He used to work for the International Trade Commission until about a year ago. The analyst who wrote this report for us said that Stanley is the brother-in-law of some big whig in the State Department. That guy supposedly got Stanley promoted to this post. Until his recent assignment to Italy, he was an Export Enforcement Policy Analyst in Washington."

"Sounds impressive."

"Not really. Commerce has a bunch of them. Anyway, the second in charge of the Rome bureau is a guy named Jason Dalton. He hasn't been around for a few days, so we haven't tailed him yet. Dalton is an International Trade Analyst. He was working at the National Institute of Standards and Technology in Gaithersburg, Maryland, prior to his assignment here. He's only been with Commerce for about a year, also. Before that, he worked in the private sector with a number of different companies."

"What kind of companies?" Kurt asked.

"Manufacturing, computers, small business consulting firms...you name it, this guy has been around."

"Computers! So this guy could know a good chip if he saw one," Kurt said.

"The other three who work out of the office are mostly administrative types. One is a receptionist slash linguist."

"Is that the good looking blonde," Kurt asked. "I'd like to see the slash part."

"Easy sailor. She helps with the wining and dining. As far as I can tell, she's the only one who speaks Italian. The other two? One's an administrative assistant. Sterling, boring background. The last guy is the one I've been checking out the last couple of days. He's a book-worm-type researcher. Spends all day scanning company statistics."

Kurt got up and went to the small table with the bottle of wine and three glasses. He was about to pour himself a glass, when he realized he still couldn't force himself to drink wine before lunch.

"We need to concentrate on Stanley and Dalton," Toni said. "Why don't you stick with Stanley?"

"Wait a minute," Kurt said. "This is Navy technology leaking out. I think I should go after Dalton, since he's the technology expert. Besides, you said yourself that Stanley is a yes man. Maybe you can convince him to talk like you did with Lt. Budd," Kurt added.

Toni glared at Kurt. "Okay, kid. Dalton is yours. But be careful. He's been gone for at least a few days, so he could have been involved with the bombing of those sailors in Genoa."

That was another reason Kurt wanted Dalton. If the sailors were selling out their country, then they deserved what they got. But if someone made them an offer for money they'd never see in a lifetime as a sailor, then they weren't all that was wrong with the equation. They were still sailors after all. Shipmates stuck together. A sentence at Leavenworth would have been far more painful than a quick blast from a bomb.

Kurt and Toni ate a scant lunch, worked out assignments and their next meeting, and then departed to observe Stanley and Dalton.

20

URMITZ, GERMANY

The green and white Polizei car slowly cornered back and forth down the switched-back hills of the West bank of the Rhine river. A morning iridescent glow filled the sky above a light fog that rose from the warmer river. The car turned left at the bottom of the hill and drove two kilometers along the curved edge of the Rhine where volcanic rock cliffs of the Neuwied Basin narrowed the road at numerous junctures. Two other Polizei cars and a medical van waited alongside the road.

Walter Kaiser slowly opened the front passenger door and lingered for a moment to observe the scene. He'd seen a number of dead bodies throughout his Polizei career. Mostly young men with too much beer and a heavy right foot destined to test the laws of physics with their Volkswagen laboratories. But this was the first time that he would have to determine the cause and reason of death and who was responsible.

"Inspector Kaiser?" asked an officer in uniform who approached from the river's edge.

Walt closed the car door and greeted the officer, "Ja."

"Sir, the body has been pulled from the river, but we don't want to move it any farther," the officer said.

Walt followed the officer to the edge of the river at a reluctant pace. He hadn't been told of the condition of the victim, but was fairly certain it wouldn't be a pretty sight.

A green plaid wool blanket lay haphazardly over the body in short grass on the bank of the river.

"How was the body found?" Inspector Kaiser asked, looking out to the river.

"A passing bicyclist on his way to work noticed it hung up in some overhanging branches," said one of the officers. "It couldn't have been there too long."

Kaiser turned and looked at the officer. "Why is that officer...Jung?" he asked reading his name tag.

"Well, the rain-swollen river reached its highest crest almost a week ago, and it receded nearly a meter in just a few days," he said apprehensively.

"So the tree is normally out of the water, and now the river is down to about normal levels," Kaiser added. "Therefore, the body must have gotten hung up in the branches less than a week ago. But, that only tells us when the body got here. How long has it been floating down the Rhine? And, where did it come from?"

Another officer stepped forward and uncovered the body. "The victim is still well preserved, so it couldn't have been in the river long."

Walt finally made himself look at the body lying at his feet. There was a bag over the victim's face, and some sort of vest strapped around his mid section. Well preserved may have been a hasty observation. Looks can be deceiving, but the smell of rotting human flesh is ingrained forever upon the nostrils of those who have had the displeasure of taking in a whiff. Walt was relieved at what he saw, but still puzzled.

"What in the hell is that?" Walt asked, pointing downward to the body's head.

"We don't know," said the first officer. "We didn't want to change anything until you got here."

Thanks guys, Walt thought. Now he'd have to open this bag and watch the brains of some poor slug ooze out. But what in the hell was that thing around his waist?

"I guess we can rule out suicide," Walt said as he tugged on a rope that had bound the body hand to feet as swine often were just before being butchered.

The men just looked at Walt not knowing if he was serious. Then Walt let out a slight chortle. "It's fine to make light of a situation, sometimes. Without a bit of humor we'd all go insane, and end up committing horrid crimes like this."

The two officers finally allowed a smile.

Walt looked up at the medical technicians and the other two Polizei who had remained at the roadside with his driver. The Polizei were in their late forties and didn't appear overly concerned with the body. The two Polizei with him at the body were in their mid-twenties and apparently eager to learn, or at least find out the truth.

"What's with those two?" Walt asked, nodding his head toward the older Polizei.

Officer Jung looked over to his partner and then back to Walter. "I hear they've been partners for the last twenty years. They do everything together. In fact, they live together. Some say they'd get married if the law allowed."

Walt looked up to the road again, then back at the young officers, and shook his head. "Oh well. More women for me," he said with a smile.

The young officers let themselves laugh.

"Did you check for identification?" Walt asked, getting back to the body.

Without further prompting, Officer Jung reached down to the body with gloved hands and carefully began to search for any sign of identification. The

victim had twelve Deutschemarks in change in his
left front pocket, and a set of keys in his right front
pocket.

"So, he was right handed," Walt said.

Officer Jung gently placed the keys into a plastic
bag held open by his partner who then relayed them
to Inspector Kaiser.

Walt looked over the keys. One key had a
Chevrolet symbol. When Walt saw that, he knew
this case would be more complex than at first
glance.

"Shit!" Walt said.

"What's wrong, sir?" Officer Jung asked.

"He's American."

"How do you know?"

"Well, not many Germans drive Chevrolets,"
Walt said.

Walt pulled a small Swiss Army Knife from his
pocket, bent over next to the body, and cut the elas-
tic tie that held the bag cinched around the man's
neck. Walt pulled his hand back as if expecting
something to jump out at him. Nothing happened.
With a small stick, he opened the mouth of the plastic bag and slid it off the victim's head.

"Camera, please," Walt said to the officers.

Officer Jung quickly ran to his green and white
Opel and returned with a camera and flash unit.

To Walt's surprise, there was very little blood visible. The man's face was pale and colorless. His

eyes were closed, but the lines around the outsides of them indicated his age must have been in the forties. Why the bag? Walt turned the man's head sideways and no-ticed dried blood inside his ear and streaks of blood coming from somewhere on the back of his head.

Officer Jung clicked off a few close up shots of the man's face.

"Let's roll him over carefully," Walt said.

The two young Polizei did as he said, rolling the man on his side and exposing the back of his head. From that view it was pretty obvious why the bag must have been used. The man's skull was split wide open. The rest of the blood must have seeped out through the bottom of the bag, Walt thought.

"What do you think?" Walt asked, looking at Officer Jung.

The young officer looked shocked to be asked his opinion by an inspector from the regional office in Koblenz. He hesitated for a moment to be sure that he said what he meant without sounding obtrusive. "I think someone crushed his head with a metal pipe or something, and then put the bag over to keep the blood from getting all over the place."

"Good! But wouldn't the blow have knocked some blood out almost instantaneously?" Walt asked. "Maybe whoever hit this guy wasn't supposed to hit him so hard. And the bag was originally intended to make sure the guy couldn't breath if he happened to wake up from the blow after hitting the water. Of course, the killer or killers had this planned out in advance. So we're talking a professional hit here."

While Walt was talking to the officers, he pulled one of the velcro strips that held a sand weight to the victim's chest, and flopped the sides of the pouch to the ground at the man's sides.

"Now we know how the man died," Walt revealed. "What we don't know is where and when he died, who killed him, and why."

Walt remembered from his training that sometimes the most obvious details were those overlooked. The search for the complex was not always appropriate. But what about the weights? Not enough to make the man sink to the bottom, but enough to keep him below the surface. Maybe the killers wanted to make sure the guy got far enough away from the murder site, yet wanted him to be found eventually.

"I found something," said Jung's partner. He slid his hand from the inside pocket of the Rhine-soaked man, and retrieved a brown leather wallet. With rubber gloves, he quickly handed it to Inspector Kaiser.

Walt carefully opened the wallet. All the contents were streaked and stained from the brown leather die. A hundred and fifty Deutschmarks in bills, a muddled photograph of a woman and two young

children in 1970s clothes, and a Visa and
Mastercard. Finally, a name for this guy, Walt
thought. And then, a retired U.S. military ID card.

"Charles M. Johnson," Walt said. "U.S. Air Force
retired. How did you get yourself into this predica-
ment, Mr. Johnson?"

Walt continued to search the contents of the wallet. From one of the side pouches, he pulled out a
business card with Charlie Johnson's name on it. In
bold green Roman letters it read: Teredata
International Semiconductors.

Immediately Walt took a double take of the card.
He remembered his conversation with Jake Adams
less than a week ago. Jake was working for the president of TIS trying to find out who was buying up
some of their computer technology. How Gunter
Schecht and his men tried to blow him away. The
man Jake was looking for.

Walt instructed the men to continue with the pho-
tographs, and to ship Johnson back to Koblenz for
an autopsy. "Bag everything," he said.

He went back up to his car and sat in the front
passenger's seat wondering what his friend Jake
was up to. But Walt had no idea where his old friend
was staying. Finding Jake would have to be his first
chore in solving this murder.

21

BONN, GERMANY

Jake got back to his house on the right bank of the Rhine after first eating breakfast at the old Bad Honnef castle. His head was still not clear after the night of beer and conversation with Herb. The sun had finally made a long awaited appearance. Jake checked over the house. Nothing looked out of the ordinary.

All of his communications equipment lay meticulously on a wooden desk in his bedroom as if it had been accumulating there for years. Time to call Milt, Jake thought.

Since it was the middle of the night in Portland, Jake realized he should call Milt at home.

The tired voice of a woman answered, "Hello."

"Sorry to disturb you, but may I speak with your husband?" Jake asked.

He could hear Milton Swenson asking his wife who it was on the phone. "I don't know!" was the terse reply.

Milt picked up the phone after apparently moving into another room and having his wife set her phone back down.

"Hello," Milt said groggily.

"It's Jake. Sorry to bother you so late."

"Shit!" Milt said. "Jake, where in the hell have you been?"

"Hey, Milt, I'm sorry I haven't kept you informed, but things have been really crazy around here."

"That's what I hear," Milt said. "I got a call from the Polizei in Koblenz just two hours ago. They found Charlie Johnson's body."

That's pretty surprising, Jake thought. The way Herb had talked, it should have taken much longer for the body to be found. "Where'd they find it?" Jake asked.

"About ten miles north of Koblenz. Jake? Do you know a guy named Walter Kaiser?" Milt asked.

"Yes. Why do you ask?"

"He's the guy who called me from Koblenz. I guess he's the investigator in charge of Charlie's murder."

Jake thought for a moment.

"He asked about you, Jake. Of course I didn't tell him shit, because I didn't know if he was who he said he was."

"He's a good friend of mine, Milt. I better give him a call."

"Wait!" Milt said. "There's more."

After a pause. "Go ahead."

"We have another problem with a technology leak," Milt said.

"Great. How serious is it?"

"Serious enough that the government already knows about it."

"Where's the leak?" Jake asked.

"In Italy...aboard the aircraft carrier Roosevelt," he said. "We have a contract for an avionics upgrade to the A-7 aircraft going on right now. The A-7 doesn't have much life left, but the Navy feels it makes a good test bed. If the new avionics system can work in that old bird, we should be able to fit it into new aircraft and sell it to the Air Force as well."

"So, how significant is this new technology?"

Milt hesitated for a moment. "Jake, some of the computer chips we use are the fastest in the world. We can't afford to allow this information to get out to anyone. In fact, our contract in Germany called for these chips to replace a slower version in a couple of months. That's why it was so urgent for you to solve that case."

"Another surprise, Milt!" Jake said callously.

"I'm sorry, Jake."

"Why did the Navy allow the aircraft to leave the states?"

"We had to test the system against NATO and French aircraft. We could only simulate so much."

"Okay, okay...so what do you want me to do about it? You said the government is already involved with the investigation."

"They haven't been keeping me informed. I don't know who's investigating what. All they said was that some of the chips and manuals were missing."

"What do you expect, Milt? There could be three or four agencies looking into it, and not one of them speaking to the other. Why in the hell do you think I left the Agency? Nobody communicated for shit."

"Could you look into it for a few days?"

Jake thought about it. Toni! She had to know about the Italian problem. Anything that happened in Italy, she knew about it.

"Milt? I'm very flexible. You've already paid me a substantial amount. I go where you want."

"Thanks, Jake," Milt said softly. "I knew I hired the right guy. So, what have you found out?"

"Well, I'm about ninety-nine percent sure that Bundenbach Electronics hired Gunter Schecht to recruit Johnson into taking your stuff. Bundenbach dropped most of its research and development staff recently, so they're looking for a cheaper way to get ahead. Maybe they've become a company of thieves. The question is why? They were slowly coming out with some decent developments of their own. Maybe the gains weren't coming fast enough. That's the only thing I need to know now, and I'm working on that. One more thing. Johnson may have gotten himself killed because he was selling out Gunter and Bundenbach."

"What do you mean?"

"Johnson may have been selling to another government and Gunter didn't like it."

"How do you know?"

"Recently, a couple of agents from Hungarian Intelligence have been hanging around Gunter. I'll let you know as soon as possible if this is true, because then we'll have to do some damage control and inform the U.S. government. That would pretty much blow my investigation all to hell."

"We haven't informed the government about our Germany leak, so you should be okay for a while."

"Hey, I better let you get back to sleep, Milt. Next time I'll try to catch you at a better time."

"No problem! Keep up the good work, and let me know how things go in Italy. I'm not sure where the Roosevelt is now, but it's big...so I'm sure you'll find it," Milt added with a slight chuckle.

"Thanks!" Jake said, and then he hung up.

Shit! What ever happened to getting in, finding the culprit taking the TIS technology, and heading back to Oregon. Maybe take a break skiing in the Cascades, or even go to Switzerland for a few days on his way back. Now he was back to jumping around to different countries...swapping currencies and cars as though he were changing underwear. Now he had no choice. He'd have to call Toni.

22

BALATON LAKE, HUNGARY

Waves from the dark water lapped ashore at a constant melodic pace echoing through the stately pines of the north shore. Ice built up into a pile at the edge of the lake forming a constantly changing sculpture. A heavy, wet snow blanketed the ground.

Isaac Lebovitz paused for a moment on the wooden porch of the cabin and turned to view the glinting light that remained in the sky above the lake. I'll have a place like this on Lake Geneva, he thought. Soon!

He entered through the heavy oak door; clamoring voices stopped, and a table of men turned to look at Isaac. Satisfied that the security lookouts had not fallen asleep or were not drunk yet, the men continued with their conversation.

Isaac retrieved a shot glass from the mantle above a stone fireplace. The fire was burning hot providing most of the light for the main room of the large log cabin. He blew out the dust and wiped out the rest with his middle finger.

"A little dirt won't hurt," said a stout man with gray hair and a long gray beard. He gestured for Isaac to join the group at the table. "Come. The schnapps will warm you as much as the fire."

Isaac sat down on the hard wood chair and slammed his glass onto the great table. The gray-haired man filled it to the top with schnapps.

With one smooth lift and twist of the wrist, Isaac devoured the contents. A hot flash streaked through his body to the furthest extremity. He slowly set the glass down in front of him.

"Have I missed anything?" Isaac asked, silencing the room. He didn't really expect an answer. "As you all know, I enjoy myself as much as the next. But we must discuss what progress has been made."

Isaac glanced around the table for a response from anyone. "Anatol, why don't we start with you," he said to the man with the gray beard.

The man finished lighting his pipe, allowing plumes of smoke to rise and join a cloud that had already formed. "Thank you, Isaac, I will," Anatol said. "My people are ready to move forward as planned. We'll be ready to go into full production in less than six months."

"Six months!" Isaac said with disbelief. "Your engineers can convert the Prague plant that quickly?"

"Yes!"

"Your people are impatient, Anatol. It won't be long...it won't be long," Isaac said patting him on the shoulder.

He looked at the men once again. Come on...this was their chance to gain back the dignity and respectability that had been denied their families for over fifty years. "Who's next? Rudolf?"

The youngest of the six men sat back in his chair and took a slow sip of schnapps. He was only a child when the great war changed his family so dramatically.

"I've just come from Berlin," Rudolf said, pausing and finding attentive ears. "The city is still not equal. We have a united Germany, but the people are sick of the jaded promises that the communists spouted for so many years. The young people want fast cars, ste-reos, computers...you name it. They've seen what the West has to offer, and they can wait no more. I agree with Anatol, we should be ready to produce in six months as well."

Isaac poured himself another schnapps and stared at it in front of him. He tapped the side of his forehead with his finger, and then grabbed the small glass with one smooth stroke and let the schnapps slowly slide down his throat until the glass was empty. The men are so eager, he thought. Energy was vital to success. But it would take more than energy for the plan to work.

The men talked into the night. One by one each revealed the agenda he had for their countries. The old world ties that bound each of the men were as strong as ever. Then, one by one they bowed out and found a place to sleep. In the end, Isaac remained with Anatol. The fire slowly faded until the flames were replaced by glowing red logs. Hope had been born, and the child would be stronger, healthier, and free.

23

BONN, GERMANY

Gunter Schecht crossed his legs with difficulty, and stared at his boss for a moment trying to read his thoughts. He found himself in the red leather hot seat again. What in the hell does he want from me, Gunter asked himself.

Finally, the president of Bundenbach Electronics shifted his large leather chair and returned Gunter's stare. "The Polizei found Charlie Johnson belly up in the Rhine this morning," the boss said.

Gunter shifted in his chair trying to come up with the right answer. "But..."

"You jumped the gun, Gunter. I needed to know who our competition was. But more importantly, I found out that Johnson didn't give us everything we needed. I won't bore you with technical terms. Let's just say Johnson failed to give us an important binding link. Without it, we'll never know what makes the chip so fast or how to mass produce it." He paused to take in a deep breath. "So, what have you come up with in the past few days?"

Gunter felt cornered and disturbed. "Plenty," he said with a clenched jaw. "I've told you that I suspected Johnson was selling to another government or company. Now I'm sure it must be Hungary."

"Why?"

"Because the last couple of days I've been trailed by a couple of Hungarian Intelligence agents."

"How do you know them?"

"I've been in this game for a long time," Gunter said brusquely. "You get to know the players. The problem I'm having, is why they're following me."

"Perhaps they saw you with Johnson."

"Perhaps! I'm not really concerned if you aren't. I can handle those two."

The Bundenbach boss leaned back in his great chair and swiveled back and forth a few times before looking directly at Gunter again. "We have another problem with Jake Adams," he said. "I've been told that Jake acquired the missing items we need." The boss smiled and lifted his eyebrows. "Have you seen Jake lately?"

Gunter shifted in his chair uneasily. "Dropped from sight. He hasn't shown up at Bitburg or any of our other locations. I don't know...maybe he returned to America."

The boss got up out of his high back chair and walked over to a large book shelf. He pulled out an old leather bound book, and turned to face Gunter. "Marx was wrong you know. History has proven that his Communist Manifesto was a baseless farce."

The two men looked at each other for a minute, and then the boss let out a slight laugh as he put the book back in its slot and returned to his chair.

"We need that data, Gunter," the boss said, becoming more serious. "You must work your contacts harder. The country is going through some growing pains. I want to be on the leading edge of technology when we get stronger. What have you promised your contacts in Berlin?"

"Just what you told me to promise."

"Are the leaders loyal?"

"Loyal? Yes! Trusting? Now that's another point," Gunter said. "As you know, they have a hard time believing anything they're told. But some of them are relatives, and those believe.

"Finding very few jobs should help our cause. And as I've told you I don't want Turks. They work hard, but there will be too much conflict at the plant. We don't need that standing in our way."

"I'll make sure that my friends in the government make it difficult for them to find jobs," Gunter said with a smile. "They'll beg us for work."

"Good! Get me more."

Gunter eased back into his chair and finally let his muscles relax. He tried to digest what his boss had just told him. How did he know that Jake Adams had his missing items? He'd find out. Gunter stood up slowly, nodded goodbye, and then left the office.

24

AUTOBAHN 61, GERMANY

A warm dry breeze out of the southwest had made the early morning seem more like May than January. But Jake wasn't complaining. The continuous cold, damp and clammy weather that he had experienced since coming back to Germany, and that he had often complained about when he lived there, could forever refrain from spoiling his days.

Driving along at over two hundred and twenty kilometers per hour was much safer with dry weather as well. Heading southeast on Autobahn 61 from Bonn to Frankfurt had always seemed to bring rain, snow or fog in the past. A clear sunny day with a warm breeze was more than Jake could have expected, but he appreciated the change nonetheless.

As he passed the Koblenz exit, he couldn't help feeling sorry for Charlie Johnson. Herb had described the murder repeatedly over the past few days, and the morbidity and inhumanity of the act seemed to intensify over time instead of becoming more detached. How could anyone commit such a horrendous crime?

Traffic on the Autobahn consisted mostly of weekend shoppers probably heading to Mainz or Frankfurt, Jake thought. The lack of slow trucks climbing the steep hills of the Idarwald made driving that magnificent highway even more enjoyable than the weather.

The fast speeds make it difficult to think of anything more than mere survival. His tense hands grasped the steering wheel. He frequently looked to the rear view mirror to ensure that nobody was trying to drive faster, and attempting to make him a hood ornament for their Mercedes. But then Jake would catch himself staring at nothing for a dangerous instant, distracted by thoughts of his conversation with Milt. He was hesitant to call Toni Contardo, but knew he needed her. His experiences in Italy weren't extensive. Toni had always been a welcome and willing guide. They had been a great team, Jake thought.

Jake took the next exit, slowing the Audi down and coming to a stop in front of an Autobahn gas station. He got out and went directly to a yellow phone booth outside a small vending area. Hopefully, Toni still lived in the same place. It had been almost a year and a half since he used the number that was still ingrained in his mind for the long term.

She's probably not home, he thought. After all, it's Saturday. The phone clicked on the other end.

"Si, Contardo," said a man on the other end.

Jake hesitated for a moment. English or Italian, he thought. "Pronto, sono il Signor Adagio. Vorrei parlare Sinorina Contardo, per favore," Jake said.

In a few seconds Toni answered. "Pronto," Toni said formally.

"Toni, can you speak freely?" Jake asked.

"Jake!" she said serenely. "Where are you?"

"I can't explain right now. Please listen. I need to call you secure in one hour. Can you make it to the office that quickly?"

"I still have the Alfa Romeo," she said. "I'll be there."

"Thanks, Toni. Ciao."

"Ciao," she said softly and hung up.

Jake hung up the receiver and walked back to his car slowly. It had been far too long. Now he knew he needed to see Toni for professional and personal reasons.

He got into his car, closed the door and put on his sun glasses. It's time for a new car, he thought. Something more Italian. He cranked over the Audi and pulled out slowly through the parking lot, and then, entering the short ramp to the Autobahn, picked up speed quickly until the car was traveling well over a hundred miles per hour.

After half an hour, he pulled into the alley behind Walter Kaiser's house and drove slowly to a parking space next to a white stucco garage.

Jake knew that Edeltrud and little Jakob would probably be off shopping in Mainz or at the vegetable market in Wiesbaden, so he and Walt would be alone.

After the third attempt at knocking on the large wooden back door, Walt finally came and opened it. He looked surprised, yet relieved to see him.

"Jake, come in," he said.

Knowing his way around the house, Jake went directly to a large plush chair in the den, sat down, and placed his briefcase next to the chair. Walt followed him and appeared anxious to start the conversation.

Jake didn't give him a chance. "I've talked with Milt Swenson, my boss, and he said you called him about me," Jake said.

Walt sat in a high back leather chair just to Jake's right. "Yes! We found Charlie Johnson. He was the guy you were hired to find?"

"Right. In fact I know who killed him. Gunter Schecht and his buddies knocked him over the head with a tire iron or something and dumped him into the Rhine at the Deutsches Eck in Koblenz over a week ago."

Walt had a puzzled look on his face. "Isn't that the guy whose license plate I ran for you last week? How do you know he did this?" Walt asked.

"A German customs agent named Herbert Kline saw the whole thing. I found out just a few days ago, but couldn't tell you about it without a body. Anyway, I just found out from Milt that the body was found and you were investigating Charlie's murder. So here I am."

"An eye witness for my first murder," Walt said. "I couldn't ask for more than that. But, why did Gunter kill Charlie? What was the motive?"

"That's the whole reason I'm here, Walt. I was hired by Teredata to find Charlie Johnson. Milt Swenson thought he might be selling some high tech hardware. I'm sure Charlie Johnson was selling to Gunter for a company in Bonn named Bundenbach Electronics. You ever hear of them?"

"Of course! There's been stories in the German press that Bundenbach is making some great breakthroughs in technology," Walt said.

Jake ran his hands through his hair and then looked into Walt's eyes. "The only breakthroughs they've made recently has been through Charlie's skull. I've looked into the company over the past week. They fired most of their research and development department. It seems easier for them to just buy and steal the technology."

"It's hard to believe that a company would have a man killed," Walt said.

"There's something I have to tell you," Jake started. "I know Gunter Schecht from when I used to work in Germany."

Walt just sat in his chair with a puzzled stare.

"You knew I was in the Air Force for three years here before moving on to a private company? In fact, we met just after I got out of the Air Force. Well, I didn't take a job with a private company, I started working for the CIA. It's no big secret now that I resigned. It's just that I feel so bad having to keep a secret from you and Edeltrud for so long. It was for your own good, and of course, the integrity of the assignments I was working. I couldn't compromise my position. I hope you understand."

Walt scratched his unshaved face. "So, is that how you know so much about electronics and computers?"

"Actually, that's the reason the CIA hired me. That and the fact that I knew Germany," Jake said. "You don't seem surprised?"

"Truthfully, Jake. Edeltrud and I wondered about all the trips you took. We couldn't figure out why your company would need you to travel so often. But we didn't suspect the CIA."

"Walt, I need another favor. I need to make a phone call."

"No problem. You can use the phone on my desk," Walt said pointing with his thumb over his shoulder.

Pulling the briefcase from the side of the chair and placing it on his lap, Jake punched in the combination to the dual locks. The case flipped open with the push of one thumb and pull from the other.

"What in the hell is that, Jake? Isn't my phone good enough?" he said smiling.

"Of course. But I need to make a secure call," Jake said.

"Are you sure you left the CIA?"

"Yes."

After a few minutes, the phone was hitched up and ready to go secure. Jake checked his watch. It was about two minutes past the hour mark when he was to call Toni. She'd love this, he thought.

Jake watched the LCD screen as he punched in the number to Toni's office in the American Embassy in Rome.

"Ciao," Toni answered.

"Ciao," Jake returned. "Don't say it. I'm two minutes late."

"It's always better to come late than early," Toni said softly.

Jake smiled. "Can't beat that argument."

"I see that you're calling from Germany," Toni said. "What are you doing there?"

"I'm here on business," Jake said, glancing at Walt.

Walt got up and headed toward the door. Jake gave him a thumbs up and a smile.

"You left the Agency. Who are you working for now?"

Jake thought for a moment, wondering how much to tell her at first. It wasn't a matter of trust, but more of a professional courtesy.

"Can you tell me anything about a technology transfer from an A-7 squadron aboard the aircraft carrier Roosevelt?" Jake asked.

From the silence on the other end of the line, Jake already had his answer.

"Jake, how in the hell do you find out about things like this?"

"If you remember Monaco, Toni, I've always been lucky." Jake paused for a moment. "I need your help."

"Jake, you know you can count on me," she said seriously. "What do you need?"

"Well, I'm working privately for Teredata International Semiconductors, the same company that has had some of its stuff come up missing from that avionics upgrade to the A-7 that I assume you're working on. TIS has some pretty important stuff missing up here on some of its contracts as well. I've been here a while now, but my boss wants me to go to Italy to see if I can plug that leak."

"You're always welcome here, Jake," she said. "When are you coming?"

"I'll be there by morning," Jake said. "I'm not sure what time. It depends on if I run into any trouble along the way."

Toni laughed out loud. "Trouble does have a tendency of following you around, Jake."

"I've got to go, Toni," he said. "I can't wait to see you...it's been far too long."

"Yes, it has," she said softly.

They both hung up gently at the same time.

Jake put the secure phone back in its case and quickly hitched up Walt's phone as normal. He turned and looked into a small mirror above the coat hangers of a wooden umbrella rack. He looked so old. He took a deep breath and released the air slowly.

* * *

A harsh voice echoed through the marble corridor of the Wiesbaden Bahnhof terminal announcing the arrival of a train from Cologne. Jake looked at his watch; exactly noon. Damn thing's on time, he thought. German efficiency.

Through a glass enclosure, Jake watched a portly man sorting Deutschmarks and punching buttons. Then a white ticket with holes popped up through a metal counter, was whisked by a chubby hand and flipped to the hole under the glass.

"Danke," the man said as he looked at the woman in line behind Jake.

Jake looked at the ticket to ensure it was for a round trip to Bremerhaven, and then stuffed it into the inside pocket of his leather coat. While inside his coat, he slid his finger across the butt of his 9mm CZ-75 as if checking his wallet to ensure it hadn't been pick pocketed.

He turned and walked down the long passageway with a high glass ceiling. His footsteps echoed in time with countless others. He stopped for a second to look at a schedule of departures and arrivals encased in a metal frame with glass front. He knew what the schedule said, but the glass was a near perfect mirror to check behind him. Gunter's two men were still there, stopped when he had, less than twenty paces behind him. Gunter was still nowhere in sight. Jake had caught them looking over Walt Kaiser's house and led them here.

Jake waited for the last call for the train to Bremerhaven, and then slowly boarded up the metal stairs. Once inside, he slipped through from car to car looking for a seat in the crowded compartments. He couldn't see his two pursuers, but he knew they were there.

When he reached the second to the last car from the engine, he quickly dropped out of the train and onto the dock before descending the stairs that led to an underground passageway beneath the tracks.

He heard the train slowly pulling away above him.

Once outside, he jumped into the first cab and directed the driver to Mainz Centrum. After he got there, he found the first downtown bank machine and withdrew money from his Luxembourg account. Then he caught another cab and went to a car rental outlet just outside the Frankfurt International Airport. Jake paid cash for a Fiat using false identification. In the parking lot, he swapped some of his gear from the Audi he had been driving for the last couple of days, and then slowly drove out onto the Autobahn and started driving south. He would have to set a fast pace to make Rome by morning.

25

BONN, GERMANY

The charcoal gray Mercedes pulled up slowly next to the curb, stopped, and the headlights went out. In a few minutes, a dark blue Fiat van pulled up behind the Mercedes and parked. Two men got out of the van, hesitated, and then proceeded to the driver's window of the Mercedes. The driver's power window came down slowly.

Parked down the road and obscured by bushes, Herbert Kline lifted a small parabolic microphone from the passenger seat of his car and aimed it through his open window toward the men at the side of the Mercedes. He adjusted the volume on his headset to bring in the conversation at over two hundred meters.

"We ran into a problem," said the Fiat driver.

"Obviously," Gunter said. "If things had gone as planned you wouldn't be here now. You'd be trailing Jake like I told you. How did he lose you?"

The men looked at each other. The thin man was content with letting the large driver explain their failure. "He bought a round trip train ticket for Bremerhaven at the Wiesbaden bahnhof and then...."

"Wait, let me guess," Gunter interrupted. "By the time you looked for him and realized that he wasn't on the train, you two were half way to Denmark."

Herb couldn't help himself. He started laughing so hard the microphone wouldn't stay put long enough to bring in the conversation. When he realized he could be missing something important, he held his breath long enough to settle down.

"Where could he be?" Gunter asked.

The men shrugged their shoulders.

"Shit! Do I have to do all the Goddamn thinking around here? Where was he when you last saw him?"

"The train," said the thin man finally.

"No, you idiot. Before that. He was at his Polizei friend's house. So, it makes sense that he might know where Adams went. Find out. But don't kill the Polizei. We don't need that kind of attention. Bring him to me at our favorite spot."

"When?" asked the fat man.

"As soon as possible. The boss needs that information now to make the plan work."

The men turned swiftly, got back into the van, and sped away. The Mercedes lights came on and the large sedan crept away from the curb and down the road.

Herb put his gear away and started driving to the nearest phone to warn Walt Kaiser. Gunter had finally made a mistake that could be exploited, Herb thought. He had every intention of taking advantage of his mistake.

26

TRIESTE, ITALY

The city lights shone across the dark Adriatic harbor glistening off the slick water. The cloudless sky brightened the fishing pier with shadows and silhouettes of men heading to the closest bar for warming spirits. The starry night brought a bitter chill with it, and frost was forming on anything not warm enough to fend it off.

Kurt Lamar crouched shivering in the shadows behind a pile of wet fishing nets. He had left Rome with only a thin short jacket, not realizing he would be out this late or this far from Toni's warm apartment. He crossed his arms, tucked his fists deep behind his biceps, and hunched his shoulders forward in a vain attempt to warm his neck.

Kurt could only wonder what Jason Dalton was doing on such a squalid pier on a Saturday night. The clothes Dalton wore as he left his Rome apartment should have alerted Kurt that something was up. The casual pants and shirt with no tie were a stark contrast to his normal expensive three piece suit. But with only one stop for gas along the way, Dalton had been easy to follow...almost too easy.

The fishing boat Dalton boarded had arrived at the precise time that Dalton had reached the end of the pier after parking his car in a small lot next to an old wooden warehouse. Kurt had allowed him to board before leaving his car for a closer look.

Kurt cupped his hand over his watch, and then pressed the light button to check the time. Eight p.m. No wonder his stomach was growling, he thought.

After Dalton had been aboard the boat for a half hour, Kurt could see movement on the stern of the boat. There were at least three men, maybe more. Then two men shook hands, one went back into the boat, and the two remaining stepped off the boat and onto the pier and started walking toward Kurt.

With a quick scan, Kurt weighed his options. Stay put and remain in the shadows and hope they didn't see him as they pass, or slowly get up now and walk back to the car nonchalantly. He looked at his clothes and realized he too would look out of place on this pier. And by now it was too late. The men had gotten too close for him to move.

He crouched down to his belly, but could still see them getting closer and closer. He didn't think they would see him as long as he remained still. One was Dalton, but who was the other one, he wondered.

When they were almost even with Kurt, they stopped dead in their tracks.

"Son of a bitch," said the other man.

Dalton slapped the man across his left shoulder and laughed. "It's only a fuckin' rat."

They started walking again.

Kurt heard a rustling to his left. He looked down toward his leg. A huge rat sat sniffing his left knee. Kurt froze and tensed his muscles tightly.

The men passed and continued on to Dalton's car. Dalton started his car and slowly pulled out of the parking lot.

Kurt slung his left leg quickly, catching the rat square across the middle and sending it flying over the pile of wet nets. Then he jumped up and quickly made his way to Toni's Alfa Romeo. He didn't understand his anxiety. Animals in the woods were no problem, but city creatures seemed to be something altogether different.

When he got to the car, he thought about Dalton and his friend. Something wasn't right. They were speaking perfect English, so the other guy must have been American. He could have just been an American businessman. But how did he get there? Not with Dalton, he thought. It had been too dark to see the man's face.

He started the car, drove to the nearest Autostrada ramp, and began the long drive back to Rome. He wasn't looking forward to driving most of the night.

ROME, ITALY

Jake pulled up behind Toni's Alfa Romeo and shut down the tired Fiat engine. The sun was still more than an hour over the horizon, but the glow from the yellow street lights gave him a hint of what was outside.

He yawned and stretched his arms above his head as far as the low roof would let him. Then he tilted the rear view mirror to see how he looked. His eyes were tired and red, and his hair could use a comb. Some fine way to impress Toni after such a long time, he thought.

Walking up to Toni's door, he turned and looked behind him for a second. Toni's car was unnaturally dirty. That only happened on intense cases or long drives.

He went through the first and second doors, and then began climbing the stairs to the second floor. The names on the mail boxes hadn't changed. An older woman owned the building and lived on the first floor alone. She was extremely quiet and spent most of her time on nice days maintaining the garden in the middle courtyard. An older gentleman lived on the third floor. Toni was sure that the older couple were having an affair. She would find one or the other sneaking back to their respective apartment in the early morning as she was on her way to work.

At the top of the stairs on the second floor, with the dark sturdy banister, Jake stood outside of Toni's door in the somber light. He began to knock, then pulled his hand away. It was early, and throughout his drive from Germany he couldn't help thinking about the man who had answered Toni's phone. Maybe he was her new boyfriend, he thought. He could be in there now. That could complicate things.

The door swung open quickly. Toni stood in the dim light looking into Jake's eyes. "Well? Are you going to come in, or would you rather stand out in the hall until morning?" Toni asked softly with a smile.

Jake couldn't think of anything to say. He stepped in, put his hand on the nape of her neck, and kissed her on both cheeks. He wanted to kiss her full on the lips, but the time wasn't right. Time would tell if she ever wanted to do that again. He quickly thought of all the times and places they had kissed. The Riviera, the Alps, and mostly in this apartment. He only hoped that her desire would match what he was feeling right now.

She closed the door quietly. When she turned,

Jake had removed his black leather jacket and taken a seat on the sofa. He looked curiously at the pillow and blankets, but didn't say a thing. He looked at her again. The small lamp on the end table behind Toni provided back lighting that revealed her tight, shapely figure through her loose night gown. He looked away, even though he had seen her many times with far less on.

"I'll explain the blankets in a minute, Jake," she offered quietly. "I see you still carry your CZ-75."

Jake reached under his left arm and tapped his 9mm automatic in its leather holster. "I'd probably walk crooked without it."

"How was your drive?"

She was nearly whispering, he noticed. Maybe the other guy was in the bedroom sleeping. "It was long and uneventful," he said. "I'd prefer to see the Alps in the daytime. Night doesn't do them justice."

Toni nodded agreement. "How about some espresso?" she asked as she walked toward the small kitchen area.

"You know the answer to that, Toni." Her graceful walk hadn't changed. Why did he ever leave her behind?

He heard her mumble something, but the sound of steam being compressed through a scoop of coffee obscured the words.

She came back with two small white cups three quarters full of thick, dark coffee. Jake picked up

his cup with his thumb and forefinger, and set it on
the table in front of him for a second to cool. The
aroma drifted up, and Jake inhaled deeply to savor
the memories that were released within his mind of
all the times that he and Toni had enjoyed espresso
together.

"Grazie," Jake said.

"Prego," she said as she sat down next to him on
the sofa and crossed her long legs.

Jake scanned the room to see what had changed.
No masculine items. That was encouraging.

"You got a new chair for your desk," Jake said.

She looked at him for a second. "Yes. I found it at
a flea market last September off Via della Lungari.
It screamed for me to barter for it. I got a good deal
on it."

Jake picked up his espresso and sucked it down
with one smooth stroke. The enrichment it brought
was nearly instantaneous. He smiled broadly.

"So, Jake, what have you been up to for the last
year and a half?" she asked.

"You know I hate to write letters," he said. "And
I know the last phone call before I left Germany for
the states was less than enlightening for you. What
can I say? Things happened quickly. I resigned and
moved to the Portland area. I took some time off.
Went hiking in the Cascades. I stayed with a few
college friends for a while, but didn't want to over-

stay my welcome. And you know how I can't stay in one place very long."

"How'd you come to work for Teredata?"

"About a year ago I was at a party in Portland, and met this corporate investigator. He was a real jerk, and couldn't find his own house without a map and pictures. Anyway, he got pretty drunk and started spouting off about how he was so busy he was turning clients away. I was looking for a job, so I told him I'd take one of his rejects. He gave me his card, and I went down to his office the next day. He had a nice place in Beaverton. He knew how to set up an office and wine and dine, but that's about all. I worked just one job for him and decided I'd rather work for myself. And here I am."

"I envy you. You always seem to know what you want. It's how you get there that's confusing at times. Of course working for Cecil is nothing like that little Hitler you worked for."

"How is Cecil?" Jake asked.

She thought for a second. "Not too good. He had a heart attack just before Christmas and hasn't returned to work yet. I'm not sure he will."

"Shit...Cecil. He was in good shape. He's one of the last old school guys."

"Yeah," she said. "That's why we're so short-handed down here. To top it off, John was transferred to the Middle East on short notice in

November and we don't expect a replacement anytime soon. I told him to lose the Arabic, but he
wouldn't listen."

Jake shook his head. He felt nervous. He looked
at his watch and around the room again. Finally, he
set his gaze on the pillow and blankets.

"Let me explain those. I have a guest who is
working on this case with me."

"The guy who answered the phone when I called
from Germany."

"Yes. His name is Kurt Lamar. He's an ensign
with the Naval Investigative Service. He was
assigned aboard the USS Roosevelt to find out how
computer chips were being pilfered from an important avionics upgrade to the A-7. It turns out a couple of technicians were working with a pilot who
carried them onboard his A-7 and then diverted to
shore complaining of some inflight emergency. We
know the pilot made a drop at Camp Darby, but
we're not sure who he sold the stuff to."

"That's similar to what was going on in Germany.
Only the guy ripping off the chips was a tech rep for
Teredata's F-15 avionics upgrade. My guy was
clonked over the head and thrown into the Rhine.
They just found him a few days ago."

Toni looked surprised. "This is crazy, Jake. The
pilot we interrogated was blown up in the Genoa
attack last week. I'm sure you heard about it."

"I haven't been listening to the news for the last

week. I've been spending most of my evenings watching the guys who killed the tech rep."

"Four sailors were killed with a remote control car loaded with plastics. Kurt had two of the four figured out, and our pilot gave us the names of the others."

"Not without your patented persuasion I'll bet," he said smiling.

Toni shrugged her shoulders. "Well? I can't help it if people try to keep secrets. Do you think the bad guys would do any less?"

"No."

"See!"

Jake felt a shiver come over him, bringing goose bumps to his arms. The long drive with no sleep must have been catching up with him. "I hate to get back to business, but I really need some sleep. I need to talk through some of this case though. You don't think that these cases are unrelated do you?"

"No. But why haven't our Agency guys in Germany contacted me yet?"

"Because I haven't told them shit. You're the only American official notified so far."

"Pride runs deep with you, doesn't it?"

"It's not just that. I don't trust those bastards. Besides, I'm working for Teredata. The company has an obligation to report lost technology, but only after they're sure it's going to a foreign government. I'm still not sure that's the case. I'm a corporate investigator. I believe this transfer has more to do with economics than politics or national security. If I find out differently, then naturally I'll report it...in due time. Like I said though, I think this is corporate espionage."

"I think you're right, Jake, but when do we draw the line between national security and a foreign company's will and desire to become more competitive?"

"I don't want to philosophize over this, Toni," Jake said as he rubbed his eyes and then stroked his fingers through his hair. It was a legitimate question. Justifying his right to remain autonomous hadn't even been a consideration in Germany. He had asked Milt Swenson if the government was aware of the technology transfer. When Milt said no, Jake hadn't even questioned his intent. He knew that the last thing any government contractor wanted was the slightest appearance of impropriety. Future contracts relied on the performance of those currently in place.

"How serious was the transfer in Germany?"

"It depends on your perspective of damage," Jake said sarcastically. "I know you're not really into computers, but I'll try to explain the problem. The chips alone are important. More so, though, is what you do with them. This is the fastest chip currently in production, and probably the fastest that anyone could expect to come out with in the foreseeable future. So they are important."

Jake paused for a second contemplating how to explain the technical details.

"So, is this technology restricted for transfer to NATO countries?"

"Currently, yes."

"Are they the same as the chips on the A-7 contract?"

"No! They're similar."

"But...."

"Wait a minute. Let me explain further. Like I said, these chips are important. Put them in your normal PC and you've got one hell of a fast computer that can out perform anything currently on the market. And that's what Teredata plans on using them for, eventually. The German company that acquired them, Bundenbach Electronics, will probably use them for that purpose...and maybe more."

"Like what?" she asked, uncrossing her legs and moving closer to Jake on the sofa.

Jake felt the shiver again. He didn't know this time if it was caused by his lack of sleep, or what he was about to reveal to Toni. "Have you ever heard of transputer technology?"

She shook her head back and forth.

"Well, it's the greatest advance the Europeans have ever made in computer technology. It's a series of chips linked in parallel sequence that integrate speed, power and communications into the fastest microprocessor ever produced at unbelievably low prices. It's turning America's best supercomputers into relics."

"Why do the Europeans need these chips then?"

"They don't , if they want to produce a half-assed computer. If they combine a bunch of these transputer chips in parallel, they come up with the fastest computer on the market. But the technology isn't perfect. It takes some complex and sophisticated software to make the big machines work at peak performance. The Americans are the world's software wizards. Also, the transputer chips lack memory direction. In other words, when a bunch of people try to use the computer at one time, the computer gets confused. It can mess up someone else's work in a heart beat."

"How will the Teredata chips help that?"

Jake got up from the sofa and walked to the window overlooking the courtyard garden. The fading moon cast a ray of light over the upper portion of the building across the square. He turned and sat against the edge of the marble sill, and crossed his legs and arms.

"The Teredata chips combined with the transputer chips would give you the perfect computing system. Speed, power, everything. And, the system would be economical. On a small scale, you could make a personal computer microprocessor about one fourth the current size with about fifty times the processing speed. On a large scale...I don't even want to think about that."

She rose from the sofa and came over to the window. "I think we have a problem." She looked out the window and placed her hands over the warmth rising from the radiator beneath the marble sill. "Kurt found out something interesting last night. In fact, he just got back a few hours ago. That's why he's sleeping in my bed instead of the sofa as normal. I knew you'd be here this morning."

"What's the problem?"

"I told you we interrogated the Navy pilot. Well, we found a telephone number on him. We traced the number to the U.S. Department of Commerce in Rome."

"Commerce? What in the hell are they doing in Rome?"

"That's the first question we asked. We found out they were chartered by Congress to help U.S. businesses currently operating in Europe, and to give technical assistance to East European countries with emerging market-based economies."

Jake rubbed the thick black stubble on his face. "I can understand the first part. American businesses are going to be at a disadvantage when the European Economic Community gets its shit together. The U.S. companies need to get their butts in gear if they plan on staying competitive. But why would they want to push to help the East European countries?"

"Kurt and I have been thinking about that. We think that the U.S. government may be looking at those countries as a cheaper labor force and an eventual market for goods. That is once they get their economies straightened out."

Jake placed his hands over the warm radiator. "That makes sense. But what did the pilot have to do with the Commerce Department?"

"That's the problem. We think we have a rogue in the department. Kurt followed Jason Dalton, the second in charge of the Rome office, to Trieste last night. Dalton dropped off something with at least two guys aboard a fishing boat. We think that Dalton was the contact for the pilot and his men and is transferring the chips to some other country."

"I see. If he made the drop here in Rome then perhaps he would be selling to a company in Italy. But he's transferring in Trieste, which is more like a Slovenian port than Italian."

"Exactly! I see your time in the private sector hasn't dulled your reasoning," Toni said.

"Ha...Ha." A shiver came over Jake again. This time he was afraid he shook visibly. He had to sleep. But more than that, he had to digest the essence of this case. It had become an enigma; two fold from what he had just left in Germany. His case there wasn't complete, yet he had this new case to work as well. It was comforting to have Toni here, and Herb would keep things moving in Germany while he was away. But how did they relate to one another, or were they even related? He'd need sleep to determine that.

"What are you thinking, Jake?"

"I'm thinking if I don't get some sleep I'm going to drop."

"The sofa is yours," she said stroking her arm slowly toward the makeshift bed.

He didn't need any further convincing. He swaggered over, plopped down on the sofa, and curled up his legs to fit on the short couch.

* * *

In a few minutes, Toni came over to the sofa and looked at Jake. She unhooked his gun from the shoulder holster and set it on the coffee table. Then she covered him with the blanket and straightened it over his body. She sat down in the chair next to the sofa and watched him sleep.

27

VARAZDIN, CROATIA

The pale morning sun seeped through the lead glass outer windows of the great foyer picture window casting elongated diamonds across the burgundy Persian rug.

Isaac Lebovitz hesitated briefly at a small wooden table to smell a grand bouquet of tiny red roses. It was but a small example of what would come, he thought. The beauty and fragrance of a San Remo villa would embrace him with pleasure, and bring tears to his eyes each and every morning. Tears of joy, not despair.

With the creak of the stairway behind him, Isaac turned. Vitaly Urbadic, his most trusted agent, made his way down the rest of the stairs slowly, and stopped to look out to the overgrown front garden. His tired, wrinkled eyes revealed the reality of his forty years, and the long nights and constant travel.

Yet, his muscular chest bulged his tight black shirt almost as it had when he was an eighteen-year-old Olympic hopeful. Only a knee injury had stopped his running career. And his twenty years with Hungarian Intelligence had kept him out of the factories.

"It's a jungle out there," Vitaly quipped.

Isaac moved over and opened the door to his large study. "I know you must be tired from the long trip last night," he said. "But I have to hear what you've learned."

Vitaly stretched his arms high above his head and yawned. "All right. But I thought we could at least make time for coffee."

"The maid will take care of that. Come, have a seat. You may be young, but time will eventually catch up to you as it has me. And then watch out. You won't be able to run around the continent from Germany to Italy and back to Croatia without a great deal of discomfort."

"The discomfort has already arrived, Isaac," he said.

"Greater discomfort than fatigue."

Vitaly sat in the chair opposite Isaac's desk.

"Did you get enough sleep?" Isaac asked.

"I guess."

Isaac tapped the side of his forehead with his index finger in time with the clock on his desk. "What did you find out?" he asked.

Vitaly shifted in his chair. "Dalton is a shrewd man."

"Besides that," Isaac said, becoming more impatient.

"He signed the contract. I countersigned to the right of your signature as you requested. He had another guy with him. I think an attorney. He had that distinguished and arrogant air to him, yet shifty eyes. His investors were eager to close the deal, so we can go forward with the plan."

"Was the money transferred?" Isaac asked directly, realizing his question was more like an accusation.

Vitaly hesitated. "Yes. In the Swiss account."

"Excellent! Things are moving ahead even faster than expected. I don't want to wait for Budapest to get off its ass. I could die of old age before that happens."

"What other choice do we have?" Vitaly asked.

Isaac rose from his chair and walked over to the window overlooking the overgrown side garden that scaled the side of the high brick outer wall. The wall had once kept the poor from peering inward, and the gentry from seeing those less fortunate. Perhaps he could move forward faster, he thought. The money was in place. The technology acquired. Why not? He turned toward Vitaly.

"We have another choice, Vitaly," he said smiling. "We can shift our first project to Germany. I know...I know, that was supposed to come later. But Germany is moving much faster than Hungary. Rudolf said his company would be ready in six months. That would give his engineers plenty of time to convert the production line."

"But...will Rudolf's workers stay?"

Isaac sat down again and tapped his forehead. "Yes," he said softly. "They must. They are loyal to Rudolf. He said he's only lost a few workers to the West. Other companies have lost up to fifty percent. Production has nearly come to a standstill some places. We could start training Rudolf's workers now, and in a few months, be ready for full production. Rudolf said six months not knowing that the money would be available this soon. I'm sure that he could push for an earlier production date."

"But what about marketing?" Vitaly asked.

"Dalton's strategy will help us out there as well. We should be able to keep labor and production costs down. We'll pump our products out to Western Europe and America at a reasonable price and great profit for us. Then, we'll be established to exploit Eastern Europe also."

Vitaly smiled broadly. "It sounds like we can't fail."

"We can't fail!" Isaac emphasized. "The chips Dalton has given us are the fastest available. Combine those with the information we are obtaining in Germany, and we'll have the most advanced product on the market at the cheapest price. They'll sell like ice cream on a hot day."

Without knocking, the maid came in with coffee and an assortment of bread, cheese and meats. She nodded to Isaac, and slowly limped out without saying a word.

Isaac motioned for Vitaly to help himself, and then got up to leave the room. "I'll be back in a minute."

Out in the foyer, the sun had intensified allowing the visibility of dust particles in its beams. Isaac met a tall man in a dark black suit. The man's eyes stared coldly at Isaac without blinking. His cratered face and steel jaw looked like a Greek statue that had succumbed to acid rain. His large hands were thick and strong. He still had his black felt hat on.

Isaac looked into the man's eyes sternly and then turned and walked toward the kitchen. The man followed. Once the door to the kitchen was closed, Isaac said, "You were supposed to get here first."

The man finally took his hat off. "Yes sir, I know. But I had to make a detour to Rome first."

Isaac raised his eyebrows. "Rome? Why Rome?"

"I watched the transaction as planned. But I wasn't alone. There was another guy who had followed Dalton to Trieste."

Isaac's interest was now rightfully peaked. He gestured for the man to sit at a small booth near a convex window with a view of the sculptured back garden and pond. It was the only garden on the estate well maintained and out of view of Varazdin's lower class. "Please, tell me more."

"I followed the man to a nice residential area in Rome. The car and apartment belong to a woman named Toni Contardo. I couldn't find out who the man was."

"Who is she?" Isaac asked quickly.

The man paused for a second. "CIA."

"What? How do you know?" Isaac asked.

"About two years ago, when I was still assigned to the Southern NATO intelligence acquisition, I ran across her path. She's one of the agents who cracked our NATO plans scheme. She planted the disinformation to our guys, who then turned it over to the KGB. When the Kremlin found out the plans were useless, our two agents were killed."

"Yes, yes...I remember," Isaac said. "So then we must assume that the other man who followed Dalton is CIA also."

The man shrugged.

Isaac tapped his forehead and then looked at his man directly. "You must make sure they don't stop Dalton. We can't have anything go wrong now. I thought that getting rid of Cecil, her boss, would be enough. But I guess we'll have to get rid of a few more. Do what you have to do. Use whatever means required. I want it done quickly, and with as little commotion as possible.

The man smiled and shook his head.

"You have a problem with that?" Isaac asked.

"No, sir. It's just that Contardo is quite the looker. It will be a terrible waste of beauty."

"That's never stopped you before. Use as many men as you need. Don't confuse her beauty with a lack of competence. The CIA doesn't hire just anyone. She has to be good."

The man needed no more guidance. He rose and departed through the back door.

When Isaac returned to the study, Vitaly was stuffing the last of the bread into his mouth. Isaac poured himself a cup of coffee and took a slow sip.

"Is everything all right?" Vitaly asked, his voice muffled by the bread.

Isaac heard the words, but neglected their meaning. He looked at Vitaly carefully. He was eager to please without question. When Isaac left Hungarian Intelligence for early retirement, his men slowly resigned with him to keep from arousing suspicion. Govern-ment service had at one time meant a prestigious position, but had quickly become a mire of bureaucratic stagnation. Vitaly should be beyond the scrutiny of question, Isaac thought. But there was far too much at stake to disregard a double-layered operation. Even Vitaly had to be watched.

"Yes, Vitaly. Everything is just fine." Isaac sat back in his chair and brought his hands together to his mouth as if praying.

28

ROME, ITALY

Jake slowly opened his eyes to a darkened room. The shades were drawn, but a glint of light seeped through; only enough to make out objects of furniture in Toni's living area. He pressed the light to his watch; sixteen ten. That was more sleep than he expected to get.

He switched on a small lamp on the table next to the sofa; his bed. Toni had left him a note. She and Kurt had gone to check on Jason Dalton, and would return by five p.m. He checked his watch again. Less than fifty minutes away. Milt should be on his third cup of coffee and halfway through the Sunday paper by now, he thought.

Jake picked up the phone and dialed Milt's number.

"Hello," Milt answered.

"Jake Adams," he said.

"Jake, where are you?"

"Italy." Jake yawned.

"You sound tired. Did you drive down?" Milt asked.

"Yeah. I just woke up. Has anything happened since we talked last?"

"Well, yes." Milt paused. "The government is giving me shit. They say the leak is still in place aboard the USS Roosevelt."

"How's that possible? I take it you've heard about the bombing in Genoa a week ago?"

"Yes."

"That may have been to cover someone's tracks. I'm not sure who. But we're working on it."

"We?" Milt asked.

"Yeah, I still have a few friends in Italy. Milt, are you alone? Is Steve Carlson there with you?"

"I'm alone. Steve took an unexpected vacation. Something about a sick aunt out East. I briefed him before he left, though."

"Sorry to hear that. Milt I'll track down the Roosevelt and see what I can come up with. Who's the tech rep onboard?"

"A guy named Burt Simpson. But he's trustworthy. Steve hired him personally about two years ago."

"I don't trust anyone," Jake said sternly. "Trust can get you killed at this stage of the game. But I'll find him and get as much information as I can from him."

"Milt, I've got a theory. Bundenbach Electronics was moving in a number of different directions up until about five months ago. At that point, they cut loose all of their research and development people except for those working on transputer technology." Jake waited for some response.

"Go ahead."

"Well, I think that Bundenbach decided to shift all its efforts to transputers, but then came up with the same problem that the other European companies have run across. The transputer processing is fast, but it comes with trade-offs. To make it truly outstanding, say a breakthrough equivalent to the Cray One back in the early eighties, they had to overcome memory direction problems. With the speed and storage capabilities of your chips, they can overcome all of their problems. They'll have a computer with an ironclad networking scheme at one fourth the price of any supercomputer. They could put a lot of companies out of business with a super transputer like that. But even more scary would be to shift production of transputers to the personal computer level. I don't even want to think about what would happen then."

Jake paused again to listen for a response.

"Milt, are you still with me?" Jake asked.

"Shit. I wish we'd thought of that. Are you sure you don't want to come to work for me permanently?"

Jake laughed. "No, thanks anyway. Computers are just a hobby with me."

"Yeah, right. I wish we had a few more hobbyists in our company."

"Do you think my theory has relevance then?"

"Yes, unfortunately," Milt said. "I wish you were wrong, but I doubt you are."

"Thanks for the confidence. Milt, this case is taking some strange twists. I'm sure that I'll have it wrapped up in no time. But...." He thought about his own motives.

"What's the matter, Jake?"

"I don't know. This case really pisses me off. And when I get pissed, I do things that may hurt others. It would be okay, but sometimes those people are close to me."

"Do what you have to do," Milt said, and then paused. "There's a lot to be said for self-preservation. Sometimes you have to hit people over their head to get their attention. Let's hope it doesn't come to that."

That's the problem. Jake had a bad feeling about this case. Getting shot at during his first days in Germany didn't help dispel that feeling. He thought things would change for the better, but keeping one step ahead of Gunter and his men had been nearly a full-time job.

"Milt, I'll do my best," Jake said with confidence.

"I know, Jake. I know."

Jake hung the phone up gently. He stroked his hands through his hair. This shit's getting long, he thought, as he pulled pieces of hair straight up. Dirty too. He rose from the sofa, quickly undressed, and went into the bathroom to take a shower.

As the shower was getting hot, Jake looked at himself in the mirror. He noticed he'd lost a few pounds. His muscles were a little less defined; probably due to his lack of working out since arriving in Europe.

After the shower, he walked out into the living room, naked, rubbing his head dry with the towel.

Toni stood at the door, watching him.

Jake finally noticed her and just stood there looking back at her. He felt a warmth rising within him.

She kept her gaze on his eyes, but had to notice him growing.

"Is Kurt with you?" Jake asked.

"No. I'll have to go pick him up in a few hours."

"That should be enough time," Jake said as he moved closer to Toni.

Her breathing became slower and deeper; her chest rising with each breath.

Jake dropped the towel, grasped the nape of her neck, and kissed her anxiously.

Squeezing his firm buttocks with both hands, she thrust him closer to her.

He released his kiss and nibbled along her strong jaw and down her neck; then back up to her ear.

She stretched her head backward. "Jake," she sighed.

He slowly unbuttoned her shirt and unleashed the front latch on her overflowing bra. Her breasts escaped into his awaiting hand. He caressed her gently, discovering her firm, rounded form, as he had so many times before.

Toni kicked off her shoes, and Jake helped her slip out of her skirt.

Their lips met again as they lowered themselves to the smooth blue tapestry.

He slowly entered her.

"Yes," she cried softly. "Pronto, pronto."

He picked up the tempo. Smoothly, quickly, forcefully.

She arched her back and forced her lips upward with each stroke.

It was as if they had never parted ways. They had always been so good together.

After a long while, they lay united, embracing, her soft face against his stubbled jaw.

29

KOBLENZ, GERMANY

The white tiles shone brightly from the overpowering florescent ceiling lights. A large nurse in white strode confidently down the corridor with a silver tray in her hands. An antiseptic odor permeated the air, enough to give a headache to the uninitiated.

Herbert Kline squinted into the small window of the hospital waiting room door. A blonde woman sat in tears. Across from her, an old man leaned forward and rested his chin on his hands cupped over the end of a wooden cane.

Herb started to push his way through the door, but hesitated. He wasn't good at comforting, he thought. That's probably why his marriage had failed. He wouldn't allow himself to lend emotional support to a woman who justly needed it.

Slowly he entered through the heavy wooden door. The old man didn't move, and the pretty blonde continued to weep.

"Entschuldigen Sie, Frau Kaiser," Herb said standing in front of the woman. "My name is Herr Kline. Jake Adams is my friend."

Finally, she looked up at Herb; tears streaking her high cheek bones. "Is Jake here?" she asked softly.

"No. I just found out that your husband, Walter, was here less than an hour ago."

"You're the Customs Officer?" she asked.

"Yes." Herb quickly flashed his identification to prove who he was, and hopefully put her at ease. "How is your husband?"

She shifted in her chair and crossed her legs in the opposite direction. "The doctors won't commit themselves one way or the other. He has a lot of internal bleeding."

Herb noticed that she found strength in talking about Walter's condition. "I'm sure he'll be fine," Herb said. "This is the best Krankenhaus in Koblenz...perhaps in all of Rhineland-Pfalz."

She nodded.

"Can you tell me what happened?"

"I don't know much. I came home with Jakob, my son, after spending the evening with my parents. Walt decided at the last minute not to come with me. He said he had some things to clear up on a case he's been working. When I came home, he was gone. His computer was on, the lights were on, but that was it. I thought he might have taken a walk. He does that from time to time. I put Jakob to bed, and then started to worry when he still wasn't home. I called his assistant to see if he had gone there, but he hadn't."

"So, how did they find him?" Herb asked softly.

"A young couple found him this morning lying in the street less than five blocks from here. I...I didn't recognize him when I saw him." She covered her eyes with her hands and shook trying to hold back the tears.

Herb placed his hand on her shoulder. "We'll find the bastards who did this." He knew that he would-n't have to look far. Gunter's men had done just what they were told. Get the information, but don't kill him, Gunter had said. What could Walter Kaiser have known to make him hold out that long? Perhaps only Jake and Walt could answer that...and maybe Gunter now.

"How did you get here then, Frau Kaiser?" Herb asked, trying to displace some of the tears.

"One of Walt's men drove me from Wiesbaden."

Herb saw a flash of white at the door through the corner of his eye. A doctor waited as Herb had, not knowing if he really wanted to enter. Herb quickly went out to greet the silver-haired doctor.

"Are you Walter Kaiser's doctor?" Herb asked anxiously.

"Yes. Are you with the Polizei?"

Herb didn't say a word. He simply flashed his credentials quickly and slid them back into his pocket. "Well? How is he?"

"Pretty banged up," the doctor said. "He lost blood internally and through numerous cuts and lacerations. He looks like somebody dragged him behind a Mercedes at high speed on the Autobahn. He has broken ribs, a broken nose and jaw. A few fingers were snapped like twigs. Whoever did this must enjoy giving pain. It appears that Herr Kaiser resisted heavily."

"Has he said anything yet?"

"Yes, he keeps mumbling something. It's hard to make out, but I think he's saying, Johnson, and Boss. I don't understand what that means. Do you?"

Herb thought for a moment. Johnson? He's dead. What could Johnson be the boss of? That makes no sense. "No, it makes no sense to me," Herb finally said. "But I'll guarantee one thing. I'll find out who did this. May I speak with him?"

"Yes, for a moment. But I'm not sure how much he'll understand."

Inside the private room, tubes protruded from nearly every opening on Walt's body. A machine pumped a bellows up and down and acted as Walt's lungs. He could have been any man, Herb thought. He had never met Walter, but was sure he looked nothing like the frail entity lying before him. Would he trust a stranger? Herb scanned the room to be certain they were alone, and then moved next to the bed.

"I'm Herbert Kline, a good friend of Jake Adams, and an agent with the German Customs Office," he started. "I know the men who did this to you, and will make them pay dearly. But first, I need some information from you."

Herb looked around again. He had to find out what, if anything, Walt told the men.

Walt's face was heavily bandaged, and his eyes were swollen nearly shut. So it was hard for Herb to know if Walt's eyes were even open. Finally, the same words that the doctor had heard came out softly. "Johnson...boss."

Damn it! What in the hell does that mean? "Johnson is dead!" Herb said adamantly.

"Boss...." Walt said desperately.

Johnson...boss. "Johnson's boss?" Herb asked.

Walt attempted to nod his head.

Who in the hell is Johnson's boss? Did he mean Gunter? "Gunter Schecht?"

Walt shook his head sideways.

A monitor the size of a lunch box kept track of Walt's pulse and heart rhythm, and was now producing an erratic and fluctuating wave setting off a buzzer.

In a few seconds, the doctor and the large nurse came barging through the door and put an end to the questioning.

Herb walked back toward the waiting room. Two uniformed Polizei were now positioned outside the door. Herb didn't want to be questioned at this time on what his involvement was in the case. Nor did he care to explain how he gained access to Walt's room. Instead, he changed directions and departed the hospital by way of the stairs.

BONN, GERMANY

Herb slammed his office door behind him. The outside hall probably reverberated from the percussion, but on Sunday nobody was there to turn their heads in disgust or complain out loud. Herb sat down hard in his swivel chair and stared at his cluttered desk. "Now what, Herbert?" he said softly to himself.

He opened the lower right desk drawer and withdrew a fresh liter of schnapps. Gently, he broke the seal with a twist and set the bottle down on the desk in front of him. The schnapps rocked back and forth against the side of the glass as a stone would do to water when dropped in a clear mountain pool. He grabbed the bottle and poured a shot glass nearly full. Then he hesitated. Jake was depending on him to keep the investigation going strong in Germany, and he had failed miserably. Jake's good friend lay battered in the hospital, and Gunter could now know where Jake was and what he was up to in

Italy. The answers remaining couldn't be found in the bottle, he realized.

Slowly, Herb picked up the shot glass and started pouring it back into the bottle. Most made it into the bottle, but in the end, his desk was splotched. "Shit!" After capping the bottle and returning it to the drawer, he cleaned the mess with paper towels.

Herb had to know why Gunter and his men were so willing to waste human lives, or at least snub them from dignity as he had with Walter Kaiser. What would Jake do? Herb closed his eyes and rubbed his face with both hands. He felt like weeping as Frau Kaiser had. But tears, like schnapps, rarely found solace in Herb's mind. Only the schnapps flowed freely regardless.

Herb pressed his fingers against his temples as if trying to squeeze an answer from his memory. He and Jake had planned for nearly every contingency. If Jake were to come up missing, Herb was to quickly turn his information over to the CIA and German Intelli-gence. Jake would do the same for Herb.

He was beginning to think that it was time to turn the case over to the Intelligence Community any-way. Why should he have to put up with Gunter and his men? But, of course, that was part of the prob-lem. Gunter had so many friends in German Intelligence that he didn't know who to turn the case over to. Who could he trust? At least now he

knew that he could trust himself and Jake...and
Kaiser if he survived. This wasn't a case of national security, but more of national direction, he
thought. It was becoming obvious that corporations
would now do most anything to survive and pros-
per. The merger of the European Economic
Community into one market made that even more
important, he thought. So, German Intelligence
would have to wait. This was a commercial and
economic case, he convinced himself. German
Customs would work this one until the end...with
the help of one American.

He rose from his chair and went to the window
overlooking the Rhine River. The current flowed
smoothly to the north. It had always been a deceiving flow to Herb. The water appeared to be stagnant, but in reality was strong and swift. Perhaps
this case had been deceiving as well. It had
appeared to be a simple case of customs violation.
The transfer of technology that was not allowed by
the United States, Germany, or NATO allies. But
now murder, kidnapping and terrorism had moved
the case forward as dangerously as the swift Rhine.

Herb returned to his desk and opened the top
drawer. He looked carefully at the brown leather
holster that contained the Walther 9mm automatic
that was issued to him, but rarely used. He took off
his jacket, wrapped the shoulder harness into place,
and clipped the pistol under his left arm. Slowly, he

put his jacket back on. Jake was counting on him, and now he'd have to prove that he could handle Gunter. Maybe not only for Jake, but for himself.

30

ROME, ITALY

A warm breeze out of North Africa streaked the temperature upward and gave the Romans hope for a short winter. The Monday streets were teamed with cars with windows down, and sidewalks with pedestrians carrying their coats over their shoulders.

Toni Contardo got out of the Fiat cab, paid the man, and walked swiftly toward a restaurant less than a block from the Colosseum. She noticed that the tables that were normally reserved for the warmer months had been pulled out on short notice to accommodate the quickly increasing noon crowd.

She didn't see her lunch date, so she went inside. After taking off her sunglasses, she quickly scanned the small room to the left and the alcove to the right. Nothing. Then back in the corner she saw a large hand waving above the crowd. Taking careful steps around the crowded tables, she finally reached the small table with two chairs against the back wall.

Bruno Gallano rose from his chair to greet her. He kissed her on both cheeks and they sat down. She looked closely at his face and read the bags under his eyes. They said he had lost far too much sleep. Probably on the Genoa bombing.

"You look fantastic, Toni," Bruno said, letting his tired eyes shift up and down Toni's body.

She hesitated. "Thanks. You look tired."

He shook his head and then took a slow sip of Chianti. "Yes, I guess I do," he said softly. "I have a lot of pressure on this case I'm working. It just doesn't make any sense. I think I've come up with a breakthrough, and then I run into a brick wall and have to backtrack." He shook his head again.

Toni looked at the full glass of Chianti in front of her that Bruno must have ordered for her. She took a long sip. Longer than normal. "I might be able to help you out."

Bruno raised his eyebrows. "How?"

"First of all, I need you to tell me what you've found out so far," she said, almost demanding.

Bruno rubbed the day old stubble on his face. "That's the strangest part of this whole case. The Americans just picked up anchor and proceeded on their schedule as if nothing happened. I expected them to leave a team of investigators behind to hound me day and night until I found out who killed their four sailors. Instead, they only asked for updates through diplomatic channels. My boss here in Rome has also shown no real concern for the case. He simply tells me from time to time to just put the blame on the Red Brigade and call it quits. But I don't see that as the solution."

"What do you think?" Toni asked, and then took another sip of wine. She knew now that the pressure Bruno felt was self-imposed.

"I don't think the Red Brigade had a thing to do with the bombing," Bruno started. "Not that they didn't have a good reason. But they usually go after the higher ranking military leaders."

Toni nodded her head in agreement. "The Red Brigade was not involved," she said smiling.

"How do you...never mind. I'm sure you have your sources."

"A fledgling member, not one of the chartered few, decided to call in responsibility. So, you can direct your efforts elsewhere," she said.

He picked up his glass, swirled the last of his wine around in circles, and then gulped the rest down. He poured himself another glass, and stared directly at Toni. "It was an American," he whispered.

Toni's eyes widened. "An American? How do you know?"

"I have an eye witness who even helped the man with the bombing. A child, actually." He smiled and drank some more wine.

"Was he another sailor? I mean, what was the possible motive?" she asked, knowing that he couldn't know the answer or he wouldn't be here with her.

"I was hoping you'd help me with that, Toni."

She knew that giving Bruno information was impossible. But he could be helpful to her later, so she didn't want to shut him out completely. She pulled out a pencil from her purse, scribbled the name Stanley Kirby on a beer coaster and handed it to Bruno.

"This guy has been in the country for a little over a month," she said. "I don't trust the guy. He might know something."

"Another brilliant hunch, Toni?"

She shrugged her shoulders and finished the last of her wine. "I've got to run, Bruno. Thanks for the wine and conversation." She rose to leave.

Bruno stood and kissed her on both cheeks again. "It was my pleasure, as always. Ciao."

"Ciao." She turned and made her way through the crowded room.

31

USS THEODORE ROOSEVELT,
NAPLES, ITALY

Jake steadied himself as the officer's liberty launch rocked with a swell from a boat heading to shore. The island of Capri glistened to the south, and Mount Vesuvius loomed to the east. He gazed with amazement as his launch got closer to the huge carrier. Aircraft lined the deck with their tails hanging over the edge nearly seventy feet above the water. The island towered even higher above the flight deck with radar circling, keeping vigilance even in the harbor.

The young boatswain's mate cranked the wheel, cut the power, and then cranked it into full reverse for a few seconds before switching to idle. The launch swelled high and parallel to the gray wall that was the starboard hull about midship. A metal ladder with a platform at the bottom awaited the passengers once the swells settled. The boatswain had to quickly shift forward and reverse and crank the wheel violently just to keep the launch close to the platform and ladder.

Jake watched closely as a few officers made graceful jumps from the launch to the platform. He wanted to ask why the launch couldn't be tied to the platform. But after watching the swells for a few minutes, he realized that the small craft would be battered to pieces in a matter of minutes without a skilled boatswain.

Jake moved to the edge of the launch. He looked down at his cowboy boots and knew that if it weren't for his cover he should have worn tennis shoes. As the launch reached the height of a swell, he leapt to the platform and landed with a slight slip.

At the top of the ladder, Jake was greeted by a lieutenant commander with a dark black mustache and bushy eyebrows. His khaki uniform was finely tailored and pressed. Probably the public affairs officer, Jake thought.

"Senator Blake?" the officer asked.

Jake nodded and noticed a petty officer standing to the edge of the quarter deck. "Thanks for having me aboard," Jake said, reaching out to shake the commander's hand.

The commander shook Jake's hand and then turned to his left and looked at the young petty officer. "Sir, this is Petty Officer Third Class Leo

Birdsong from Denver." The commander turned
and winked at Jake, knowing that the Senator had
requested Leo by name since he was from
Colorado.

"Glad to meet you, Leo," Jake said reaching his
hand out to shake as if campaigning. "I hear you can
get lost on one of these big bird farms, so I asked for
a guide. Sorry if it's an inconvenience to you."

"No problem, sir," Leo said, attempting to smile.

"Well, I'll leave you two to wander the ship," the
commander said. "You can go just about anywhere.
You won't have access to the secure areas, but
they're not very interesting anyway. Petty Officer
Birdsong knows the flight deck area—that's what
most people like to see."

Jake looked sternly at the commander for his con-
descending expressions. "I'm sure we'll do just
fine."

Leo started out at a fairly slow pace winding his
way through passageways, over knee knockers, and
up ladders. Then he picked up the pace to what must
have been his normal stride. Jake kept up with difficulty as his hard cowboy boots echoed through the
empty corridors.

"Leo," Jake finally said.

Leo stopped and turned to look at Jake. "Yes,
sir?"

"I'm not on a short schedule. We can take our
time...if that's all right with you?" Jake grinned.

Leo didn't seem overly amused. Kurt had told Jake that Leo was one to be trusted, but who would take some time to trust others. Jake had to break through to Leo quickly. Gain his confidence.

"I'm sorry, sir. But I was supposed to have liberty today. I could give a shit about Naples, but I really need a beer," Leo said, with apparent relief.

Jake moved closer to Leo. "Is there a place we can talk freely?"

"About what?" Leo asked skeptically, obviously searching his mind for a motive.

"I'll tell you in a minute."

Leo turned and went through a few more compartments, opened a hatch with a Z on it, and directioned Jake to enter. Once inside, Leo battened the hatch and dogged it tight with a metal tube. It was a small compartment with two work benches, a gray metal desk, a file cabinet, and a book shelf with Navy Regulations in black binders. A few aircraft black boxes sat on the benches among an array of test equipment and tools.

Jake sat down on an old pilot's ready room chair that had probably been replaced by something much better. The blue vinyl cover had cracked and been repaired with wide green duct tape. Leo remained standing with his arms crossed.

"Tell me about your friend, Kurt Lamar," Jake said, looking up at the tall, black sailor.

Leo was caught off guard. That had to be the last

name he expected to come out of the Senator's mouth.

"Sir, what the hell does Kurt have to do with Denver or Colorado? Shit, he's from Wisconsin. In fact, he's probably back there right now freezing his ass off." Leo laughed at the thought.

Jake laughed too. "No...no he's not in Wisconsin," Jake said shaking his head. "Not that he probably doesn't wish he were there from time to time."

Leo looked more seriously at Jake now. "Do you know Kurt?"

"Yeah, and I know you. At least I've had a thorough background check done on you."

Leo looked more concerned. "What the hell do you want from me?"

"Information. Just information. Without it, your friend Kurt could be in a lot of trouble. In fact, he could be charged with four counts of murder."

"Murder? What in the hell are you talking about? Kurt got hit by a fuckin' car in Naples while we were in port in Genoa."

"Why did he go all the way to Naples if he wasn't trying to set up an alibi? A bit convenient wouldn't you say?" Jake asked, stretching his legs out and crossing his boots.

"Convenient? Even Kurt isn't crazy enough to let himself get hit by a car. I mean, we might not like living aboard this floating city working twelve-hour shifts 'till we drop, but I sure as hell ain't going to let some car fuck up my body just to get out of it. And I know Kurt wouldn't either. Who the fuck are you anyway? You ain't no Goddamn senator."

Jake didn't want to push any farther, but knew he had to. He had to be sure that Leo was a safe risk. "Your buddy didn't get hit by a car. I saw him in Rome this morning."

"You're fulla shit," Leo shouted. "I saw the message saying he went home on convalescent leave." He was becoming visibly angry now.

"He must have had it sent," Jake said, fighting to keep a straight face. "The Italians have questioned him more than once about the Genoa bombing. They think he did it, and won't allow him to leave Italy until someone proves otherwise." Jake paused for a minute to think of which direction to move next. The entire conversation was extemporaneous. He had planned the concept, but not the details. "What can you tell me to prove that your buddy is innocent?"

"Out at sea, it doesn't take long to get to know people. You have to trust your shipmates. You choose those who you feel you can count on. Kurt is that kind of guy."

Kurt was right. Leo could be trusted. Judging character was the most important aspect of human intelligence. Schools can only partially prepare someone for this work, Jake thought. But experience is what really counted. Time to come clean.

"Sit down, Leo," Jake said. Leo sat in a chair across the small compartment. "My name is Jake Adams. I'm not a senator from Denver. I'm a corporate investigator from Oregon. I'm working with Ensign Kurt Lamar of the Naval Investigative Service." Jake paused for a response.

"Kurt's NIS? Ensign?"

Jake nodded. "Yes. He was working undercover in your squadron to find out who was taking computer technology from the new avionics retrofit."

"Son of a bitch. That's why he kept looking over the supply records."

"That's right," Jake said. "He had the leak figured out to a certain level before his services became more important in Italy. Petty Officer Shelby Taylor, Lt. Stephen Budd, and those two others who died in the bombing in Genoa were all involved with the transfer of technology to an unknown source."

"Shelby was a spy? Shit, he couldn't even keep his own shoes tied," Leo said with a slight laugh.

"Maybe so, but he was the one putting the stuff aboard the A-7s for Lt. Budd to bring ashore."

"What kind of stuff are you talking about?" Leo asked.

Jake thought for a moment about the elaborate diversion by Lt. Budd. "Leo, I came aboard without being searched. Is that normal practice?" Jake asked, and then pressed his left arm against his CZ-75.

"No! They assumed you were a senator, so wouldn't dare search you. I've been strip searched, spread the cheeks and all, coming aboard and going ashore. The Marines do the searching, and seem to enjoy pissing you off with the inconvenience. They don't search everyone. It's mostly random. So you never know when it might happen."

"That makes sense with six thousand people coming and going," Jake said. "But what about civilians? Do they get searched?"

"Yes! At least I think so. I haven't actually seen one picked to be searched, but I'm guessing they could be."

"I've got a problem, Leo. I need to talk with the Teredata tech rep, Burt Simpson. Do you know him?" Jake asked.

"Yeah, I know him," Leo said derisively. "He doesn't know shit about electronics."

"Why's that?"

"Every time I ask him a technical question, he doesn't have the answer. He just says he doesn't have time, and he'll get back with me. What that means to me is he doesn't know shit. If he ever gets back to me at all, he gives me some bullshit answer that I could have gotten out of the tech manual."

Jake smiled. He could see why Kurt liked Leo. "I need to talk with him. Could you bring me to his shop?"

"No problem."

Leo unlatched the hatch and led Jake through the winding passageways, up and down ladders, and finally to a hatch with a sign that read: "Teredata International Semiconductors."

"He's probably inside," Leo said. "Otherwise the hatch would be locked."

Jake looked closely at Leo. He didn't want to get him involved. "Stay out here, Leo. I need to talk with him alone."

Jake entered through the hatch and closed it snugly behind him. A man sitting in a gray metal chair looked up at Jake, obviously startled by his presence. Neither said a word. The man glanced toward a small wooden box on the desk next to him.

"May I help you?" the man finally asked.

Jake noticed he was wearing an expensive leather coat and black pants with a recent crease. He was younger than Jake expected. Probably early thirties. His long, thin face and skinny nose made him look like a rat. "Are you Burt Simpson?"

"Yes! Who are you?" he asked bluntly, his eyes shifting from Jake to the box on the bench.

"I'm with NIS investigating the deaths of the four sailors blown up in Genoa," Jake lied.

"I've already answered all the questions from your buddies," Simpson said, rising from his chair, and squaring himself to Jake.

"That's nice...but I want the truth."

"Fuck you. You squids don't have any jurisdiction over me."

"That's true. But people do have a tendency of slipping on the wet deck on dark, cold evenings. The Mediterranean may seem warm compared to the air at first, but after bobbing around for a half hour or so, it becomes quite cold."

Simpson looked directly at Jake.

"What's the matter, smart ass, you can't come up with a quick answer now?" Jake said.

"I don't know shit about the bombing," Simpson said, and then turned toward the work bench, picked up the small box and placed it gently in a small black satchel.

Jake quietly stepped a few feet to his right. He was across the shop, but still only about ten feet from Simpson.

Without warning, Simpson turned and shot toward Jake. The sound of the gun echoed loudly throughout the small compartment.

Jake hit the ground. The world around him blackened for a moment as he lay on the cold, gray metal. His face, smashed against the deck, felt the percussion of steps as Simpson ran to the hatch. And then the hatch slammed with a hard clang and reverberated back and forth against the steel walls as if some giant had blown through a metal pipe. Jake tried to lift his head, but couldn't.

Finally, he opened his eyes and stared directly at a pair of black leather boots.

"Son of a bitch," Leo said, standing over Jake. "He shot your ass."

Jake wanted to talk, to say anything, to know he was still among the living and not just dreaming Leo standing in front of him. But his lips wouldn't move yet either. Then he felt strong hands grab him under his arms and pull him to his feet and hold him in place until he could stand on his own.

Jake felt the side of his head. There was barely enough blood to feel moist. But his head ached and he could still see stars. His knees buckled slightly. It seemed as though the ship was swaying back and forth in heavy seas, but he knew that his equilibrium must have been disjointed. He remembered the last time he felt this way. He was a running back in high school. He hit a hole at full speed, stuck his head down at the last second, and bashed head on with a linebacker helmet to helmet. The next thing he knew, he was on the sidelines sniffing some nasty chemical. He had hoped that feeling would never return.

"Are you okay?" Leo asked, still holding onto Jake.

"I think so. Where is the bastard?"

"He came flying out the hatch, nearly knocked me to my ass. I heard what I thought was a shot. So I was getting ready to open the hatch. Come on. He's probably heading off the ship."

Jake shook his head and started to follow Leo through the passageways. Leo was wasting no time. It was as if he too had been shot at and felt violated.

"I know a short cut," Leo said.

They had to be at least two or three minutes behind Simpson. Jake had no idea how long he had been lying on the deck before Leo picked him up, nor did he have time to ask the question.

When they reached the first downward ladder, Leo swung his arms outward over the railings and quickly slid to the bottom. Jake tried this too, but his leather jacket stuck to the railings slowing him down. Heading aft, Jake followed Leo through a long passageway with open hatches. Jake felt as he had running the low hurdles in his youth. The difference was the unforgiving knee knockers and the low metal overhead. One mistake, one slight lifting of the head at the wrong second, and he knew that the pain from the bullet hitting his left temple would be minor in comparison to his head bashing into the heavy curved door frame.

Leo stopped quickly. He turned to Jake and put his index finger to his lips.

Jake heard the pounding of footsteps coming from a cross passageway. He slid his hand inside his jacket and pulled out his 9mm automatic. Leo looked surprised.

Jake pushed Leo behind a door frame and motioned for him to stay put.

Jake jumped through the door to the cross passageway with his pistol pointed ahead. "Stop, Simpson!"

Simpson stopped dead in his tracks looking shocked to see Jake. He slid to the nearest bulkhead behind a narrow door frame. Then Simpson's pistol appeared and shot once.

The bullet echoed loudly and pinged as it ricocheted down the passageway. Jake smashed himself against the gray bulkhead and took cover. There was a hatch about six feet in front of him. He knew he had to reach that, or he would be an easy target. He slithered along the bulkhead to the wide hatch. The hatch was hooked to the wall with a small metal latch. Jake unhooked it and waited for a second. Peeking around the edge, it appeared to Jake that Simpson was reloading. He could make out just part of his body, not enough to place a bullet, but maybe enough to force return fire.

Jake shot once, narrowly missing Simpson's jacket. Then he quickly closed the hatch halfway.

Simpson returned fire, hitting the hatch.

Jake checked his side of the hatch for damage. Nothing. Nice shield, he thought. Now came the waiting game. Who had more bullets and the better aim? Just as Jake was about to take another shot, he heard the swishing sound like that of water smashing against a hard surface. He poked his head around the hatch and saw a thick stream of water plastering Simpson, and the muffled sound of a man being battered from the salt water of an inch and a half fire hose opened wide. The hose went from Simpson's lower body then quickly upward bashing his skull against the hard metal bulkhead. Then the water stopped.

"Take that, mother fucker," Leo said smiling. He had gone up the nearest ladder and slid up behind Simpson.

Jake quickly ran out and pushed Simpson's gun away from his wet, crumpled form lying in the corner unconscious.

"Quick," Jake said. "We've got to get him out of here."

"Why? NIS will take it from here," Leo assured him.

"No. It will take too much time to fill them in on the case, and Kurt said that the Navy wasn't sure who was involved. We can't trust anyone. I can only trust you, Leo. Please?" Jake knew he had no jurisdiction to conduct an investigation onboard a U.S. Navy ship, and his false entry aboard the ship could land him in the brig.

"What the fuck. I haven't had this much fun in a long time," Leo said.

Jake and Leo carried Simpson back to the Teredata shop and found some dry clothes for him. Then Jake pulled a small brown wallet from inside

his leather jacket. Flipping the wallet open, Jake
exposed what looked like a set of three darts. He
unscrewed the tip from one and replaced it with a
needle from a different pouch in the wallet. Then,
pushing on one of the metal vanes on the other end
that was supposed to be the dart's feather, a small
amount of liquid squirted out.

Jake examined Simpson's limp body lying on the
cold metal surface that his own body had already
been introduced to. Simpson had a large bump on
the back of his head with a small amount of blood
already drying to form a clump in his hair. Jake
pulled Simpson's mouth open, curled his lip over,
and shot the needle and the drug into his already
flaccid body.

"Shit! I'm glad we're on the same side," Leo said.

Jake smiled. "The needle is so small he shouldn't
even feel the hole when he wakes up for good. And,
it won't leave a mark like it would on an arm or
leg."

"Maybe. But it sure looks crude."

"Leo, could you hand me that bag," Jake said,
pointing to Simpson's small satchel.

Leo handed it to Jake. He looked through it. A
pair of leather gloves, a watch hat, a change of
underwear and socks, and the small wooden box.
He opened the box. It was empty. Something didn't
fit, Jake thought. The depth of the box seemed too
shallow. He shook it. Nothing. The bottom looked

normal. Then he twisted the latch ninety degrees and the bottom popped up. Jake pried the false bottom upward to reveal the hidden contents. Four computer chips were encased in styrofoam, and a computer disk lay over the top of them. Jake knew that he had found the source of the Italian link, but he still had no idea who Simpson worked for, or whom he was selling the chips and information to. He had to interrogate Simpson.

"What did you find?" Leo asked.

Jake looked up slowly, feeling a little weak still from the bullet graze to his temple. "Nothing much, Leo. Just the fastest chip in Europe." Jake closed the box and placed it back in the bag. "How can I get Simpson off the ship without waking him?"

Leo thought for a second and then smiled. "You're the senator. You outrank the captain of the ship. We should be able to just walk off onto a liberty launch with any bullshit story."

Jake realized that Leo was probably right. His cover had worked to get aboard, so pulling this off should be fairly easy. Jake and Leo prepared their story, and then set out with Simpson's semi-limp body between the two of them.

32

BONN, GERMANY

The cobbled streets of the old town were crowd-ed with raucous people heading from one Gasthaus Fashing party to the next. Half of the people were in costume. A lion, Cowboys, a voluptuous wench, and the others wore nice slacks and sweaters. But they all weaved as though they were slightly drunk.

Herbert Kline watched the fat man slide from the driver's side of the dark blue Fiat van and swing the door shut. When the door failed to latch complete-ly, the man slammed his shoulder into it.

"Bastard's already drunk," Herb said softly to himself. He reached into the glove box and pulled out his standard issue Walther 9mm automatic. He slid the bolt back slowly and then released it allow-ing a round to set firmly into the chamber. Then he disengaged the hammer and let it slide forward carefully. After placing the gun in its brown leather case, he clipped it to the Polizei belt on his right hip.

He grasped the green hat with short black brim and placed it squarely on his head. Not a perfect fit, but it would have to do.

Herb was convinced that most of the people on the sidewalk wouldn't take a second glance at his mustard yellow shirt and dark green trousers that signified he was a Polizei. He walked with authority to the door of the Gasthaus that the fat man had entered. Then he hesitated for a moment to assure his mind that what he was about to do was not only necessary, but essential to his case. To sleep with swine you had to get used to the smell, he thought.

He entered through the glass door and stood for another moment in the foyer. Large floor plants lined the walls and accented thick tan ceramic tiles. Loud voices echoed through the brick walls. Herb pulled open the heavy wooden inner door and a cloud of smoke bil-lowed from the crowded bar area. He walked over to the end of the bar and searched for his target.

"Bier?" the bartender asked, pointing to Herb.

"Nay, danke. Ich mochte, aber haben Sie arbeit."

"Schade!"

Herb nodded his head in agreement, playing the dedicated Polizei. Then he saw the fat man at the far corner of the bar quaffing a large mug of beer. Be patient. A few more beers.

The fat man ordered one after another and drank them faster than the bartender could draw the next one. Finally the man slid off the wooden stool, grabbed his belt and pants waist and pulled them upward, and then walked toward the men's room.

Herb casually followed the fat man out of the bar to the foyer area and then into the men's room. The man stood with his chubby hand against the wall over the open urinal and was relieving himself in a grand fashion.

Herb pulled his leather gloves over his fingers tighter and quietly walked up to the fat man. Just as the man shook off any residual urine and zipped his pants, Herb gave him a strong, quick kidney punch.

The fat man crumpled hard to the floor immediately with a release of air as the wind was knocked out of him. Herb grabbed him by his jacket collar and dragged him away from the urinal. He rolled him to his back, pulled his head from the ground by his hair, and then punched him in the nose and mouth. He punched him again and again. Blood oozed from the man's nose, lip, and a cut under his left eye.

Stop. Herb's heart raced. He wanted to swing and swing until all the life was out of the fat bastard. After all, he was the one who had clonked the pipe across Johnson's head and then wrapped him and threw him in the swift Rhine. The one who had sent a flurry of bullets Jake's way. And undoubtedly one of the cowards who had battered Kaiser senseless. He didn't deserve to live, Herb thought.

The door swung open quickly and a skinhead walked in, stepped over the fat man's legs, and then relieved himself. Without concern, he simply walked out.

Herb shook his head in disbelief. He dropped the fat man's head and let it slam to the ceramic floor. Quickly he emptied the contents of the man's pockets onto the floor. A handful of Deutschmarks, a small knife, two paper clips, a pen, a slimy comb; nothing out of the ordinary. Inside his jacket was a gun and shoulder holster. The right inside jacket pocket contained a small piece of paper.

Herb looked behind him to the door, and then unfolded the paper. The initials F.I. and the number 0920 were at the top. Then Rome and Lufthansa were scribbled quickly. He folded the note and returned it to the man's right pocket. Frankfurt International, Luf-thansa from Rome arriving at 0920. That's nice, Herb though, but what fucking day.

The fat man lay with a stupid smirk on his face. Unfortunately, he probably didn't even feel the blows to his face. Maybe the pain would come in the morning.

Herb started to leave the men's room, but stopped. He came back and rolled the fat man on his side, tugged his wallet from his pocket, took all the money out, and returned the wallet to his pocket. Robbery was reason enough to beat a man.

Outside the Gasthaus, back in his car, Herb wondered what day that flight would arrive and whether there was even any significance in the information. Something had to work. Somehow, he had to prove to Jake, to himself, to the rest of the customs office, that he was worthy of the best assignments. That he still had what it takes to run a proper investigation. Some way he had to bring this whole thing together. Make sense of it all. Somebody would have to make a mistake eventually. And the fat man lying on the men's room floor might be that somebody.

Herb gripped the shift knob and quickly pulled it back against his chest in pain. Even through the leather glove, he could tell that his hand would be bruised from smashing the fat man's face. A small price to pay, he thought.

FRANKFURT INTERNATIONAL AIRPORT

The large black board ticked away feverishly updating the arrival schedule of flights from across the globe. Herb watched as Lufthansa Flight 86 from Rome clicked up in bold white letters, Arrived. The large crowd of people pushed and shoved closer to a metal railing that separated them from four doors leading to a ramped customs area. A pair of U.S. Army Military Police stood staunchly side by side surveying the crowded scene. Two German Polizei, armed with Uzis, strolled over to the edge of the crowd and parked themselves next to the corridor that led from the International Terminal to the parking ramps and the main terminal.

Finding the right day for the Lufthansa flight had been easier than Herb had expected. The airlines changed times of their flights frequently to deter terrorists from becoming overly familiar with their routes. It was laughable reasoning, but just one small effort out of many to curb the possibility of a bombing. So the flight had been the day after the fat man found his face against the men's room tile.

A soft female voice echoed over the public address system in German, English and French the gate where the Rome passengers would descend through. Herb scanned the shifting crowd for Gunter and his men. Nothing. It had to be the right day, he thought.

A fat woman walked over with a small poodle on a leash and sat in the chair next to Herb. He pretended not to notice her, but her body odor would have chased a room full of weight lifters from a gym.

Then he saw the fat man at the far edge of the awaiting crowd on the opposite side of the Polizei with Uzis. The fat man's face looked like it had gone through a car windshield in an accident. His left eye was swollen shut, his nose looked twice the normal size, and his upper lip would take days to get back to its proper dimensions. Herb smiled as he looked down to his own bruised hand.

Passengers started streaming down the ramp and through the four open doors to the terminal waiting area. Some carried only brief cases, but others pushed carts loaded with suitcases. Herb kept his eyes open for Gunter Schecht. He had to be there somewhere.

Then the fat man moved forward quickly to greet a man in a blue suit with a black and gray beard. He only had one thin suit bag slung over his shoulder, and a small brown attaché case. Who the hell was that? Herb reached to his ankles and pulled up his socks, then he sat up again to watch for Gunter.

The two Polizei, seeing Herb's signal, approached the fat man and the bearded passenger. The man, apparently disturbed, set down his attaché case, pulled a blue passport from his inside coat pocket and flipped it open for the armed men. Satisfied, the Polizei slowly strolled over to a young couple and asked to see their passports as well.

Herb got up and followed the men to the exit. Outside, the men waited next to the curb. Herb lingered and watched from the window next to the automatic sliding doors.

The early morning fog had actually gotten worse. The large multi-level parking ramp only a short distance across the loading road, taxi area, and bus stop was barely visible. In a few seconds, a silver

Mercedes pulled up and stopped in front of the two
men. It was Gunter's car. The fat man opened the
rear door for the bearded man, closed it behind him,
and then got into the front passenger seat. Swiftly
the car pulled away and was lost in the fog.

Herb wandered outside and watched as passengers and friends boarded buses and taxis and awaiting cars. The cold moist air seemed to move right
through Herb's body as if a ghost had enveloped
him and then departed to another victim. He shiv-
ered and pulled his thick cloth collar up around his
neck.

The electronic doors slid open behind him and the
two Polizei walked toward Herb. They chatted
about the lousy weather as they brushed up beside
Herb and passed a small note into his open left
pocket. He put his hands into his pockets and held
on tightly to the piece of paper. He knew that his
break had finally come. Following Gunter was of no
consequence to him. Whoever this man was, he had
to be important to his case. The fat man acted as
though he were somebody. Gunter wasted no time
picking him up. Normally, his arrogance made him
late. The distinguished bearded man had to be
important. He had to be a key to Bundenbach's
plans.

Finally, Herb pulled out his wallet with his right
hand and placed the note inside among his
Deutschmarks as if seeing how much money he

had. "Steven Carlson" is all that was written. The name sounded familiar, but he couldn't place where he had heard it. It wouldn't take too long to find out more about this man, but he'd need Jake's help. He missed the days that he and Jake had worked side by side. He felt as though Jake was the only one who believed in him. The only one to see him for what he was. Not perfect, not the best, but a fellow human who needed to feel viable once in a while. Jake took him seriously. He listened to his ideas and cared.

Herb went back inside through the doors. He strolled back toward the parking ramp. Passing close to a smoke-filled airport bar, he felt the urge to go in and shoot down a few shots of schnapps to celebrate his small victory. He even stopped for a second and started to turn in. But then he changed directions and continued on toward his car. He stopped at a yellow enclosed phone booth, called Italy, and left a message for Jake.

Back at his car, he planned his next move. He would drive back to Bonn and keep track of Gunter and Steve Carlson until Jake got back. Carlson had to be the key, Herb was convinced.

33

BUDAPEST, HUNGARY

Isaac Lebovitz sat quietly in his dingy office and stared at the government clock that he took with him when he left Hungarian Intelligence. He knew it was a useless State product that had only about a fifty percent chance of being on time, but it reminded him of all the time he had spent surveying Western targets. Who cares? In no time, only Swiss clocks would let him know that he didn't really have to be anywhere special at any special time. Besides, the warm San Remo beaches of the Italian Riviera would remain faithful to his tardy ways.

He sifted through page after page of economic reports that Dalton had provided him. Some were marked NATO Restricted by the U.S. Commerce Department. That brought a special smile from Isaac.

Vitaly Urbanic walked in unannounced and took a seat on the other side of Isaac's desk.

"Is everything coming together?" Isaac asked. He felt guilty not telling Vitaly everything about his plan. He was convinced that the less Vitaly knew about certain aspects of the operation the better off he'd be in the long run.

"Yes, sir."

"I expect nothing less from you," Isaac complimented.

Vitaly shifted in his chair. "I'm a bit confused. I don't understand how we can produce and market this computer without the help of our government?"

Isaac smiled as he rose from his chair. "Vitaly, Vitaly, you're still thinking like a Communist." He patted his old friend on the shoulder. "Think like a Capitalist. I realize that you haven't had as much exposure to the West as I, but get away from the old thinking. Or back to the older thinking."

He loomed over Vitaly as a teacher scolding his pupil. "You were too young to remember anything prior to World War II. As a young boy my father told me stories of how great the Austro-Hungarian Empire was. We had a strong navy. Great wealth. World esteem. Power. Now look at us. A dog that slobbers for table scraps from Russians. But change is moving forward swiftly. Soon we will be strong again. Soon the Russians will be begging us for food, and we shall be powerful like our European cousins. The time for action is now. We'll make mistakes, stumble as a child does when he first learns to walk, but eventually we will stand tall and walk...run with the other economic powers. With or without our government."

Isaac drifted slowly to his chair and sat down behind his desk. His breathing and heart rate had increased. He tapped the side of his head with his index finger.

"How will we make this work?" Vitaly asked.

"Smooooothly." Isaac quipped, finally smiling.

"But..."

"Are you worried about the technical support?" Isaac asked.

"Yes. But also the marketing arrangement."

"It's a risk. I admit it," Isaac said. "But every great entrepreneur has to take risks. It's the nature of the game. Technical support will be no problem. Dalton has given us nearly everything we need to produce his chip. I'm waiting for the last piece of information from him and we'll be set to start producing the chips in Germany. We'll have the leading edge of our network ready to exploit the European Community's single market. In less than six months, we'll produce the computers and chips here as well. And then six months later in Prague. You see, we're nearly ready."

"And the German technology?"

Isaac hesitated. "Rudolf assures me that his technicians can handle the transputer conversion."

"Is Rudolf loyal?"

Isaac laughed. "Of course. He's family. Married to my niece. She's quite good looking. Our family network is important, Vitaly. We've had nothing else for the past fifty years."

"But I thought we still needed the remainder of the transputer relay schematics?"

"That's true. In fact, that's why you're here. The American will be in Germany soon. I need you to take the rest of your men to Bonn and confront him. You explain to him that we had a deal with his man, Johnson." Isaac's eyes became wide and his voice deepened. "Don't take no for an answer. He'll have access to the German technology we need."

Vitaly shifted nervously in his chair. Isaac knew that this was the first time since leaving Hungarian Intelligence he had asked his good friend to go beyond the normal means of persuasion. Yet, he also knew that he would never ask his top man to do something he himself was not willing to do.

"What if the American is stronger than we think?" Vitaly asked, knowing the answer already.

Isaac hesitated. He tapped his finger against his temple and stared directly at Vitaly. "Take all of your best men," Isaac said. "We need this information now. If the American hands over the last of the chip technology to Bundenbach Electronics, they could reach the market much sooner than us. We could still produce a quality product much cheaper, but we can't afford that kind of competition.

Bundenbach has massive resources compared to us. So then you must do two things, Vitaly. Get the German technology, and stop the American from turning over his information."

Vitaly nodded. "Yes, sir." He got up from his chair and slowly walked out of the room.

Isaac slid his front desk drawer open. Inside, a beautiful postcard of the Italian Riviera lay among a pile of stark white papers. He picked up the card, brought it to his lips, and kissed it gently. Bright red, yellow and green sailboats were moored in the San Remo harbor. The sun shone brightly. Colorful flowers canvassed the foreground. And Isaac saw himself bend over to take a deep whiff. He closed his eyes and smiled.

34

ROME, ITALY

Toni paced from the refrigerator to the sink and stood with her hand on the faucet not remembering why she was even in the kitchen. She noticed her hand tremble.

Kurt came into the kitchen from the living room. "I guess I'll get my own beer, Toni, but thanks for offering anyway," he said, pulling a liter bottle of Peroni from her refrigerator.

"I'm sorry, Kurt. I guess I'm drifting off a bit tonight," Toni said. She stroked her long fingers through her thick black hair.

Kurt opened the bottle and took a slow gulp. "Jake should be back any minute."

Toni knew that Kurt was trying to play down the fact that Jake was later than they had planned.

"He should have been here two hours ago," she said. "This is really rare for Jake. When he says he's going to be someplace at a certain time, he's there dammit. I can't remember him being more than a few minutes late for any occasion."

Kurt took another sip. "Maybe so. But an aircraft carrier can take your breath away and make you lose track of time."

"That wouldn't matter," she said, and then walked into the living room.

Kurt was right behind her. "I don't understand what the problem is. I'm sure everything is all right."

Toni peered through the decorative sheers of the window overlooking the courtyard. A new dusk had darkened the garden greenery into one melded mass. She pulled the nylon cord next to the window and lowered the rolladen all the way to the bottom, and then turned toward Kurt. "Is everything all right? We have four people dead, at least one person with the U.S. Customs office transferring restricted technology to another country, and who knows what else. Jake has a similar technology transfer in Germany by the same company, at least one person dead, and a former German Intelligence agent and his men trying to shoot Jake full of holes. Other than that, everything is just fine."

Kurt plopped into the plush living room chair and took another long sip of beer. It was obvious to Toni that Kurt's long day watching Dalton had taken its toll on him.

Toni turned her head quickly with the sound of a key in the door lock.

Jake entered slowly and quietly closed the door behind him. He looked over at Toni next to the window, and then to Kurt sitting in the chair. "It's like a fuckin' morgue in here," Jake said. "Who died?"

"Where the hell have you been?" Toni asked.

Jake unsnapped his leather coat, pulled it off, and set it gently on a chair. "Working, dear," he answered, smiling.

Toni gasped when she noticed the dried blood on Jake's left temple. "What happened to you?" She came over to Jake and pushed his head sideways as a mother would to inspect her son's road rash after taking a spill on his bicycle.

"I had a little misunderstanding with Burt Simpson. He thought my sideburns were a bit too long."

"Go ahead and make fun," Toni said.

"Okay, truthfully, I'm pretty damn sick of getting shot at. And I don't see that the end is near. By the way, Kurt, your buddy Leo is a good guy."

"He's a character, though," Kurt said, as he rose from the deep chair. "You want a beer, Jake?"

"Thanks, I could use one."

Toni twirled her hands toward herself. "Go on. What else happened."

Kurt returned from the kitchen with a few beers and handed one to Jake.

"Hungarians," Jake stated, and then took a satisfying chug of beer.

"Hungarians?" Toni asked. "What about Hungarians?"

"In Germany Herb and I ran into a few Hungarians. At the time I wasn't sure what they were looking for. But today my new friend Burt told me a good story about Hungarians. That's who Dalton and Simpson were selling to."

"Why sell to the Hungarian government?" Kurt asked.

"I don't think they were selling to the government. Simpson isn't the most intelligent guy in the world. He saw dollar signs in his eyes and could have just as easily been selling to the Pope as far as he knew. Dalton is the brains behind the Roosevelt chips, but I don't think he handled what took place in Germany. I'm not sure who's behind that. I know what Bundenbach Electronics is trying to do, but I don't know who wants them to succeed."

"What about the Genoa bombing?" Kurt asked.

"Shit! I almost forgot. Toni, give your friend Bruno a call and have him pick up Burt Simpson at the Hotel Capri, room 303, in Naples," Jake said.

"Simpson bombed those four guys?"

"Kind of. He delivered the car to the young boy. Simpson told me that a strange, tall Hungarian gave the bomb to him with the instructions. I didn't have time to get more, even though I enjoyed the effort. I'm sure Bruno will get everything he needs. I've softened Simpson considerably."

"Thanks, Jake. I owe Bruno."

Jake shrugged his shoulders. "No problem."

Toni picked up the phone and instinctively punched in Bruno Gallano's number. In her quickest Italian, Toni explained as much as she could to her old friend. When she finished, she said "Ciao" and then pursed her lips in a mock kiss through the phone and hung up. She paused for a moment with her hand still on the phone.

"What's the matter?" Jake asked.

She thought for a second. "Herb!" Toni said, as she picked up Jake's message beeper on the table next to the phone. "Herb sent you a message through the Italian switch of the European Messaging Service."

Jake gently received the small beeper from Toni. "I love these gadgets."

Jake had purposely left the device behind because he knew he couldn't get a signal onboard the aircraft carrier. Herb's message was simple but revealing: "Lassen Sie sich Zeit."

"What does that mean?" Toni asked, leaning over Jake's shoulder.

"It means take your time. But what he means is, get your ass in gear back to Germany. I'll have to call him."

"Does he have secure capability?" Toni asked.

Jake smiled. "No. Herb's a German Customs Agent working out of a tiny office in Bonn. He's close to retirement, and the agency doesn't have much use for his investigative approach. When he first found out about the technology transfer, his superiors thought he was full of shit. In fact, they only humor him now because they don't fully understand the possible impact, and they don't think he's capable of uncovering anything significant."

"Do you?"

Jake hesitated. "I've known Herb for quite a few years. Not well, but we've worked together. I trust his judgment. I trust him. Besides, his disdain for bureaucrats is equal to mine."

"So, I guess you'll have to call like normal people," Toni said smiling.

Jake smiled as he propped the phone against his ear and punched in Herb's home number. "Herb? Yeah." A pause. "No shit? Yeah I know the slimy bastard. I had a feeling about him from the first time I met him. From Rome? What was he doing here? He's from Portland. He's an executive vice president with Teredata. Yes, this does change things. I'm not sure how yet. No, don't confront him. Keep an eye on him until I get there. Okay. What?" Jake listened intently. "Who the fuck did it? Gunter? I'm going to kick his ass this time. Yeah, thanks, I'll try to. See you in the morning."

Jake hung up the phone with a crash and then looked toward Toni and Kurt. Toni had moved closer to him and Kurt had gotten up from his chair.

"Well?" Toni asked.

"Not good!" Jake pinched his nose. He knew he had to maintain his strength up front. Whatever his feelings, whatever weaknesses, he had to get stronger and not let anything get in his way.

"Is everything all right?" Toni asked softly, putting her hand on Jake's shoulder.

"Do you remember my friend Walt Kaiser, the Polizei out of Wiesbaden"?

"Yes. We met once at that New Year's party a few years back. The one in Frankfurt."

"Yeah, well Gunter and his men have put him in the hospital in Koblenz."

"How?" Toni asked.

"I don't know. He and his men beat him up pretty bad. Herb said he'll make it. But I've about had it with Gunter. I never liked the bastard. And now I've got a good reason to kick his fat ass." Jake felt his ears warm and his face become flush as though he were still a school boy enamored by some beautiful new girl. But he knew this heat was not from passion. A pain wrenched in his stomach as he took a sip of his beer and tried to enjoy it.

All three stood there, not knowing what to say.

Finally, Kurt said, "Do you need some help, Jake?"

Jake looked at him. "I'm sure I could use you, Kurt, but we still have to keep an eye on Dalton here. We know he's pretty much in charge of this operation. We need to close him down for good. Besides, I'd like to know who he's selling to, and what else he might be giving away. You need to stay here and finish your case. Toni's office really needs you. Since Cecil has been gone, they've been short handed."

Kurt nodded his head as if taking an order from his superior.

"What about..." Toni stopped short.

Jake knew that she could go to Germany if she wanted. She could work anywhere in Europe. Even if he said no, she could shadow and back him up.

"Kurt could use your help, Toni," Jake said, before she could get her question out. "The Hungarian bomber is still out there. I'm sure Bruno will catch him, but what about before he does? It's better to have two sets of eyes." Before Toni or Kurt could respond, Jake swirled his leather jacket on. He felt the butt of his gun and then ensured the two extra fifteen-round clips were in his inside pocket. "I've got to go," he said bluntly.

Jake noticed Toni staring into his eyes. He wanted to kiss her and hold her tight and then make love through the night. But that would have to wait, he thought. He zipped and snapped his coat half way and then started toward the door. He stopped with his hand on the curved door latch and turned to Toni. What the hell. Romans never waste an opportunity to kiss a pretty girl. He walked over to Toni, kissed her gently on both cheeks, and then meshed his lips firmly with Toni's moist red lips. Toni's chest heaved with a slow deep breath. Finally, Jake slowly released his lips and looked into Toni's eyes.

"I'll come back to Rome if you want me," Jake whispered softly.

Toni smiled. "I want. Be careful."

"Always."

Jake shook Kurt's hand. "Get Dalton."

"You can count on it, Jake."

Jake slowly closed Toni's door and started walking down the stairs. He got to the bottom and stopped. Someone was following him down the stairs. He quickly moved to the side of the wooden banister and waited.

The steps were slow but deliberate. It wasn't Toni or Kurt, he thought. A shadow preceded the figure and came farther and farther and closer to the bottom of the stairs.

Jake slid his CZ-75 out of its holster quietly. The figure came into Jake's view. It was the old man from the third floor in his night clothes with a pillow under his right arm as if going to a slumber party. Jake quickly holstered his gun and watched the man walk right into the first floor apartment. Finally, he sighed with relief and went out the door.

Once outside and walking toward his car, he realized how presumptuous he had been. It was never bad to be too careful, he reassured himself.

There was a chill in the darkness. The dim yellow street lights made Jake's eyes work overtime trying to adjust.

He got to his car and stopped for a second pretending to look for his keys. Jake had noticed a blue BMW, similar to Herb's, with two dark shapes a block down the street, but the figures had disappeared. He was sure they had both crouched down. He got in and thought for a moment. What if those were the Hungarians and they just planted a bomb in his car? But why would they want to kill him?

He shook his head, started the car, and slowly pulled from the curb. He looked into the rear view mirror, but the car was still there.

After a few blocks, he turned right and continued driving slower than normal. He couldn't help wonder why those two men were outside Toni's apartment. Or were they even there? Were his eyes playing tricks on him? He had been up since before the sun rose, driven to Naples and back, and encountered Burt Simpson on the USS Roosevelt and then interrogated him. He had every right to be tired. His eyes had every right to be deceiving him. The bullet graze to his head still brought pain and dizziness.

He turned right again down a one way street. He shook his head to break loose his blurred vision. But he couldn't get those two men out of his mind. Why were they there? He had to find out.

Turning right again, he headed back toward

Toni's apartment. Just before he turned back on
Toni's street, he pulled over to the curb and stopped.
How you going to play this one? Scanning his
memory, he tried to remember the best way to confront trained terrorists, if that's who they were. If it
came to firepower, he knew he'd be out-gunned
without Toni and Kurt. But there was no phone in
the area to call Toni, so he had to move fast.

Jake pulled away from the curb and turned right
onto Toni's street. The car was still there. No heads
though. He stopped just two car lengths behind the
BMW and turned off his lights.

The darkness made it difficult to make out anything. To the right of the car, across the sidewalk,
was a high metal fence that ran for nearly the length
of the block. The multi-unit apartment building on
the other side of the fence had a security system
with a speaker box on the fence gate. Jake could see
from the fence to the building, so he felt fairly sure
that the two men couldn't lurk in the shadows there
and ambush him.

He sat and waited. It had only taken him a few
minutes to drive around the block and come back.
Long enough for the two men to leave their car.

"Shit!" he said aloud. Jake popped the seat belt
and got out of his car. He pulled his gun, cocked the
hammer, and ran up to the blue BMW. Nobody
there. Terrible thoughts ran through his mind as he
ran toward Toni's apartment. He should have

known something was wrong. Shut up. Just get the bastards.

Jake reached the front door of Toni's building and slowly and quietly entered. If they had knocked on Toni's door she might have thought it was him having forgotten something. She could have just swung the door open. And then. Shut up.

With his gun leading the way up the stairs, Jake smoothly stepped upward. He knew every creak in the hardwood stairs. Every spot to watch for. His eyes quickly jutted downward and then back up again. His steps were sure. He listened carefully for any sound above. It was as if he were in the woods stalking a deer. Senses against senses. But deer didn't carry Uzis.

Then he stopped. He thought he heard whispering for just a second. Just a few words, but he couldn't make them out. Hungarian?

He froze. His gun pointed up to the last corner just outside Toni's door. Did they know he was there? That's it. Draw their fire to allow Toni and Kurt enough time to react.

Then Jake heard the sound of the door slowly swishing shut below him. Who the hell is that? Redundancy! An East Bloc trademark. If two could do the job, send four. Now he was trapped just above the ninety degree turn in the stairs. A team of Hungarians above him, and probably a back up team below him. He had to make the first move.

Now!

He aimed his gun to the corner of the ceiling above him and fired a shot. The sound reverberated throughout the stairwell. He heard the men above him stir. Below there was no sound. Toni and Kurt had to hear that.

"Ciao," Jake screamed.

Around the corner above him came a flurry of flashes without sound. He dodged to his left and hugged the wall. Plaster flew from the wall where he had been standing.

Jake pumped off a couple rounds toward the flashing barrel.

Then Jake thought of the others below him. Did they know he knew they were there? He smashed his body as close to the wall as he could. Sweat streaked down the sides of his face. His heart pounded uncontrollably. What if those below were just visiting the old man on the third floor? Then the shots would have made them move, and they won't be there. You've gotta move. They've got you, Jake.

Now!

Jake swung around the corner, fired five shots quickly downward, and returned to his position on the wall. Two men. One hit for sure. Come on Toni, Kurt, I could use some help here.

Two shots rang out above him. And then the sound of heavy footsteps moving up to the third floor.

"Jake, is that you?" Toni yelled.

"Shit, yeah," Jake said. "Who else would shoot up your apartment. Is it clear up there?"

"Yes, hurry."

Jake ran up toward Toni's apartment. She and Kurt were standing with the door wide open, guns drawn.

Jake signaled with his hands that there were two upstairs and two downstairs. And that he had hit at least one downstairs. Jake popped his clip out and replaced it with a full one.

The door to the third floor apartment smashed in. Toni gasped and put her hand over her mouth.

Jake shook his head. "He's down on the first floor apartment," he whispered. "Kurt, stay here and hold those two from getting any closer. Toni, let's go."

Jake and Toni quickly ran up the stairs. Jake peaked around the corner. The old man's door hung open. He moved forward quickly with his gun cocked and ready to fire. He felt Toni just behind him. Jake had been in the apartment a couple of times, so he knew the lay-out. But the rooms were dark.

Now!

Jake flung himself through the open door to the living room carpet. Instantly, a barrage of flashes from behind where the sofa normally sat lit the room. Bullets thumped against the wall behind Jake.

Jake shot three times toward the flashes. He heard the distinct thud of bullet penetrating flesh. He rolled across the carpet a few feet.

Then from the kitchen came another barrage. Toni instantly fired four times and then scooted back behind the door.

Jake crawled behind a large, thick lounge chair. Had he killed the man he hit? He thought he heard a body hit the ground, but he wasn't sure. Now what?

Shots echoed up the stairway from Kurt's gun. It had to be his 45 automatic, Jake thought. The sound was much louder than all the 9mm shots fired so far.

Then at least five more shots came from downstairs. Not Kurt this time.

One more shot from Kurt. Then silence.

Jake looked to where Toni was positioned. He couldn't see her. The darkness was complete. He picked up a small ash tray from a table next to the chair and flung it across the room. Flashes came from the kitchen, followed by Toni firing three times.

As they fired, Jake crawled across toward where he had shot the first guy. He slithered around the outside of the large sofa. He listened for breathing. Nothing.

Then Toni shot twice. With the light from the flashing Uzi, Jake peeked around the sofa. The man he shot lay face up just two feet from him. Jake reached his hand around the corner of the sofa and felt the man's neck. Nothing. Lifeless. His neck was still warm, but no pulse. Then he felt a moist, stickiness that had to be blood. He slid his hand up to the man's face. His nose was nearly gone. Jake quickly pulled his hand away and wiped it on the carpet. A shiver came over him. Control Jake. Control.

Jake scooted forward far enough for his gun to clear the edge of the sofa.

"Your friends are dead, give it up." More flashes came from the kitchen. Jake could feel the sofa taking hits, and the wall next to the door near Toni.

Jake and Toni fired a salvo. And then the louder sound of Kurt's 45 auto. Jake moved out farther from behind the sofa and opened fire through the thin kitchen wall until his gun was empty. Quickly, he popped in his last clip. But the flashes ended.

Then silence. The smell of gun powder filled the air. And the hard, cold iron smell of blood from the man next to Jake.

"Toni?"

"Yeah?"

"Hit the lights."

Finally, the overhead light lit the room. Jake looked over to the door. Toni was crouched on one side and Kurt on the other.

Toni pointed toward the kitchen. "I can see his feet on the floor."

Jake got up and charged toward the kitchen. The man lay face down in a pool of blood. "All clear."

Toni and Kurt drifted slowly into the room. Jake watched as Kurt winced when he saw the man with no nose. In the light, Jake could see that the back of the man's head had been shattered and splintered and was stuck to the wall about six feet behind the sofa.

The last to die was riddled with at least five bullets. It was hard to tell through all the blood.

Jake turned the man over. He had a strong jaw and pock marked face. Even lifeless he looked mean.

Toni moved over closer and crouched down for a better look. "I know him. Well, I don't know him, but I've had a few run-ins with him and his buddies over the years. I nailed a few of his friends about two years ago."

"I remember," Jake said. "I was in England for a few months at the time."

Toni nodded.

Kurt came and stood near the entrance to the kitchen. "I could use a beer," he said. "By the way, I got the guy on the first floor. But one of them got away."

"There were only two," Jake said, moving out of the kitchen and across the living room.

Toni and Kurt followed Jake down the stairs to the first floor. A man lay crumpled at the midway point between the second and first floors.

On the first floor, Jake crouched down to the hard wood floor and pointed to a small spot of blood. "There! I thought I hit one," Jake said, with the eagerness of a hunter on the trail of a wounded animal.

Polizia sirens alternated in higher and lower tones off in the distance. Jake cocked his head. He checked his watch. Time had stood still for less than ten minutes as the Hungarians chose their destiny, Jake thought.

Toni squeezed Jake's shoulder. "You've got to get out of here. Now!"

Jake knew that it would be hard to explain his presence. Toni had a diplomatic passport, and Kurt his military identification. They could convince the authorities of nearly anything. And Toni had many friends. But his story would sound much too contrived. He had to leave. He rose and started to open the door. He hesitated.

"Go! I'll explain everything." Toni said. Her eyes sparkled as if tears had started to form.

"I'll let you know how things go in Germany," Jake said. He flung the door open and swiftly ran toward his car.

The sirens were getting closer. Jake cranked over the engine, made a U-turn, and sped away. He wound through back streets for a few kilometers and then entered the Autostrada and headed north toward Germany. He'd have to drive through the night to make it there by morning.

35

BALATON LAKE, HUNGARY

Isaac Lebovitz opened the heavy wooden door to the large cabin and ushered in two men with a gust of cold rain. He slammed the door hard and turned to view his guests. One had a bandage around his left shoulder. Blood was escaping regardless of the futile effort. The other, Jason Dalton, slipped his coat off and shook the rain from it.

"A few more degrees, Jason, and we'd have snow instead of that blasted freezing rain." Isaac said, moving closer to the two men. "Would you like a shot of schnapps?"

They both nodded their heads. Isaac sat down at the large wooden table and poured three shots of clear schnapps. Isaac knew there was no cause for celebration. No time to waste. But he also knew that sometimes it was easier to get information, the right information, with a comfortable glass of schnapps.

All three quickly tilted their heads and downed the contents of the small glasses.

"Ah! Now, what do you have for me gentlemen?" Isaac asked.

The man with the bandage appeared to be in a great deal of pain. His eyes would close from time to time, and he grimaced when he moved wrong.

Dalton looked at the injured man and then back to Isaac. "We've got a little problem."

"We wouldn't be here if that weren't the case," Isaac said. "I heard through some of my sources that there was a terrorist attack in Rome yesterday. Even the news had something to say about three dead Hungarians and a whole lot of bullets shooting up a nice neighborhood. What happened?" Isaac eyed the injured man.

"We had the CIA agents cold," the man said with a weak, raspy voice. "Then this other guy showed up out of nowhere."

"Who? Did you get a good look at him?" Isaac inquired.

"Dark hair, mustache, medium height, athletic walk. He was an American. At first I thought he might have been Italian."

"How do you know?"

"The girl, Toni, called out his name. Jake," the man said. He coughed a few times. "He answered back in English."

Isaac thought for a moment. "Shit!" He poured another round of schnapps and didn't hesitate to be the first to drink. "Why in the hell does this have to happen to me?"

Dalton and the wounded man looked confused.

"The man, Jake? That's Jake Adams. He was CIA, but I heard he left the agency about a year ago. Did he shoot you?" Isaac asked, pointing at the wounded man.

"Yes."

"Then you are truly a lucky son of a bitch," Isaac said. "You should be dead now. Jake Adams doesn't miss much."

Isaac went to the door and yelled to his driver. In a few seconds, the wounded man was escorted out of the cabin.

"He'll bring him to a doctor in Budapest," Isaac explained to Dalton. Deep down he knew the man wouldn't make the trip alive.

Dalton shot down his glass of schnapps and set his glass on the heavy table gently. "We have another problem. My man on the USS Roosevelt is missing. As you know, he was supposed to deliver our last bit of information on the computer chips."

"Missing?" Isaac asked, clenching his fists. "How could he be missing?"

"I don't know for sure," Dalton said. "I got word from diplomatic sources that there was a little trouble aboard the carrier. Maybe even a shooting.

These are mostly rumors that I didn't have time to check into. All I know is my man didn't show as planned."

"Probably Jake Adams," Isaac said. "Now we'll have to depend totally on Carlson in Germany."

Dalton's eye brows rose sharply. "Carlson? Why?"

Isaac tapped the side of his head. "I guess you have a right to know. Maybe you could even help me out. His name is Steve Carlson. He works for the company you were getting the computer technology from. Do you know him?"

Dalton's face became red. "That son of a bitch. You've been working with him out of Germany?"

They stared at each other.

"Then you do know him?" Isaac asked.

"Yes! He's my supplier."

Isaac shook his head. "I guess Carlson has been playing both of us. I didn't know that he was your boss."

"Yeah, sort of. He planned the Italy scheme. He's also most of my funding source for this partnership. Why was he selling to your men in Germany?"

Isaac smiled. "He wasn't . One of his men sold him out."

"What do you mean?"

"Steve Carlson is selling the same technology you've been selling to me to a German company called Bundenbach Electronics. His middle man, a guy named Johnson, decided to sell to us as well."

"That asshole," Dalton said, pouring himself another glass of schnapps. "I trusted him. It was Carlson's idea in the first place to set up our arrangement. He wanted to get in on the ground floor of Europe's monetary union. He expected great profits. But he also as-sumed great risk, and felt comfortable with those risks. Now I know why. He was padding his risk by diversifying. The German company was far more secure. No offense."

"Jason, I have complete confidence in you," Isaac said. "When you sold me on the partnership, I was-n't buying only technology. I was buying into you. Your concern for our plight. You were a good sales-man. I only hope we can continue working togeth-er."

"What do I have to offer you now? If Carlson drops out, I'll have to scurry for investors. I can find them. I'm sure of that. But it would take a little longer. I still have Wall Street connections."

Isaac poured and drank another glass of schnapps. "I've got a better idea. Carlson is in Germany right now. Go to him and get the information we need."

"What makes you think he has the information there?"

"I'm guessing. But if I were him, I'd hold out that last bit of information to the Germans the same as he's done to us."

Dalton gulped his schnapps. "Okay."

Isaac slid a small folder across the table to Dalton. "Plane tickets to Frankfurt and then Bonn. There are instructions inside on where to meet. I've also signed a coded message saying who you are and why you are there. Give that to Vitaly when you get there. Any questions?"

Dalton picked up the small folder the size of a plane ticket and slid it inside his coat pocket. "No."

"Then good luck."

Isaac sat at the great table alone. The door slammed behind Dalton. He scanned the empty chairs and dreamt of his friends sitting there with him and drinking to his health. Smoke would billow and linger in the air. Languages would switch from Hungarian to German to Czech to Slovak in a single sentence. No one seemed to notice the intermingled and eclectic changes.

He poured another glass of schnapps and raised it up in front of himself in a mock toast. Then he downed it quickly and smiled.

36

BONN, GERMANY

The Alfa Romeo hugged the corner without slip-ping as it quickly decelerated off the Autobahn at the Centrum exit. A light mist was freezing as soon as it hit the pavement. Early morning had failed to produce even a glimmer of light from the sun.

Jake Adams yawned as he turned right onto Kaiserstrasse and ran through the gears up to third, making each green light. The trip to Italy and back had given him a chance to become familiar with the new rental Alfa. It was a year newer than Toni Contardo's, but none of the instruments had changed.

He turned left and drove along the Rhine. He checked his watch again; 1105. He was five minutes late. This was starting to become a habit, he thought. Glancing to the rear view mirror, he noticed his eyes were red and the lids drooped. He found little control over them. They would drop shut and he'd shake his head to make them rise temporarily.

Jake pulled over to the curb a block from the parking area for the public park that butted up to the Rhine and provided government employees a diversion for a lunch time stroll, or a place to eat and feed the ducks and swans.

When Jake set up the meeting with Herb Kline in the middle of the night from Switzerland, Herb must have forgotten that the freezing drizzle was in the forecast. Maybe the cold rain would keep him awake, he concluded.

From the bushes near the passenger side of the Alfa Romeo, Jake saw a slight movement. Then Herb appeared and approached the door. Jake unlocked the door for him.

"This is a change," Jake said, gesturing for Herb to get in.

Herb brushed off as much rain as he could before getting in and sitting down. He put his briefcase on his lap and wiped the drops of water from the top. "Yeah, I thought I'd leave my car at the office to make it look like I'm there. I even left the office lights on. How was the drive?"

Jake paused for the right words. "Fast! I never like to see Switzerland that way."

"I haven't been there in years myself. Maybe I'll get out and travel more when I retire."

Jake nodded agreement. He started the engine and slowly drove away from the curb. Headlights were required with the dreary lighting. And the only thing keeping the windshield from icing over and the wipers from collecting ice, was a hot, blowing defroster.

"Where are they?" Jake asked brashly, not even looking toward Herb.

"Bundenbach Electronics."

"How long have they been there?"

"All morning. I put a motion sensitive tracker on Gunter's car. It hasn't moved an inch," Herb said, patting his briefcase with his right hand.

"Left?"

"Yes! Bachstrasse"

"I thought so. I know I haven't been gone that long, but I've been through so many cities in the last week."

Jake could sense a tension from Herb that he hadn't noticed before going to Italy. It was as if he had lost his confidence again, forgotten how important this case was. And what it meant to his self esteem, more than anything else. Something had changed him, Jake was sure. But what?

"So...what happened while I was gone?" Jake searched for an expression; a clue. Apprehension perhaps. Maybe concern. That would be understandable.

"I told you most everything on the phone."

Jake made a right on Kolnstrasse and picked up speed slowly. He was in no real hurry, yet.

"How did you find out about Carlson coming?" Jake asked.

Herb glanced toward Jake. "The fat guy got a little careless. I've never felt like killing anyone, really. My ex-wife once or twice, maybe. But that was different. With the fat man, I had the opportunity and the actual desire to follow through. I had him cold. Beating him senseless as he had surely done to Walt. I don't know what stopped me."

Jake felt a flush over his body. Almost a new-found realization of his friend. Sure he knew that Herb had a special desire to succeed this one last time. He needed to take a case from beginning to end and come out the winner, like he had as a young rising star. But even with that burden or inner ambition, he had the self-control to stay within the limits of the law. That was admirable, Jake thought.

"Herb! That's what separates you from the Gunters of the world."

"Maybe."

Jake stopped along the curb with a long view of Bundenbach Electronics. The grass was dark green and the reflective glass glimmered even in the overcast darkness.

"You don't have to follow through with this," Jake said. "I'll understand."

"No! I had a feeling it would come to this. My

boss is still too busy to see anything wrong. I don't understand how anyone can be so blind in a position like his. I don't trust him either."

"Does he know anything about this?" Jake inquired.

"No, no. I stopped keeping him informed before you left for Rome. And he hasn't even asked me for an update. If that isn't irresponsible."

"I've had assholes like that for bosses. They're so caught up in their own little world they won't take the time to see what you're doing. Fucking bureaucrats."

Herb laughed. "What exactly do we need to do now? I mean, how do the Hungarians fit into this?"

"Well, I have a theory. Remember I've been driving all night. I've had a lot of time to think about this. I believe that Carlson has been pulling the puppet strings all along both here and in Italy. He set up Johnson to transfer the technology to Gunter and Bundenbach Electronics. At the same time, he set up Burt Simpson and his guys aboard the USS Roosevelt to drop off the same stuff to Jason Dalton. Simpson gave me Dalton's name but didn't mention Steve Carlson. I didn't push him as far as I could have, though."

"Why is Carlson here?"

"That bothered me for quite awhile. Carlson couldn't risk carrying the chips and all the technical information into Germany without getting caught.

He needed a way to isolate himself from the entire process. So he had the U.S. Air Force fly everything into Bitburg Air Base. Customs doesn't check military supply planes. Besides, that equipment was part of an approved retrofit. It was NATO restricted, but as long as the technology didn't get into German hands, no problem."

"But why come now?" Herb asked.

Jake pointed at Herb. "Because Gunter fucked up. Gunter found out that Johnson was selling out to the Hungarians, right?"

"Yeah, that's what I thought."

"Well, Gunter jumped the gun a bit. He was only supposed to rough him up a bit to get the information. But Gunter is a sick son of a bitch. He doesn't like someone taking advantage of him. So he does in Johnson. The problem is, Johnson hasn't sold everything that Bundenbach needs to make their super transputer."

"So then Carlson is stuck. He can't start over from scratch. He has to come here himself."

"Exactly. Also, when I started working the case, we cut off Johnson's supply chain. So Carlson couldn't even send the information by military channels and pick it up once he got here. He had to carry whatever was left personally. Teredata had shut him down. Carl-son tried to get me off the case before I was even hired."

"Wasn't Carlson afraid you'd see him with Gunter?"

"I told Milt Swenson I was going to Italy. He must have told Carlson. But they didn't know about my ace in the hole."

"What?" Herb looked confused.

"You! Carlson didn't know you were here on the case."

"What's keeping Gunter from killing Carlson after Bundenbach gets the last bit of information?"

"I don't know. But I'm sure he hasn't left himself open for that."

"His ace in the hole?" Herb smiled.

He seemed more comfortable now. Almost relaxed.

"This shit is getting crazy." Jake rubbed his eyes and yawned. "I pulled over at an Autobahn stop in Switzerland for about two hours. Definitely not enough sleep. When I get back to Oregon, I'm going to sleep for a week."

Freezing rain pelted the windshield and started to pile up on the wipers. Jake just watched. The weather would be a problem, he thought.

"We had a little problem in Italy just before I left," Jake said solemnly.

Herb was silent.

"At least four Hungarians tried to hit Toni's apartment. I had to leave in a hurry, without finding out who they were really after, and why. I could only speculate."

"You couldn't ask a few questions?" Herb asked.

"No. They weren't able to talk."

"Ah...."

"Unfortunately one of them got away. I don't know why they would want Toni or Kurt killed. I assume they were getting too close to Dalton, and he ordered it. Maybe not though."

They both sat in silence. The rhythmic sound of rain on the roof fluctuated from time to time as gusts of wind intensified and then became calm again. Bundenbach looked abandoned—nobody in sight. The rain must have kept only the hardy from coming and going, Jake thought.

"I missed having the company while you were gone," Herb said. "I'm sorry about your friend, Walt. I should have been able to help him. I really blew it."

Jake faced Herb. "Even if you could have gotten to him, Gunter wouldn't have made it easy for you. His two men are heavily armed at all times. Numbers tend to enhance effectiveness. I got lucky. They had me cold. I could have been back in some Oregon deep freeze."

"But..."

"Forget it!" Jake said, becoming angry. "We can't dwell on what's passed. We have to look forward and get these bastards. It's more than just the tech-

nology transfer now. Gunter has gone too far. The
Hungarians have gone too far. Carlson has gone too
far. These fuckers have pissed me off for the last
time."

Jake knew that getting angry was counterproduc-
tive. Yet, he needed his anger. His senses became
more sharp; more aware of his surroundings. Maybe
it was the lack of sleep. Maybe he knew that Gunter
wouldn't give up Carlson's last bit of information
without a fight.

"You know, Herb, if Bundenbach can produce
this super transputer, and a mini version for personal computing, it will completely change the world
computer market? They'll have a corner on the market. It could take other companies years to recover,
if ever."

"It's that important?" Herb asked.

"I'm afraid so. I'm assuming that Carlson has
held out the most important information until the
end. Probably some hidden factor that makes the
chip so fast. It could be as simple as a chemical formula or special metal relay. I don't know. Anything.
But whatever it is, Carlson is probably in there right
now explaining its function and effect." Jake pointed toward the Bundenbach headquarters.

"But I still don't understand the Hungarian plan,"
Herb said.

Jake rubbed his eyes and shook his head to try to
wake up. "I don't know for sure. Simpson gave me

some information. About as much as he really
knew. After all, he was only a middle man. Carlson
is an insecure guy. He doesn't totally trust anyone.
The Germans are no exception. He figures if the
Germans hose him over, he'll have a backup plan."

"So he hires Dalton and Simpson to set up the
Hungarian connection?" Herb asked.

Jake thought for a second. "Sort of. You see,
Carlson didn't know that Johnson was also selling
out to the Hungarians. I think Carlson wanted some
other relationship with the Hungarians."

"Like what?"

"Dalton works for the U.S. Commerce
Department. He's privy to some pretty sensitive
economic information. Maybe Dalton was giving
the Hungarians more than just computer technology. He might have been handing over economic
forecasts and U.S. strategic economic plans for
Europe, based on the new Euro currency."

"What good would that do for the Hungarians?"

"It could do a lot. If the Hungarians not only have
the technology to produce a fast computer, but also
the marketing strategy to go with it, the Hungarians
could have a winning combination. They could be
in a position to produce a computer, with cheap
labor costs, and market it throughout Western
Europe and eventually Eastern Europe. That would
put them at a distinct advantage to exploit those
markets."

Jake covered his face with his hands and stroked his hair. He knew that what he had just told Herb was close enough to the truth to be scary. If he was right, and he was pretty sure of that, then corporations had started to go too far. Killing people for secrets. Bombing people to keep them quiet. Where would it end? How far would they go to succeed? Carlson had gone too far. Bundenbach had gone too far. The Hungarians had gone too far. And Jake knew that only he and Herb could help reverse what had been set in motion.

Jake looked at his watch.

"We have to move!" Herb said anxiously.

Jake checked his watch one last time. "Let's go."

They got out of the car into the bitter wind and rain. Drops of rain driven by the heavy wind prickled the back of Jake's neck like tiny needles. He flipped up the collar on his jacket. They shuffled quickly toward the entrance to Bundenbach Electronics.

37

BONN, GERMANY

A gust of wind and rain followed Jake and Herb into a small foyer between two sets of doors at the entrance to Bundenbach Electronics. Jake shook the rain from his leather coat as he looked into the bright lobby that awaited. He pressed his arm against the butt of his gun.

Herb looked nervously to the street. "Did you see the car across the street as we walked up?"

Jake strained, but couldn't see the car from the entrance way. "Yeah. Looked like it might be the Hungarian twins."

"That's what I was thinking."

"The place looks like a morgue in here," Jake said, pointing toward the lobby. "Let's go."

They walked past an information desk, as if they knew where they were going, and waited for an elevator.

Rising to the top floor, they stood together in silence. They got out and looked down both hallways. To their left was a passageway with only one door at the far end on the left with an exit sign at the top. Large plants sat at the end of the hall beneath a window. Not much natural light supplemented the florescent overhead lights today, Jake thought.

The passageway to the right had a number of doors on both sides of the hall. Workers came and went from one door to the next.

Just in front of the elevators was a small waiting area with a large overhead skylight and well-kept plants. A convex window extended outward with a view of the Rhine below.

A blonde receptionist sat talking unofficial business with a soft voice. She didn't seem to notice Jake and Herb.

Jake took a better look at her. He smiled. She was the one who had lulled him when he first got to Germany. The lookout for Gunter and his friends with the Uzis.

"Wie bitte," Jake said, forcing a smile. "Ist Herr Bundenbach frei?"

The woman looked up at Jake and seemed surprised. She must not have been told that he had survived. Gunter was always one to emphasize success and ignore failure, Jake thought.

The woman hung up the phone with a quick good-bye. "A moment," she said, keeping her eyes on Jake as she buzzed her boss.

Jake glanced at Herb. He was watching the elevator and the hall.

"He'll see you Mr. Adams," she finally said.

"Explain to your boss that Herr Kline is with the German Customs office, and has a few questions to ask as well."

She didn't relay the message. Instead she got up and escorted the two of them to a large set of carved wooden doors. She inserted an electronically coded key and the doors swung open.

"I hope it's not that hard to get out," Herb whispered to Jake as they entered the office.

Jake scanned the room. Obviously the boss sitting behind the desk. Gunter sat to the man's right in a red leather chair with studs. His fat goon with the rearranged face stood behind him against the wall next to the window. To the left of the boss, another man, even larger than Gunter's beaten sidekick, stood with his arms crossed. No Carlson though.

The boss sat back in his high chair. His dark gray suit looked nearly perfect. His dark hair with silver along the temples was meticulously combed. Not a hair out of place.

"So, Jake Adams. Gunter has told me so much about you, I feel I know you already," the boss said with a politician smile. Smug confidence.

"You have me at a disadvantage then," Jake said. "I can only assume that you are Herr Bundenbach."

The man nodded his head. "Yes. What can I do for you?"

Jake started to feel the urge to explode. It was one thing for a secretary to ignore Herb, but this son of a bitch should have a little more respect.

"First of all, this is Herr Kline with the German Customs office," Jake said, as he put his hand on Herb's shoulder. "I'm looking for a man named Steve Carlson. I understand he's here, and he works for you?"

"What do you want with this man?"

Jake started to pull something from an inside coat pocket and the large men quickly pulled toward their guns. The boss raised his hands to keep them from drawing the guns to view. Jake flashed a black leather case open to expose a gold oval badge.

"I'm a special agent with the United States International Trade Commission. I have reason to believe that Steve Carlson has been providing your company with congressionally restricted computer technology." Jake put his badge back in his pocket, but refused to look at Gunter.

Gunter stood up quickly. "Bullshit, Jake! You're just an overpaid corporate investigator."

"According to who?" Jake asked, staring at Gunter.

Gunter looked at his boss.

"Adams, you have no jurisdiction in Germany," Bundenbach said, his hands together almost as if he were praying.

"Ah, but you're wrong. You see, the U.S. Trade Commission has a reciprocity agreement with the NATO Council. The NATO Council and German Customs also have agreements. But I think you know this. So why don't we quit with the bullshit and produce Carl-son?"

The boss shifted his eyes toward Gunter's man and lifted his head slightly. The fat beaten man went to a private door and let Steve Carlson in. Carlson immediately gave Jake a harsh stare as he walked in with his briefcase dangling from his left arm.

"What's the matter? Wasn't Milt paying you enough?" Jake asked callously.

"Fuck you!" Carlson said. "You wouldn't understand."

"You're right. I wouldn't."

Jake felt Herb's hand on his right arm. Jake knew he needed to maintain control. But he was tired. He was mad. And the pain from his bullet wound increased with his blood pressure and was now throbbing uncontrollably.

* * *

Downstairs, four men entered the lobby. Vitally Urbanic was in the lead, followed closely by the Hungarian Twins. A few steps back was the American, Jason Dalton. They stepped into the elevator and the door closed them in.

They were at a stand-still and Jake knew it. He kept his eyes piercing through Carlson. It was his move.

"What's this Trade Commission shit, Jake?" Carlson asked.

"That's right. And I'm here to bring you and the last bit of Teredata information back to America."

Carlson laughed aloud. Gunter and the two large men joined in as well.

Suddenly, Jake drew his gun and aimed it directly at Carlson's head. Herb pulled his out now and trained it on Gunter.

"Go ahead...laugh," Jake said. He stepped up to Carlson and grabbed ahold of his collar, pulling him toward the door.

The largest of Gunter's men went for his gun, so Herb swung around and shot him, sending him to the carpet in a heap. Backing toward the door, Jake, Herb, and the struggling Carlson headed out into the reception area.

The elevator dinged, followed by the doors opening. When Jake saw the Hungarians with Dalton, there was a period of misunderstanding in everyone's eyes. The Hungarians went for their guns, but Herb was faster. He fired a round into the elevator, sending the four men scrambling to the corners.

Jake pulled Carlson down the corridor to the stairwell, the briefcase clanking against the wall.

Herb followed closely behind, his gun aimed back at the elevator.

Shots sprayed down after them. One hit Herb in the shoulder, sending him sprawling to the floor. Jake let go of Carlson for a second as he pulled Herb into the stairwell. Carlson made a break down the stairs.

Herb looked up at Jake. "I'm all right. Go! Get Carlson."

Reluctantly, Jake turned and rushed down the stairs after Carlson. Herb leaned against the door frame, his gun aimed down the hallway.

* * *

Back in Bundenbach's office, Gunter and his man were at the edge of the door.

"Get Carlson back!" Bundenbach yelled at Gunter.

Gunter shoved the door open. His man sprayed the Hungarians with his Uzi, dropping one of the twins and Dalton. Vitaly and the other twin returned fire and scooted back into the elevator, punching the down button. Gunter peppered the door, and then turned to find his man dead at his side.

"Damn it!" Gunter yelled. He rushed around the corner toward the stairwell, but jumped back when Herb sent a few rounds after him. Gunter retreated back into the office and slammed the door.

Bundenbach pointed toward the back door. "Take the back stairs. We need Carlson."

Gunter rushed out.

* * *

The back door burst open and Steve Carlson ran out into the biting rain whipping across the trees and side of the building. He glanced around and then hurried toward a park along the Rhine River.

Seconds later, Jake flew out the door into the squall, his gun aimed in each direction. Then he saw Carlson, so he took off after him through the wet grass.

* * *

Coming out the front door, Vitaly and the remaining twin ran around the side of the building. They stopped at the corner, glancing around through the driving rain.

Vitaly pointed his gun toward the river park. "There they are!"

The two of them sprinted off after Carlson and Jake.

* * *

Gunter stepped out the private door. He noticed the two Hungarians sloshing through the wet grass, and farther on toward the river, Carlson and Adams. Rain lashed down on him, and he wiped the water from his eyes before running off after the four of them.

* * *

By now Jake had closed in on Carlson. They were running parallel to the Rhine, the grass lashing out at their legs. The briefcase dangled from Carlson's hand.

Jake was closer now. With one quick motion, he dove at Carlson, catching him in the legs and tackling him to the wet weeds. They rolled around on the muddy ground. Jake punched Carlson in the face, sending his head flinging back to the ground.

Suddenly, shots rang out in the hollow wind.

Jake rolled over, drew his gun. He spotted the source, aimed, and fired three times, dropping the

second Hungarian twin. Then Jake saw Vitaly dive
behind a tree. A hand appeared with a gun, followed
by two shots in Jake's direction.

Silence. Only the wind and rain.

"I just want the briefcase, Adams!" Vitaly yelled.

Jake, on his belly, rolled a few times to a safer
position.

"That's not gonna happen, pal," Jake hollered
back at him.

Behind Jake, he could hear Carlson crawling
away toward the river. But he was worried more
about the man with the gun.

A single shot echoed through the trees. But not
toward Jake, he thought.

Silence again. But Jake could see another figure
making his way through the trees perhaps thirty
meters to the left of the Hungarian. Who was that?

"Shoot him!" Carlson yelled behind Jake. He was
standing now, at the edge of the river.

Jake turned his head just as a single shot ripped
through Carlson's chest, sending him flailing backwards into the Rhine with a tremendous splash. The
dark river swallowed him. The briefcase suddenly
rose to the surface and floated downstream.

Starting to rise, Jake was forced back down with
a flurry of rounds cutting up a tree next to him.

Jake returned fire. Three times.

More bullets flew toward Jake.

Jake fired again and ducked back down.

More shots at Jake.

He waited now, hearing footfalls through the trees. Jake pulled up and fired three times at the figure.

Silence.

Jake swapped out a new clip. After a short while, he got up and crept toward the area he shot last, his gun leading the way. Freezing rain beat down on him, making him shiver. He cleared the bushes away and glanced down toward the ground. Gunter was on his back in the wet grass, a bullet hole in his forehead.

* * *

Polizei were everywhere, along with EMTs checking bodies in the woods and strapping them to stretchers, hauling them down from Bundenbach's office.

Jake had made his way to the front of the building, and was sitting on a retaining wall in the entranceway when two men in white pulled a gurney toward him.

Strapped down and patched up was Herb. He had the two men stop next to Jake.

"You gonna live, Herb?" Jake asked.

"I have to. I'm too close to retirement."

Just then two of the uniformed Polizei hauled Herr Bundenbach out of the elevator, his hands cuffed behind his back. He looked defeated and dejected as they whisked him past Jake and Herb.

Jake turned back toward Herb. "You take it easy."

With that, the EMTs pushed the gurney out into the driving rain.

A moment later, Jake went out into the freezing downpour and got behind the wheel of his car. He looked into his mirror at his tired eyes and hoped the airplane would have a terrible movie.

38

PORTLAND, OREGON

Jake sat in the informal area of Milt Swenson's office.

Milt came in and sat down on the sofa. "How was your flight?"

"Pretty normal. Screaming kids. Obnoxious assholes trying to strike up conversations." Jake smiled.

Milt seemed uneasy, shifting from legs crossed to open and then crossed again.

"What's the matter, Milt?"

"I had no idea Steve was involved. You have to believe me."

"Why shouldn't I? You had nothing to gain by knowing what he was up to."

Milt shifted again. "The Senate Armed Services Committee comes here tomorrow. I plan on pitching our Joint Strike Fighter proposal at that time."

Jake didn't say a thing.

"I'm really satisfied with your results," Milt said. "I mean, you could have just let Steve sell my company out to the Germans and the Hungarians. You took the extra step for me. I appreciate it."

Jake didn't know what to say. Had he really done anything out of the ordinary? After all, he was hired to do a job. Reputation was important for future cases. Without references, how could he expect to continue in this business. No. He had done what needed to be done. Sure he could have sold out his principles. Given in to greed. But looking in the mirror each morning would have been far too difficult.

"I got lucky. Had some good help, also."

"Luck? I doubt it. You seem to have a penchant for being in the right place at the right time. I call that experience."

Jake wondered where the praise was leading.

"Jake, I could use you here at Teredata," Milt said.

Jake shifted in his chair. "I don't think so. You've compensated me nicely. I've made more in the last month than in six months with the agency. That's the good part. But I've found that I like working for myself. I know I'll always have a boss. But at least I can choose who that boss is."

"You've saved us a lot of money, Jake. If the Germans had picked up on our chip design, the European market would have been flooded with our technology. And we wouldn't have made a dime off all our research expenses. Besides that, we wouldn't have a chance in hell of getting the Joint Strike Fighter contract."

Jake got up from the chair and went to the window overlooking the city. It was a bright, sunny day. The Willamette River sparkled from the direct sun and the reflection off the tall, mirrored skyline.

"Not only did you save us money," Milt continued. "But you're going to make us a lot of money."

Jake studied the river. "How?"

"That transputer theory you talked about. Our engineers feel they can make it work with the right information."

Jake still didn't turn to Milt.

"We need a few things that would take us years to come up with on our own," Milt pleaded.

"I can't help you with that. I have only a limited knowledge of the theory," Jake said.

"True. But the Germans have it. You could get it from them."

Jake turned toward Milt. "What do you want from me? I've just been shot at how many times trying to keep your information from reaching the Germans and Hungarians? And now you want me to go back there and get the transputer information? I don't think so."

"You're the only one who can do this for me, Jake."

Jake turned back toward the window and the river. Beneath the surface flows swift water, Jake thought. Uncertain eddies. Whirlpools. People were no different. Bundenbach had his agenda. Lebovitz had his. Even Milt now.

Jake turned back toward Milt. "Bundenbach is in no position to deal," Jake explained. "He'll be wrapped up in a legal battle for quite a while. Besides, I wouldn't trust him."

Wait a minute. With Bundenbach severely hampered, Teredata could exploit his markets. Come on line with the fastest transputer at a far lower cost than any other super computer. More importantly, the personal transputer would revolutionize the industry. Exactly what Bundenbach was trying to do. Exactly what Lebovitz was trying to do. So, how was Milt any different from the Germans or Hungarians? Shit! Did Milt know what Steve Carlson was up to? Did he actually set up the entire scheme? Or did he just now come up with the idea now that the opportunity presented itself?

"You're thinking it over, Jake?"

"I'll give you one last bit of information and then I'm out of here," Jake said, perniciously. "Lebovitz."

"Lebovitz? What about Lebovitz?"

"Do you know him?"

"No."

"He's the Hungarian Carlson was dealing with indirectly," Jake said.

"What about him?"

"He has most of the transputer information. I'm sure you can work with him. But I won't help you. Lebovitz can supply cheap, skilled labor and the transputer technology. You'll need to provide your chips, engineers, and a little capital and marketing strategy."

"But Jake, I need you to make the deal."

Jake walked slowly toward the door. "Find someone else, Milt. I have a date."

Jake left and closed the door behind him. A part of him wanted to help. He knew Lebovitz. Knew it would be easy to pick up some cash at Milt's expense. But what about the price? The men who had died had paid a price. Who could pay that price without a conscience? And what price would Jake have to pay? Conscience wasn't cheap.

As the elevator closed him in and he drifted toward the ground floor, he reached to the inside pocket of his leather jacket and pulled out an airline ticket. He studied the open ticket to Rome carefully, smiled, and then placed it back in his pocket. He felt his temple where the bullet had grazed him, shook his head, took in a deep breath and let it out slowly.

Jake left the building and climbed into a cab waiting for him.

The cab driver turned to Jake for a destination.

Jake looked at the man and smiled. "The airport."

ABOUT THE AUTHOR

TREVOR SCOTT is the author of the international thrillers Fatal Network, Extreme Faction, The Dolomite Solution, and Hypershot. He was a weapons expert working the flight deck of aircraft carriers in the Navy, and was a captain in the Air Force, where he was stationed in Germany for three years in a tactical missile unit. He holds a Bacheloris Degree in English from the University of Minnesota, and a Masteris in creative writing from Northern Michigan University. He currently resides in Oregon with his wife and two sons.

COMING JULY 2005

EXTREME FACTION

**A JAKE ADAMS
INTERNATIONAL THRILLER
by Trevor Scott**

Jake Adams, former CIA officer and Air Force Intelligence captain, is back with a new thrilling adventure. This time, Jake is hired by a Portland, Oregon company as a private security agent during an international agriculture conference in Odessa, Ukraine. When a world-renowned biochemist is murdered, Jake seeks his killer. The scientist had been the foremost authority on chemical and biological weapons, developing the most deadly agents for the former Soviet Union. But now he was supposed to be a staunch opponent of those weapons. Was he still secretly developing those deadly weapons?

Extreme Faction brings all the old agents from the U.S., England, Israel and Russia back together again. The names might have changed, but the games remain the same . . .